THE DATING DISASTER

FRANKLIN U #2

SAXON JAMES

D1411467

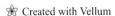 Created with Vellum

ABOUT THIS BOOK

Thousands of students on this campus, and I keep being set up with the roommate I can't stand.

Felix

One date.

That's how long it takes for Marshall Harrows to end up on my bad side.

Luckily, I have no plans to see the giant teddy bear again. Except when he shows up as my new roommate, I can't escape him, and he's just as irritating as I thought he'd be.

He leaves cupboards ajar and puts empty milk cartons back in the fridge. His bedroom door is always open, I find his underwear on the laundry floor, and he has this whole bashful sweetheart thing going on that I just … can't … stand.

But the most completely, *horribly irritating* thing about him is that he's totally my type.

And my friends won't stop setting us up on blind dates.

Marshall

One date.

That's how long it took for Felix Andrews to steal my heart. The sparky little spitfire is everything I'm not. Confident, adorable, and completely outspoken.

He also wants nothing to do with me. Which is a real problem when I want to give him everything. Including my virginity. But the more I try to gain his attention, the more I see the real him. The one who doesn't feel worthy of being treated like anything other than a one-night stand. So I decide to take matters into my own hands.

A total do-over. One night. One date. Where hopefully I can steal his heart too.

AUTHOR'S NOTE

These FUKing books are total stand alones and you don't need to have read the others to enjoy this one (though you should, because they're awesome).

If you are following the recommended reading order, this one takes place at roughly the same time as *Playing Games* and *Mr. Romance*. Neither couple in those books are together … yet.

Happy reading!

PROLOGUE

Felix

Two months ago

THE GUY—NO, MAN—NO, *BEEFCAKE* ACROSS FROM ME SHOULD have been a slam dunk. Blue/gray eyes, dark brown hair, five-o'clock shadow, and arms that could break me in half. He has to be over six foot and is the exact mix of strong and soft-bellied that makes all my limbs weak—well, except the one in my pants.

And yet this entire date has been more painful than anal bleaching post-crack wax.

My gaze keeps slipping to the Christmas decorations adorning the bar, and I remind myself *again* to focus.

Marshall's deliciously big hands twist and twist over the table. "Ah …" He swallows. "So … you're from Massachusetts."

"We did cover that, yeah," I say, trying not to laugh. The thing is, he seems like a total sweetheart, but—and it's a *big* but—there's no way someone like him would be able to handle someone like me.

He's so … *wholesome*. Which is a pity because he's hot as fuck, and I'd do anything to be *handled* by him.

"Huh. Right." He's squinting, which is really ruining the eye candy, and blinks way too much to be healthy. And I swear he hasn't looked at me directly once. His eyes keep darting around the bar like he'd rather be anywhere else.

All my expectations that had skyrocketed at seeing him are shriveling. It's not his fault though. It's mine for putting so much pressure on this date. Sure, I love me some sex, every night of the week if I can get it, but after seeing my dad and godfather get married last year and watching some of my friends start to find their someones, I'm craving that connection too.

I've put my friends on Operation Find Felix a Boyfriend, and so far, they're failing. Though, to be fair to them, none of them actually know about their mission. As far as they're concerned, I'm on the hunt for more guys to sleep with.

And yeah, I'll probably end up in bed with the teddy bear across from me, but the disappointment is setting in thick. He's not my Mr. Right, and it's really starting to wear on me that I can't find *one* guy who's halfway decent and wants me for more than a quickie.

I really like me, and I happen to be someone who likes a lot of sex, but I'm not an idiot. I know the word some guys call me. Even *after* they've been with me.

Most of the time, I don't let it get to me, but times like these —sitting across from a guy who makes my heart feel all funny just from looking at him—it hurts to know I'll never be good enough.

"What do you do on the weekends?" Marshall asks, hurrying to take a sip from his beer and dripping some down the front of his shirt. His *Shenanigans* polo, to be exact. Because apparently, he finished his shift five minutes before our date time and thought us meeting in the college bar where he works would be a smooth move. After I spent literally hours obsessing over what to wear. For him. To make him *like* me.

I put in effort for him, and he clearly didn't think I was worth doing the same.

Determined to shake off my funk, I lift a shoulder and try to smile. "Fuck around, mostly," I say. Because hey, if he's not future boyfriend material, he can at least bang me senseless before the night is over. Might as well get *something* out of this date.

"Yeah, me too." He nods, looking suddenly relieved. "My weekends are really low-key when I'm not working. Video games with the guys, reading, maybe some—"

"*Oh*, you think I meant fucking around as in relaxing?"

His eyebrows jump up. "Umm … is that *not* …"

"Bless … I meant literally."

His mouth forms an O even as his cheeks redden. "That's, uh, cool," he stutters out.

And *great*, now he's judging me.

I hold back my sigh, not wanting to go off on a rant about sex positivity. How long should I leave this thing before we're both happy to admit it isn't working? Dating is new to me, so I'm not sure if there's an etiquette here, but after being closeted the entirety of my high school years, I'm determined to never hide who I am again. And there's no way I'm letting this guy make me feel like less than him because I like a bit of sex.

And even with the gross feelings swirling in my gut, my cock is still on board for the after-party. He wouldn't be the first guy to hate fuck me.

Marshall lifts a hand to run through his shaggy hair, revealing a huge sweat patch and an enormous bicep. My stare follows the line of his shoulder, up along his thick neck to his solid jaw, and when my gaze flicks up to meet his, there's a flare of heat between us.

He clears his throat and glances down into his lap. "Do you ... do you, uh, what do you study?"

My eyes narrow at the way he asked that, and I crane my neck to try and confirm my suspicions. I can't see his lap from here, but I take a stab in the dark.

"Please tell me you're looking at your cock and not a list of conversation starters."

His head jerks up, and the guilty expression he's wearing immediately gives him away. "I'm ..."

"Am I really that hard to talk to?"

"What? No. No, I—"

That settles it, then. There's no natural connection here. We're too different. I remind myself that's okay and try to shove the feelings of disappointment and worthlessness way down deep. He's not my person. He'll never be my person.

Well, no reason why he can't be my person *tonight*.

My chair squeals against the hardwood as I stand.

Marshall's mouth gapes at the movement, but I'm determined to make the most of the night. It's already close to eleven, and the bar is busy, but it's still too early to hook up in the alley out back. Which means we're going to have to go somewhere, and I'd rather it not be my place because then it's up to *him* to leave instead of the other way around. I learned that lesson the hard way.

Before he can say a word, I grab his giant hand, link my fingers through his, and drag him through the crowd. He follows me easily, and it's not until I push through the back door into the dark alleyway that he gives me some resistance.

"Ah, Felix, what are you ..."

I turn and press him into the wall. With his legs parted enough for me to step between, he's still taller than me by a lot, and even if everything in there was a total write-off, I can already tell how we end the night will be burned into my memory for a long time.

His eyes are wide as he rests those sexy hands on my waist. "What are you doing?"

"I want to kiss you."

A shuddery breath. A deep swallow. A nod. "Okay."

I press onto my tiptoes and bring our lips together. At first, I'm not expecting much, but the second our mouths make contact is explosive. He opens for me instantly, tongue pressing against mine with a confidence that's been missing the rest of the night, and the warmth from his mouth, the tightening grip on my back, the press of his solid chest against mine, gives me butterflies.

Full-on winged little bastards doing laps in my gut.

Marshall reaches up to cup my face, a soft hum leaving him. He keeps the kiss slow, deep, and it's incredible and knee-melting, but I need more. I need to feel his solid body naked against me, his cock stretching me open, and see the awkward person who's sat across from me all night sweat-slicked and desperate.

I grunt, fingers digging into his shoulders, before I trail them down his chest to tweak his nipple through his stupid polo shirt.

I'm breathing deeply when I break our kiss and press my lips to his ear instead. "I want you to fuck me," I whisper.

The shift in him is immediate.

Marshall's whole body goes tense, and his head jerks back. "I ... I ..."

"It's okay," I assure him. "The date was a fail, but we might as well get an orgasm out of it, right?"

The bewildered expression he's wearing tightens, and he shakes his head. "That's not for me." And there's that confidence I'd been looking for. At the worst possible moment.

My gut clenches at the implication, and I hurriedly take a step back. "Say no more." I'm not going to force him to do me. In fact, if he doesn't want me, the asshole doesn't deserve me.

Hurt clenches around my chest, and I try to brush it off.

"I'm sorry, I just … I'm … I'm not …"

"That kind of guy," I finish for him, having heard this shit before. He either thinks he's too good for a quickie with me, or he's a total closet case. Either way, I want off this ride. "Don't worry. Message received."

I pat my pockets to make sure I have everything with me before turning to leave.

Marshall's hand snakes out to grab my arm, and I shoot him a glare.

"Want to let go there, big guy?"

He jerks back like he's been shocked. "Sorry. Please. I'm confused."

Closeted it is. "Don't worry about it," I brush him off and spare a genuine smile. I went through the closeted, confused self-discovery myself. I step in to brush a kiss over his cheek, then start to back away. "Thanks for the date."

"You're leaving?"

"I think it's for the best."

His face falls, but I turn and block it out, reminding myself it's pathetic to cry over a little rejection. Marshall isn't my Prince Charming, but that doesn't mean I won't find him.

One day.

Eventually.

Still, when I reach the parking lot, I can't help but glance back over my shoulder. He's slumped against the wall, watching me leave, and even though I can't see his expression with the shadows over his face, this knot has lodged in my gut. Too bad for him.

He didn't want all this, he doesn't get to make me feel bad about walking away. I don't have time for games, and I especially don't have time for guys who make me doubt my self-worth. I've gone through that enough in the last few years.

I leave, the sound of the beach behind me a dull roar, the smell of salt water heavy on the air, and make the familiar walk home.

Alone.

IF I NEVER SEE MARSHALL HARROWS AGAIN, IT WILL BE TOO soon.

That's the last thought I have before falling asleep, and apparently, it's the wrong one to put out into the universe. I wake to Jason, one of my roommates, talking to someone with an unnervingly familiar voice. Considering Jason rarely stays here as it is, hearing him so early is weird enough, but …

I kick off my covers and go to investigate.

And as soon as I descend the short staircase to the next level, I wish I'd stayed in bed.

Standing in the middle of our currently vacant room is Jason … and Marshall.

My gut swoops as his eyes immediately drop to my tiny pajama pants, and I kick myself for not getting dressed first, but what are the chances?

"Hey, Fe," Jason says. "You're just in time to meet our new roommate."

Ohh, fucking fuck no.

"Marshall, this is Felix," Jason continues as if the ground hasn't just caved out from right under me.

Instead of the earlier delightful swoop, my gut churns. My home is the place I can be me. I don't have to tone down or act like someone I'm not, and now here's this six-foot-something, sexy-eyed, scruffy, judgmental closet case, moving in.

"Ah, hi." He offers me a confused kind of smile.

"Hi. Umm … how is this happening?" *Whoa*, that sounded high-pitched even by my standard.

"Bowser asked if I wanted the room …" His gaze flicks to Jason, like he's checking for permission.

"So glad he did," Jason says. "Some of the guys who applied were … well, they didn't exactly come highly recommended."

Marshall sniggers. "You won't get any issues from me. I usually just hang out with Bowser, anyway."

"How do you know him?" I ask, trying not to sound panicked or snappy, but fuck. Fucking fuck.

"We're best friends."

Well, that explains why Bowser was the one who set our date up. He's lucky he's already gone home for the holidays because otherwise, I'd have some very stern words for him. *Very* stern. Like who the hell sets someone up with their roommate-to-be?

"I need to go," I say abruptly.

Jason throws me a concerned look, and I swear Marshall goes pale. His eyes are as wide as damn plates, and even though I'm borderline freaking out, I know what that look is. *Don't worry, buddy, I'm not going to out you.*

"You good, Fe?"

Am I? Cue hysterical laughter, because what the hell?

I get to live with the guy who turned me down and made me feel just as small as I worry I am. Now whenever I look at him, I get to see my insecurities staring me back in the face.

The kicked puppy look he's wearing *really* isn't helping matters.

"Just fucking peachy."

1

Marshall

"How's this?" my best friend, Bowser, asks.

I look around the room that's larger than my half of the shared dorm I moved out of. Bowser left early for Christmas break, so he wasn't around when I moved in a few weeks ago, and I only got back here from break this morning. "Private."

"Private?" he gasps with mock offense. "You have a view of the fucking beach from here, man."

"Yeah, but it's a longer walk to work."

"You ungrateful sod."

"Been watching British sitcoms again?"

He shrugs. "The Brits are hilarious, dude. I'm telling you, there's this one—"

"Hard pass."

"But—"

I laugh and give him a light nudge. "The limited time I get for

TV isn't going to be spent watching people from Scotland Yard find Jack the Ripper."

"That's not—" He stops himself, knowing I'm giving him shit. "How long do I have to stick with you before I can trade you in for a new best friend?"

I gesture to the room. "Hey, we're roommates now. I think that buys me at least another few months."

Bowser grumbles under his breath and hauls over the rug he found at a thrift shop to spread out on the floor. The room is basic and more expensive than my shared dorm, but I had to get out of there. A roommate who's up all night talking to himself about Mercury in retrograde and mapping out star paths isn't a good fit for me. While he's looking skyward, I'm constantly looking back. History is so fucking cool and wildly terrifying. There's more we can learn from the years behind us than the guesswork of astrology.

"We'll kit the room out like mine," Bowser says. "Xbox and TV over there, we'll pick up a secondhand desk from somewhere, and—ooh! Fish tank, dude. We'll put it on that wall—"

"I'm vetoing anything living in here. So don't buy me a plant either."

"*Uh-oh.*" He ducks out of my room and disappears into his across the hall before coming back with a tiny pot. "You wouldn't expect me to take Cactus Everdeen back, would you?"

"Cactus Ever … what?"

Bowser crosses to place the terra-cotta pot on my windowsill, and I move in for a closer look. It's a fuzzy white ball.

"That's maybe the ugliest cactus I've ever seen."

"It's an Old Man Cactus." He winks. "Reminded me of you."

I puff out a breath.

"Don't worry, once it grows, it'll lose the ball shape and turn into a big fuzzy dick."

"Perfect. I always wanted phallic-shaped plants."

"See? I know you too well."

I leave him to admire the ugly thing and move to unpack my clothes. Relief is hitting me hard. I've been working as a barback at Shenanigans for the past few months in order to save up and move out of the dorms senior year, but when Bowser called me to say his roommate was dropping out before the spring semester, I moved up my timeline. It's going to be tight with money, but fuck it. At least now I can study without a background of constant muttering.

Mom and Dad were great when I told them I might need help now and then with money. They've sent me home from Christmas with a new budget and promises to chip in for food and utilities. Hopefully, I won't need them to though.

"Hey, you never told me how your date with Felix went," Bowser says.

I groan, suddenly on high alert. Bowser might not have been here before Christmas, but running into Felix the day I moved in here made for a very uncomfortable conversation. I swear Felix's eyes almost shot from his head when he realized we'd be living together, and the week leading up to Christmas only got more and more tense.

"Terribly."

"What?" Bowser's jaw drops. "I thought it was a sure thing."

Goddammit, I know what he means. The second I realized the cute guy with the reddish-golden hair was there for *me*, I'd almost pissed myself. I'd wanted to back out and pretend I was sick. I should have too. Because sitting across from him, getting more and more nervous under his blue stare, I was only too aware of how much I was blowing things.

"How the hell did you screw it up? You're both each other's perfect types." He sounds personally offended.

"Why do you assume *I* blew it?"

"Because I know you." When I don't answer, he flops down onto the bed and tucks his hands behind his head. His dark red hair is covered by a backward cap. "Felix simps over big dudes—there's no way in hell he wouldn't have tried to sleep with you."

My face heats right out to my ears. "He, uh, did."

"Oh."

"Yep."

Bowser licks his lips, gaze pinned to the wall overhead, and I know where the conversation is going before he opens his mouth. "This virgin thing—"

"It's not a thing." I hate having this conversation. "It's not some huge deal. I just don't want to sleep around."

"Okay, but you know having sex with *one* person isn't sleeping around, right?"

"I do understand words, yes." I also understand the word *demisexual.* When it comes to sex … it's not something I've ever been excited about. Sometimes I joke—to myself—that my brother Robbie got my share of a sex drive, given all the stories he used to tell me. There's been one person in my entire life who I've actually *wanted* to have sex with, but unfortunately, she didn't want me back. And so now I have a giant V over my head that apparently Bowser thinks he needs to help me "fix." I love the guy—he reminds me of Robbie in some ways—but that's one aspect of his supportiveness I could do without.

"Maybe you're too in your head about it. You should go out and find a hottie to get it over and done with. Then the pressure will be off. I'd offer to do it for you if I thought I could get it up with a dude, but I've tried, mate, and nothing's happening down there."

"I don't *want* to get it over and done with."

He lifts his hands in surrender. "Okay, no need for the tone. I only thought if you wanted to fuck anyone that Felix was a good choice."

"And why is that?"

"He's your type. He's eager. And he's the kind of guy who can do the one-night hookup thing without making it weird when you see him again."

I narrow my eyes at Bowser. "Have *you* slept with him?"

He laughs. "No. Well, he tried, but seriously, *nothing* down there."

I try to shake away that unsettling imagery as I dump a pile of folded clothes into the closet. "Well, none of that matters anyway. We didn't have sex, and I don't want anything casual, and Felix never wants to see me again."

And to be honest, I'm not in a hurry to see him again either. Those few days before I left for Christmas were awkward as hell. I push my glasses further up my face, knowing how impossible that hope is. As gorgeous as the guy might be, I don't need the reminder of completely choking with him, and yet there's a good chance I'm going to run into him a lot now.

"Actually I don't think *Felix* ever said that."

I freeze at the familiar voice. My gut twists as I debate stepping out from behind my closet door to face Felix or hiding here until he goes away.

Bowser smirks, ignoring my panicked look, and waves a hand in my direction. "Felix, you know our new roommate, right?"

Shit. The bastard's smirk only gets wider when I make a slashing motion at my throat. Tongue feeling way too big for my mouth, I relax my expression and step out to face him. "Hey …"

Felix's unnerving blue eyes narrow. It's been almost two weeks since I've seen him, but I'm reminded again that with my glasses on … goddamn.

He's even hotter when he's not all blurry. Those unrelenting nerves hit me out of nowhere, and I shove my clammy fists into my pockets. Shake hands? No, thank you.

"Still moving in, huh?" he asks, pretty face screwed up.

I nod. "Looks like it."

"Just keep the noise down."

Bowser laughs. "I'm so glad your date went great because you're going to be spending a whole lot of time together now."

My eyes fall closed, and when I dare open them again, Felix has his arms crossed tight.

"Call me crazy, but I don't class ending the night on rejection as successful." Then he spins on his heel and leaves.

It takes all my energy not to hang my head in my hands.

Bowser sits up. "Okay, not only did you blow it, you blew it *big*-time. How did you piss off the kitty?"

"Kitty?"

"Yeah." He gestures to where Felix was standing. "He's a flirty little spitfire. I legitimately thought it was impossible for Fe to hate someone, but the look you got from him …" He cringes. "You're gonna have to tell me what went down on this date."

"So you can judge me some more?"

"So I can figure out how bad this is. Duh." He shrugs. "And also to judge you some more. Because, come on."

Well, shit. I drag my hand over my face before crossing to sit on the windowsill beside Everdeen. Directly outside is a stretch of white, flat roof I'll be able to easily climb out onto and sit on to watch the sunset over the beach. Bowser's room overlooks Liberty Court, which is the courtyard this group of share houses surrounds, and in the afternoons, he hangs out of his window, talking to the groups of people who are always out there. The quiet on this side of the house suits me perfectly.

I fill Bowser in on the date. Everything from being called in to work overtime right before it, to stinking like sweat and stale beer, to accidentally leaving my glasses in the bathroom and not wanting to draw attention by going back to get them.

"I was *so* fucking nervous."

"You? Nervous?" Bowser asks.

"Yeah, I don't get it either." Devolving into a bumbling mess isn't my style. I might not be the most confident guy in the world, but I can usually hold my own with new people.

Felix … unsettles me. Big-time. Even now, knowing he's in the house, that I might bump into him again, is stirring up all of these *oh shit* feelings. "Maybe I should go back to the dorms?"

Bowser snorts. "We both know your roommate is probably doing a séance on your old bed as we speak. Now, *maybe* you should keep going with your story and tell me how it ended with you rejecting Felix."

"He kissed me."

"Right."

"Then asked me to fuck him."

"Ah." Bowser clears his throat, and a laugh hiccups from him. "Right. Well, I can see how that wouldn't have worked out."

"Is it *my* turn to upgrade best friends?"

"Nope, I got you this room, so I figure that buys me until the end of college, at least."

The bastard is right.

"Please tell me you let Fe down easy."

"Of course." I mean, I'm *sure* I did. But if that was the case, would he have been as annoyed with me as he is, then?

"What exactly did you say?"

And now I'm drawing a blank. "I can't remember. Something about that not being possible … or not being into that, or …"

This time, his laughter rips free. "Bloody hell. No wonder you're single."

"It's not my fault that all anyone ever seems to want is sex."

He gives me a genuine smile. "I can't relate. Look … if I'd

known things had gone sideways, I would have given you the heads-up. But neither of you mentioned anything, and I know how badly you wanted out of that dorm ..."

"It's fine."

He still looks unsure.

"*Really*. It's a big house, and we live with two other guys. I probably won't run into him much anyway."

2

Felix

FOR A FIVE-BEDROOM HOUSE WITH MULTIPLE LIVING AREAS, THE space is entirely too small. Since I got back here from Massachusetts, it's as though Marshall's *everywhere*. I see him in the kitchen before class or bump into him leaving the bathroom. Even when he's not *right there*, he leaves reminders of himself all over the house.

The navy towels that are always screwed up and flung over the rail instead of spread out neatly. His spray deodorant that he never puts back in the cupboard and lingers for longer than anyone else's in the bathroom. The tiny mouthful of milk he leaves in the carton, and his ridiculous habit of never fully closing cupboards, so the doors are always slightly ajar.

Not to mention, he leaves his bedroom door wide open when he goes out.

Open.

Just exposing his room and his things for anyone to walk by and stick their head inside. It's too trusting. He makes me suspicious.

And I'm thinking of the guy again when I came out here specifically to stop that.

The hammock closest to our house is free, so I climb into it and burrow into the fabric. I've got a decent view of the whole courtyard from here. Our house, Freidman, is one of four that surround this large courtyard, and if I'm honest, it's what sold me on moving in.

I love hanging out here in the afternoons. There are always people around, which my social side adores, and it's a far cry from small-town Massachusetts where I grew up. Burned-orange stone tile takes up any space that isn't filled with palm trees, cacti, and spikey ferns, and climbing vines creep up the sides of the white stucco buildings. The whole place smells like sun with a hint of weed, thanks to the stoner house, and most afternoons, someone is either playing music or firing up the grill.

I take a long breath, absorbing the atmosphere, and pull out my phone. I'm caught up on most of my coursework, so might as well have a little fun tonight. Only when I open Grindr and start to flick through the options, I'm pickier than usual. Normally I'll message the first decently attractive beefy guy I find, but tonight … nope. Nope. And … *nope.*

After my parents' divorce, I'd decided that love wasn't worth it. Seeing two people I'd always believed were perfect for each other fall apart sent me on a spiral I regret in a big way. I barely got through my freshman-year courses, had a lot of casual and sometimes unsafe sex, and experimented with whatever substances I was offered. It was stupid, and I was acting out, maybe even trying to punish Mom and Dad for the split, but … now they're with their new partners, it's really driven home how unhappy they were together.

I'm so grateful I had Brady around to help me pull my head out of my ass.

I sigh and drop my phone onto my chest before staring across at the arched entrance that leads to the road outside. And of course the second I look up, Marshall walks in.

Dammit.

How can one guy be so irritating … and so gorgeous?

He's staring at his phone, backpack high on his shoulders, which only shows off his barrel chest in a taunting way. Like it's highlighting the things my tongue will never be acquainted with. Damn Bowser being friends with this titan.

Marshall glances up before he walks by, and we lock eyes for a second. There's something about his stare that pins me in place. It's at complete odds with the squinting, blinking mess he was on our date, but then the moment passes, and he disappears inside.

I puff out a long breath and grab my phone again to text Brady.

Me: *Feel like some SEAL fun tonight?*

Brady: *Always*

Well, that will solve my restlessness, at least. There's nothing better than having a best friend with shared interests, and those shared interests happen to be big men who can throw us around. Which, in Brady's case, is much harder to find since he's one of those guys himself.

I throw my legs over the side of the hammock and pause, wondering if enough time has passed to go inside and not run into Marshall.

"'Sup, Fe."

I look up to where Bowser is sitting on his windowsill, one long, muscled leg hanging over the side of the house. Fucking hell, it's a hard life. Big, beefy guys everywhere, and none of them are interested in me climbing them. "Not much. I thought you were in class."

"Nah, I finished early today. You going out tonight?"

"Sure am." I shoulder shimmy. "Hoping to reel me in a SEAL."

He barks a laugh. "Of course you are." There's a pause, and I can tell he wants to say something else.

"Out with it."

"Out with what?"

I pin him with a look. "We're playing that game, are we?"

He glances over his shoulder into his room before he turns back to me. "So ... you and Marshall."

"Nope."

"What happened?"

"Are you really going to pretend he didn't tell you already?"

"I'm a gossip." He shrugs like *what can you do?* "But mostly, I want to make sure things aren't too uncomfortable for you guys to be living together."

I rake my hand back through my curls, trying to look unbothered. "Why would it be uncomfortable?"

"Because of the whole rejection thing."

"Like I care about that. If he doesn't want me, there are plenty of other men who do." Pity none of them want me for more than sex though. I jump down from the hammock and make a big deal out of straightening my cutoffs. "Now, if you'll excuse me, I'm going to get ready to meet one of them."

"Hey," he calls before I can make it a few steps. "You know that's not it, right? Marshall thinks you're gorgeous."

Nerves tremble through me, but I brush them aside and flick my curls away from my face. "He'd have to be blind not to think that."

"Or straight," Bowser says.

"Please. You're straight, and you think I'm gorgeous." I bat my eyelashes playfully.

"Damn, you caught me." He winks. "I'm just saying, give the guy a second chance. I don't think he was on top form that night."

"Geez, you're talking as though I hate him."

"Don't you?" I can tell he wants to laugh again. "Because the tension when you two are in a room together is ridiculous."

I scowl. "There's no tension between us. There's nothing. Literally nothing. Because that's all your guy wanted. Now, I'm going to continue keeping out of his way and being my awesome self."

"Like you can be anything else," he teases.

I blow Bowser a kiss and head inside, but as soon as I step into the Moroccan-tiled foyer, all that false bravado evaporates. I might be a little set in my way and hate change like my dad, but I pride myself on being friendly. Would giving Marshall a second chance really be so bad?

What did he do, *really*?

Our date was a solid never-to-be-repeated experience, but the worst part of that night was the impact on my pride. If he *is* confused about his sexuality, like he said, shouldn't I try to be a supportive roommate?

Admit that I was a tinge dramatic and maybe wrong? Gaaah. It's painful.

I close my eyes and force some steady, calming breaths.

I will be kind and supportive and understanding.

Yes. The next time I see Marshall, I'm going to magically let go of the disappointment that he doesn't want to tear my clothes off as desperately as I want to do to him. Eeeeasy.

With the forced pep in my step, I turn the corner into the kitchen—and my organs immediately try to rearrange themselves at the sight of Marshall standing there. He's taken off his sweaty T-shirt and tucked it into the side of his gym shorts while he leans against the counter, eating a bowl of cereal.

I swallow, trying with every bit of strength I have not to check him out, even as my eyes fight to dip and take in his gorgeous, thick body for the first time. I'm practically vibrating with the effort, and it takes a moment for me to realize I'm blatantly staring.

His dark eyebrows hook upward. "You okay?"

I almost swoon at his deep voice, but instead, I clear my throat and manage a smile. "Are you eating cereal?" probably shouldn't be the first words out of my mouth.

He tips the bowl so I can see. "Yeah, and?"

"It's the afternoon. Cereal is a breakfast food."

"Are you the food police?"

"I'm just—" I cut off that line of conversation—even if it *is* unnatural—and switch speeds. "Look, we got off on the wrong foot, and I wanted to say … well, I know what it's like to be confused, and if you need to talk, I'm here for you."

Instead of the thanks I'm expecting, he tilts his head. "Confused?"

"Yeah, you know, about your …" I check none of our other roommates are around, in case he's not out yet. "*Sexuality.*"

His stormy blue eyes run over me, lingering on the bottoms of my cutoff shorts. "I'm not confused about my sexuality."

What? I frown. "But you said you were."

"When?"

"When I asked you to fuck me. And excuse me for saying this, but that kiss didn't feel very confused."

He chuckles softly. "That's because I'm not confused. I'm bi —I haven't bothered to hide it."

"So …" If he didn't reject me due to some internal battle about liking dick, then … he just straight up rejected me. After *that* kiss. What the hell did I do to him? I can't manage words. This weird, hurt laugh fills the silence. "I'm not good enough for you, then? Because Bowser already said I was your type, so you can't even use that excuse."

Marshall's jaw ticks. "You're really offended by this."

"You think I'm not good enough for you. How do I *not* be offended?"

"Did I say that?"

I plant my hands on my hips. "Then what was the reason?"

"For?"

I snarl and throw my hands up. "Never mind."

"No." He places his bowl on the counter. "You're really pissed. We should talk about this."

"Yeah, pass. That doesn't sound like a fun conversation for me."

"You're acting like I owed you sex or something because of one date."

The words pull me up short. I open my mouth a few times to tell him how very, very wrong he is, but the words don't come. Instead, the seed of hurt embedded in my chest spreads outward. I never once said he *owed* it to me, but not being someone he wanted to have sex with *sucks*. I refuse to get into the whys for the reason it's hitting me so hard, but every guy I've ever gone out with or met up with has always wanted to end the night one way. Knowing they can't keep their hands off me makes me feel powerful in a world where I don't have a whole lot of that.

I swallow thickly and push all the hurt down again. I don't have time to feel that shit when I'm busy being awesome instead.

Forcing the nonchalance I'm supposed to feel, I say, "Whatever. It's over now. Just because we live together doesn't mean we have to be friends."

He stares at me, and for some reason, I can't storm away like I want to. "That's what you want?"

"Obviously. I don't put time into people who don't have time for me."

"I think you're making assumptions again."

"And I think your milk is going warm." I flick my curls back and leave the room, popping my hip against the open cupboard to close it again.

Living with Marshall is going to be a trial.

But I'm up for the challenge.

3

Marshall

THAT DIDN'T GO WELL. I DRAG MY FEET AS I CLIMB THE STAIRS TO the second floor, hoping I've left enough time for Felix to disappear. If I'd known it'd be this much of a headache to turn him down, I might have just gone through with it to bypass this awkwardness. Maybe that's not a healthy way to view sex, but I don't care all that much.

Mostly. There's a small, romantic part of me that figures since I've gone so long, the first time I do it, I want it to be special. I want to be able to look back on my first time sharing that with someone and remember how amazing it was.

I've a little over an hour before my shift, but I'm going to have to factor in the walk time from here instead of the dorms. Getting there should be faster since it's mostly downhill, but walking home will be a bitch. Thankfully it'll be close to midnight by then, and being the end of winter means the heat will be long gone.

Instead of kicking back on my bed like I desperately want, I pick up my ukulele and rest against the window. I have an awesome view from here. The road, a part of campus, the bar I work at in the distance, and the beach stretched out beyond that.

After only a week, I know I want to stay here for senior year too. But to do that … I really should make nice with Felix.

The crazy thing is, he's adorable, and if it wasn't for us having wildly different views on sex, we probably would get along. I pluck out a quick tune on the strings, picturing his bright eyes and wild curls, my mouth going dry all over again. Whenever he's around, I struggle to get words out. He's really fucking pretty, but not only that, there's something about his personality that screams *big* for such a tiny guy.

I zone out for a while, playing idle tunes, letting my mind wander through the awkward encounters over the last week. I hate conflict. Whether Felix likes me or not, I want us to at least be at a level where we can be relaxed around each other.

My lips twitch with a smile. Plus, he's really, really, *really* pretty.

Oh well, that can be future Marshall's problem.

It's still hard to believe I'm out of that dorm. There's a constant buzz of energy here that's happier and more relaxed than the frazzled vibes I left behind. I feel like I fit. Belong. Which isn't something I've maybe ever felt before in my life. Sure, my family are awesome, but I'm so different from all of them. My parents and brothers are loud and complete extroverts; they don't understand my need for downtime to power up again. Well, none of them understand except Robbie. He's oddly perceptive for a loud monster of chaos.

I tuck the ukulele back between my secondhand desk and the wall, then hunt down my work uniform and get changed. My bladder is bugging me, so I make a bathroom stop before I leave, but when I get there, the door's open, and Felix is at the counter.

His eyes meet mine in the mirror, and I have a moment where I want to back up and disappear, but that's definitely not a move that's going to help us get past this.

So I suck up my nerves and do what I'd do if it was any of the other guys in here. I send him a quick upnod and pull up at the toilet. Even with my back to him, I can feel his stare, and knowing I have his full attention makes it hard to get started.

A second of silence.

Two.

Fuck, come on ...

Any longer and he's going to think I'm having—

Oh, thank god.

I rein in the fist pump I'm tempted to throw out and focus on finishing my piss and tucking myself away. Then I flush and cross to the sink to wash my hands, where ... Felix doesn't shift.

I point to the tap. "I need to get in there."

"Did you seriously take a leak in front of me?"

My forehead crumples. "That not allowed?"

"By my friends, sure." The guarded way he says that is kind of adorable.

I point to the tap. "Still need to wash my hands."

Reluctantly, he takes a step to the side, but it's not far enough. When I step in, he's so close I can smell ... whatever that is. Something citrusy ... fruity ... I don't know. But the rattling in my gut kinda makes me want to lean in for another sniff.

"K. Bye," I say, brushing him as I sidestep to get to my towel. I can still feel him watching me, so I make it fast and then bail.

It's not until I'm out of the bathroom again that I realize how shallowly I was breathing. Acting normal around him is going to be harder than I thought when my own damn body won't even get on board.

Somehow, I'm blessed by partial cloud coverage and a cool sea breeze, so I manage to arrive at work in an okay state. Not that it matters. Since my shift is mostly spent hauling stock, I won't finish up that way, but by that point, even the bartenders have worked up a sweat.

Gwen, our head bartender, is up front, and I throw her an upnod on my way to the staffroom, where another bartender, Brax, is hanging out.

"Hey," I say.

"Hey, man."

"Not started yet?"

"I'll grace Gwen with my presence in five." He's a bit of a cocky shit, but he's not as loud as the others, and we've gotten along since I first started here.

"How is she so on all the time?" I muse. "She works more hours than either of us combined."

"Yep, but she's also a five-foot-two hurricane who never stops." His gaze suddenly pings away from mine. "Oscar hired a newbie too. Lacrosse kid as a dish bitch. I give it two weeks."

I'm not sure what's weirder: Brax's sudden awkwardness or him acting like that's information I need to have when I normally stick to myself.

I give him a muttered "Cool," then dump my bag in my cubby, throw him a wave, and clock in for another long shift.

As well as keeping the back rooms full of supplies and organized, I have to make sure they have everything they need up front as well. It's a lot of back-and-forth, a lot of lifting and carrying. But while it's labor-intensive, what I don't have to do is talk to people, which makes it kinda perfect for me.

I don't *not* like people. When I'm around friends, there's no issue. It's strangers who intimidate me. Thankfully, Friday nights pass quickly due to the busy two-hour "happy hour" for college students, and I'm so busy I tune out almost everything but the steady back-and-forth of moving stock.

Until I make another trip back up front and almost trip over my feet.

Felix is standing beside a booth just down from where we had our date the other week and … wow. He'd dressed nicely in jeans and a T-shirt when we met, but tonight … I swallow thickly. His curls are pinned up messily, and he's wearing a crop top that hangs off his shoulder and leather pants—which he's probably dying in, but damn do they look good. I'm struggling to pull my eyes away from his ass.

And even though sex isn't high on my list of needs, I can appreciate a sexy sight when it's right there in my face.

I'm barely even aware of the big guy with him as they slide into their seats. I dump the crate of bottles on the counter behind the bar and continue over toward them. My mouth is dry, but I can't tear my eyes away from him. He's so pretty.

It's not until I've stopped beside their table that … *fuck*. I need to actually say something.

Felix blinks confused blue eyes up at me, and the lack of a bright over-twenty-one band around his thin wrist catches my attention.

I point at his usual bracelets. "No happy hour for you."

He turns his attention to his wrist and then back to his friend. "Umm, yeah. Obviously."

Abort, abort. "Cool." I dart a look toward the guy with him. He's tall with light brown hair and an easy confidence that comes through in his smile. Because of course he is. Sitting with Felix, who's dressed unbelievably sexy … I put the pieces together. "Shit. I didn't mean to interrupt your date," I stumble out.

Mr. Confidence's smile drops. "Oh, we're not—"

"Well, you are," Felix says, reaching across and linking his fingers through the other guy's. "My very, *very* successful date."

Successful? Well, I know what Felix means by that. My ears

heat up, and an awkward sound slips out. "Okay. Sorry. Have fun."

"Oh, we will," Felix says.

I ignore the twist in my gut when I glance at the other guy for a second before leaving. Bowser was right—Felix does have a type. A *big* type. It's ... unsettling. I mean, yeah, I look like I could take anyone down in a fight, but I wouldn't know the first thing about throwing a punch. I'd try though, if I needed to, and could probably hold my own. But if that dude wanted to get one over on Felix, the little guy wouldn't stand a chance.

I push my glasses further up my nose, trying to convince myself to keep walking and not give in to my urge to go back over there.

"You okay, Marshall?" Gwen calls out, snapping me from my thoughts.

I glance back to where Felix and his date are laughing over something and remind myself that it isn't my business. I'm sure Felix has the numbers of countless people he can call if he gets stuck—he's not exactly short on friends—so the last thing he needs is a roommate he can't stand interrupting ... *that* for the second time tonight.

"I'm fine," I finally answer, pushing all my protective instincts down and getting back to work.

They're gone by the time I make another trip up front, and I ignore my regret at letting him walk out of here without making sure he was okay.

Then ... I mentally kick myself. Because who am I to think Felix needs looking after? I hardly know him—I'm sure he's got a hookup routine down pat by now.

I collect a bunch of empty glasses from under the bar to take out back and refuse to acknowledge the lump of worry building with concern over a certain little twink.

4

Felix

BRADY STUFFS HIS HANDS IN HIS POCKETS AND WHISTLES obnoxiously as we leave Shenanigans. I know exactly what he's waiting for, but he's not going to get it. Because I wasn't lying when I said us pretend-dating was nothing.

It *was* nothing.

Mostly.

I smile innocently at him.

Brady lifts his eyebrows and whistles louder.

I bat my lashes.

And he cuts all pretenses and pins me with a look. "Sticking to your guns, huh?"

"Not sure what you mean."

"Yeah, of course. Because you always tell random people that we're dating. Nothing new there."

"I don't think your sarcasm was heavy enough," I point out.

He doesn't stop staring at me, and when Brady is onto something, he doesn't let it drop. The smug smirk he's wearing just screams that he knows I'm going to cave eventually.

"Gah. *Fine.* Has anyone ever told you that you're the most annoying person alive?"

He laughs. "You and my brother are tied for first place on that, but there are at least a dozen others on the list. So, out with it. Who was he?"

"My new roommate."

"Damn, Fe. Let me guess, you fucked him, and now things are awkward."

"The opposite, actually."

Brady screws up his face as he puzzles that out. "You didn't fuck, and now things *aren't* awkward ... nah, that doesn't sound right."

I swear he's messing with me. "Marshall turned me down, and so now things *are* awkward, doubly so after he just ... hovered like that."

"I think he likes you."

"Sure, because guys regularly turn down eager guys when they like them."

"I don't think your sarcasm was heavy enough," he mocks. "But yeah, that's definitely not my experience. So what are you going to do?"

I send a flirty smile his way. "*We* are going to go out, dance, play *hello, sailor*, and then hopefully end the night filled by some seamen."

"Perfect plan to me." We jump into the ride he ordered to take us to the bar.

Brady and I have been friends for a year, and we knew the second we met that we clicked. He was introduced as *Brady Talon —you know,* the *Marcus Talon's son*, and I was so turned off by him trying to get ahead on his dad's name that I'd sneered and asked if he thought that made him special.

Turns out, Brady isn't *actually* a douche canoe. And the fact I didn't fawn all over him made him love me forever. The fact he's built like his football player family made *me* love *him* forever until we figured out we both went for the same type of guy.

Though having someone to go out dancing with, who thinks it's funny when I flirt with his brother and dads, is good enough payoff for not getting to sleep with him.

Besides, people might not get our insults-as-a-love-language relationship, but we get each other. He helped me out of the kind of wild time that only leads to STDs and the bad types of drugs, and I listen when he needs to vent about the expectations attached to his last name.

We're dropped at Bottoms Up, a gay bar in Coronado, and it was a good choice to go out tonight because from the looks of things, a ship must have come in yesterday or today because I spy a lot of military-grade haircuts in the crowd.

It's going to be a good night for fishing.

Brady and I post up on the dance floor, starting the night dancing together like usual. It's still early, and neither of us is desperate with so many men around.

I have no idea how much time passes while we dance together, joined every other song by random men, until I turn in some guy's arms and find Brady's been swallowed by the crowd. It's how our nights always go. He's either still dancing or on his knees in the bathrooms—we make sure we give the other the heads-up before we leave.

I'm horny and have worked up a sweat by the time I make my way to the bar for a drink. While I'm waiting, warm hands close over my waist, and the "bah!" in my ear makes me jump.

"Asshole," I say, swinging around to Brady. I can barely hear his laugh over the music.

"Gonna take off," he says, leaning in a little.

I gasp. "Who? Where?"

He jerks a thumb over his shoulder, and I follow the movement to a gorgeous-looking navy man down the other end of the bar. *Damn*, he's a good find.

"Holy shit, yes. Oh, the filthy, filthy things I'd let him do to—"

"*And* the guy beside him," he says.

My jaw drops as my attention slides to the tank beside hottie navy man. I turn back to Brady and place a hand over his heart, pretending to blink back tears. "I'm *so* proud. May you have the spit-roasting you truly deserve."

He barks a laugh and smacks a kiss on the top of my head. "Be safe."

"You too. And text me addresses, mister," I shout as he walks away.

I'm still smiling when they disappear from sight and the bartender asks what I want. I grab a water, ignoring the guy beside me who I can feel watching with interest, and pull out my phone when it vibrates.

I don't know the number, but I read it anyway, and when I do …

The bartender plonks my drink in front of me and moves away, but I suddenly don't feel like drinking it.

Unknown: *Hey, it's Marshall. I hope it's okay to text, I just wanted to check in. That guy with you looked … big. So, yeah. Just thought I'd check you're okay*

My face pulls into a frown as I read it through again, trying to ignore that teeny, tiny sliver of guilt over lying to him. Okay, so, maybe it's kinda possibly possible that Marshall came over tonight to be a good guy … and then was totally weird about it. Just like this message.

I have no fucking clue what I'm supposed to type back, *lolol all good he was my best friend and I lied to you because you unsettle me and make me feel a bit shitty honestly, but it's cool because I'm fine?*

Yeah, no go.

I'm still debating myself when a hand slips onto my waist that I know instantly isn't Brady's.

"Hey, cutie."

Where normally I welcome this kind of easy hookup, something about Marshall's text has thrown me and left me off-balance. I suddenly really, really want out.

I turn a sweet smile on the guy and lift my phone. "I have to go outside and take this."

He lets me leave without another word, and it's that, more than anything, that leaves me feeling … cheap.

Sure, I don't expect romance from these guys. I don't even need a name. But I'd at least like to know I'm sucking their dick because *I'm* the one they want at that moment, I'm not just the most convenient option.

I sigh and step outside into the cooling night. Even thinking that much is probably too generous for a hookup.

What's gotten into me lately?

Getting sex wherever and whenever I could was my thing. Even after Brady helped me out of my unhealthy spiral, it's always been something I enjoy and am good at. Seeing a guy worship my body is the best kind of high, but … it's not enough anymore.

I'd thought finding a boyfriend was what I needed, but dating guys is harder than finding someone to have a quickie with. I haven't found that *click*, that one guy who makes me feel like *I'm* the one they choose because no other option measures up for them.

When my parents divorced, I didn't understand how they could give that up. I'd assumed that if they couldn't make it, no one could, and then Dad married Heath. My godfather, his best friend for decades, and even though I originally hated it, seeing them together … I got it. There was never a choice.

I want that.

The whole ride home, Marshall's text is burning a hole in my pocket. I just can't place why. It was a casual check-in and definitely not his place, but …

Well, I can't remember the last time someone did that.

Brady cares, I'd never doubt that, but with my other friends, I don't think any of them have ever checked in on me to make sure I was okay. That realization is like being doused under cold water.

With every minute, I'm becoming more and more irritated. Being hit over the head with the idea that your friends aren't really your friends will do that to you. Especially when you've just been cockblocked by a stupid text.

And it's all Marshall's fault.

Stupid, sweet, can't-close-a-cupboard Marshall. Who had to send a text over something that's none of his business.

I'm grumpy when I get back and pass through Liberty Court to the house. It's almost one, and when I duck into the kitchen to grab a water since I never drank my one at the bar, I find the cup cupboard ajar. He's already home.

Probably upstairs in his room.

Will the door be open?

Did he send the text and then wait up to see if I'd write back? Or did he hit Send, then go to sleep, content with the knowledge that he'd ruined my whole night?

I huff and slam the cupboard closed, then drink straight from the tap before climbing the stairs to my room.

Marshall's door is closed, and I linger, straining my ears, but it's quiet. So he's either not a snorer, or he's not asleep. Either way, I'm *not* interested.

I climb the stairs to the split level above. Only Darian's room and mine are up here, and I swear he's out half the time anyway, so I basically have the space to myself. There's a landing between the rooms, holding double doors that open onto a small rooftop garden. Bowser's the only one of us who gives enough of a damn to maintain it, but even I can admit that it's peaceful out there.

Instead of going to bed, I walk outside and sit on the small bench tucked under my bedroom window. It's stuffed between two huge garden beds and has a view of the water when it's not cloudy like it is tonight. And as I sit there, I pick up the faintest sound of music. It's not the usual top hits that come from the stoner house or the country music that the guys in Mundell house like to blare … It's kinda nice. Relaxing. Not harsh enough to be a guitar, but similar.

I hug my knees to my chest as I listen and pull my phone out to read the message again. Fucking Marshall.

If I thought he had even the slightest clue how much impact that dumb message would have on me, I'd be pissed. But it's hard to mesh the big, nervous guy I've met with someone who would go out of their way to find my number and text me.

I don't get it.

And even though I want to hold on to my annoyance and let it simmer into a flame, it's impossible to do while I'm out here. Surrounded by nature, feeling small, being lulled by that soothing music. My relaxed state has to be the only reason I text back.

Felix: *Thanks for checking up on me, but I can take care of myself*

It's not a lie, but the response doesn't make me feel any better. At least it's a solid *back off* that even he should pick up on.

I sit here, stewing over it for a while longer. I'm so zoned out that I jump when another message comes through, and even though I definitely, completely, do not want it to be Marshall, I can't help the disappointment when I see it's Brady, telling me where he is.

I send him back the thumbs-up and try not to sulk about him enjoying his night while I'm wallowing—needlessly—over mine.

This isn't the Felix I'm used to.

The music has stopped, so I unfold my legs and head inside to change and climb into bed. It's just as I'm drifting off that my phone lights up my room, and my eyes snap open, worried Brady needs me. But it's not him this time.

Marshall: *Just because you can, doesn't mean you have to. Sweet dreams*

I stare at the words, hating that with so few, he can send my mind racing again. A spiral of overanalyzing, a pang of yearning for someone, and the knowledge that all I have is scraps. Before I can stop myself, I delete the messages and his number from my phone since I know I can't be trusted not to write back with them there tempting me.

There's no possible way to have sweet dreams after that.

5

Marshall

"I SWEAR, THE GUY MY MATE DESCRIBED IS PERFECT FOR YOU."

I groan at Bowser's words. The last time he set me up with someone *perfect* for me, I'd ended up with an uncomfortable living situation. Hence my studying at a picnic table in the court-yard rather than the large study room that's been set up in the house.

Bowser leans back against the blue-tiled fountain that's never on and turns his face toward the sun. "I can tell him no."

I chew on my lip as I look down at the paper I'm scribbling notes on. The whole going on some dates thing was mostly his idea, but it intrigued me. Am I really going to put a stop to it after one shitty experience? "Fine," I relent. "Set it up."

"Yes." He punches the air, and I try not to smile and encourage him.

"Should I be concerned you're *this* invested in my love life?"

"You should be flattered I love you this much."

"Noted."

"I take it you and Fe are still a no-go zone."

"Nothing's changed since you last asked." Even if I'd hoped it would have. If I could go back to the other night, there's no way I would have sent that text. I'd had a hunch it was overstepping, and he obviously didn't appreciate it, but all night, I kept thinking that if something happened and I *didn't* reach out that I'd be the biggest asshole in history.

Even though that's not true.

I … damn. It's so hard to stop thinking about him. This date is probably coming at the perfect time.

"Where do you want to meet him?" Bowser asks.

I guess suggesting the dining hall is a no go, and I've learned my lesson about meeting anyone at work. "Umm … the Food Café?"

"Are you asking or telling me?"

I laugh. "Telling, asshole. I'll meet him there."

"Tomorrow night?"

"Better make it Friday. I have a study group tomorrow."

He makes an affirmative noise and sends the text.

"So what about this guy is perfect?" I ask.

"Cute, kinda sassy, apparently. Huge flirt."

All things that had me agreeing to go on the date with Felix. Maybe I need to adjust my type. "What if I fuck this date up as well?"

"Just be your usual sweet self and you won't have any issues."

"Pretty sure that's the exact advice you gave me last time."

"And you bombed out last time." He shrugs. "So this time, you'll be fine."

"And you really don't know this guy's name?" I check.

Bowser shakes his head, already looking distracted. "Nah, my mate mentioned he had a friend who wanted to start dating and asked if I knew any queer dudes who'd be interested."

"And of course you immediately thought of me: queer and desperate."

"Should I be thinking of you some other way?" he asks, sounding genuine.

I flip him off and pack up my shit. "I need to head down the street to pick up groceries."

"Like the milk you polished off?"

I smile sheepishly. "I keep buying my own, but it gets used as well."

"I told you, milk is shared. Just make sure if you drink it, you stock it. That shit isn't hard, man."

Says *him*. I'm not used to living with people, and I hate being the one to finish off anything on the shared shelves in the fridge or cupboard. I panic and always try to leave something for my roommates, in case any of them desperately needs milk or bread or whatever. Thanks to my older brothers, I know how frustrating it is to not have something be where you were expecting it. "So, Friday night?" I ask, steering him back to the better conversation.

"Yep, just texted back. Meet at eight for dinner."

"Can do." I hand over my bag. "Take this inside for me? I'll be back in half an hour."

"Too easy, man. Don't forget the milk."

I wave him off as I leave, trying not to focus on yet another date that I'm probably going to mess up. All I have to do is make sure the pressure doesn't get to me this time. My date is just another guy. Just like me.

There's nothing at all for me to worry about.

THERE'S SOMETHING TO WORRY ABOUT.

The second I glimpse Felix walking into the Food Café, I all but duck behind my menu. I curse my luck that he's here when

I'm about to have another date because I can't think of anything more awkward. I mean, yeah, I saw *him* on a date, but unlike me, he looked hot as fuck and was clearly holding his own.

I've at least dressed nicely tonight, but that's about as much credit as I'm willing to give myself. Despite the air-conditioning, a prickling heat is climbing over my skin at seeing him, and I try to focus on breathing and calming down before I sweat through my shirt.

I count backward from three, then risk a glance over the top of the menu. Felix is a table away, his back turned to me, so I have a perfect view of those gorgeous curls. A quick flash of them crushed between my fingers flickers through my mind, and I shove it away.

How do I play this?

He's close enough I could reach over and tap his shoulder, so he'd definitely notice if I got up and tried to move. I'm stuck. And it's already five past, so it's way too late to text Bowser, to text his friend, to text my date that I'm leaving. I should have insisted they give me his number instead of relying on the vague assurance that it would be fine.

I nudge my glasses higher up my nose and lift the menu again.

Okay, two choices. Leave, or have my date and ignore Felix is even here.

Well, three choices, I guess, since I could acknowledge his existence and maybe even try for a friendly conversation.

Right … I internally eye roll. He doesn't say a thing to me at home, so he'd definitely want to make small talk in public. Where the hell did I go so wrong with him?

Slowly, I lower the menu and try to act normal. He's clearly not going anywhere, and I have as much of a right to be here as he does. With a really deep breath, I lean toward him.

"Hey, Felix."

He jumps and whirls around, gorgeous smile on his face—until he sees me. "Oh. I thought you were someone else."

"Sorry to disappoint."

"Then why do you do it so often?"

I chuckle, even though I know he meant to offend me. The thing about Felix is he's about as dangerous as a kitten, and when he tries to hit me where it hurts, I can't help finding it kinda cute. "Think that's why my date isn't here yet?"

Surprise flashes over his face. "What do you mean?"

"Maybe they saw me and were disappointed."

This cute little frown pulls at his face as he looks me over. "I wouldn't be surprised."

And for something that's supposed to be an insult, it's half-hearted at best. Especially since he hasn't stopped checking me out. I swing around to face him and rest my arm across the backrest. "Okay, then what about this"—I wave a hand over myself—"would you change to not be disappointing?"

"We are so not playing that game."

"Why? You've never been worried about offending me before."

He cocks his head in surprise, and then, as though making a split-second decision, he turns his chair to face me too. Our knees have an inch of space between them, and for some reason, I'm overly aware of the distance. "Fine. You shouldn't have worn black because you're basically screaming that you either want to cover sweat patches or are anxious about your body."

He's right about the sweat patches but not the rest. I might not be some jacked gym bro, but I'm happy with who I am. "Gotta keep them guessing about that six-pack," I say dryly, patting my soft stomach.

Felix snorts. "Six-packs are overrated."

"You have one," I point out. He's not overly muscled, more

thin and lean than anything, but I definitely noticed his abs when he was wearing that crop top last weekend.

"Barely, and only because it's everyone else's type, but it's not mine."

"You like big guys, right? You don't want them ripped?" The guy he was with last weekend looked muscly.

"No."

"Then you prefer …"

His eyes drop, slowly running over me, before he jerks them away. Interesting. If I didn't know better, I'd think maybe I'm exactly Felix's type. The way he kissed me supports that theory.

Before he can get up and leave—or go back to ignoring me—I ask, "So what color should I have worn, then?"

"Royal blue." There's no hesitation in his answer.

"I don't think I own anything that color."

"Yes, you do. That button-up with the subtle pineapple pri—" He cuts off, and I lift my eyebrows. That got specific.

"Pineapple shirt for my next date. Got it."

He reluctantly meets my eyes.

"Anything else?" I ask. "To make sure my date shows up."

"Yes, don't slick your hair back like that. You remind me of my dad."

I bark a loud laugh that sounds closer to my brother's usual laugh than mine. "I look like a dad, got it."

"And …"

"Yeah?" Might as well get it all out there.

"Well … maybe *don't* shave. Possibly. Just my opinion."

I reach up and run my hand over my smooth jaw. It's not something I normally do, but it grows fast and looked too long for meeting someone for the first time. "I didn't want to look like a mountain man."

His exhale is short and shaky. "Some of us like mountain men."

"So that's your type?"

Felix fidgets with the wood-and-leather bracelets at his wrist. "My type is cute and available," he says, and then his eyes narrow in a stare. "*And* interested. I don't need your pity."

"Not trying to give it to you."

We're quiet for a moment, and I'm anxiously straining to try and find something else for us to talk about. I know if it ends now, that's probably it—at least until I get the courage up to start a conversation again. Felix is intimidating, because he's so gorgeous, or outspoken, or put together—I don't know. All I know is that when he's around, my tongue feels twenty pounds heavier.

"What are you doing here?" I ask.

His attention darts to the time on his phone. "I *was* supposed to have a date, but it looks like I've been stood up as well."

I smirk. "Worried they saw *you* and were disappointed?"

"Please." He crosses his arms. "I'm everyone's type. Well, except *yours*, apparently."

Damn, he's really hung up on that. I'm not sure *why* me not wanting to sleep with him pissed him off so badly, but I really don't want that being a constant wedge between us. "Who said you weren't my type?"

"You didn't need to say it. I basically offered myself up as a buffet for you, and you weren't interested."

"Did it occur to you that maybe I don't like all-you-can-eat?"

His mouth drops. "*Everyone* likes all-you-can-eat."

And there's the problem, right there. I'm a guy, so I must want sex. Always. Because if I don't, there's something wrong with me. I tap the menu I've left on the table, debating how much to tell him. My sexuality is my own business, and from the little I know about Felix, he's wrapped himself into a sex-loving-twink package that's directly tied to his own self-worth. Society has a lot to answer for.

But maybe if I can show him that I think he's worth more than sex, the sting of me turning him down might not hurt as much. That's an easier option than going into what being demi means for me and avoiding the standard suggestions of maybe I haven't met the right person. Given how Felix views sex, I can't be sure that won't be the first thing out of his mouth.

So I start with an apology.

"I'm sorry that I hurt your feelings."

Apparently, it's the wrong thing to say because Felix scowls. "I'm pissed that you gave me blue balls. Don't think it's anything more than that."

I hold up my hands. "My mistake."

"Good." But through his hostility, a crack of vulnerability sneaks out. "Just so we're clear."

"We're clear."

He looks suddenly wrong-footed, like he can't work out what to say next. I watch him struggle, loving the shifts in his expressive face.

"I need to call my date," he says suddenly. "You should probably do the same."

"Didn't get his number."

"You came on a date without the person's number?" He sounds scandalized.

"It's a blind date. We knew where we were meeting, and since he obviously chose not to show up, I think it's probably a good thing I don't have his name or contact details."

Felix blinks like that never occurred to him, then shakes it off and lifts his phone to his ear.

Whatever. All I know is that if Felix's date is still coming, I'm getting out of here before I can see them together. The last thing I need is another image of Felix and a date that I can torture myself with.

If I'd been more confident when we met, more myself, would it have turned out differently?

I'll never know. All I can do now is deflect the attitude he gives me and show him I'm not the nervous, sweaty mess he thinks I am.

My phone rings, so I scoop it up and answer automatically. "Hello?"

There's silence on the line before, "M-Marshall?"

Ohhh no. I know that voice. Turning back to him, I find Felix already staring at me. My gut swoops. "Ah, hey."

"Motherfucker." He hangs up. "Did you know?"

"Did *you*? You're the one who got your date's details."

"Only his number." Felix's face drops. "Right. Well. That's two failed dates. Let's not do it again."

He jumps up, and I go to catch his wrist but think better of it.

"You don't have to go," I say.

"Well, we're not going to *actually* have a date, so there's no other reason to stay."

"We could have dinner," I point out. "Not a date, just … dinner."

The defensive mask he keeps in place slips, and his tone is soft with confusion. "Umm …"

"Come on." I try for a confident smile. "We're roommates."

He takes a step back. "No, I … no. Sorry. I'm … no." Then he turns on his heel and leaves as fast as he can without running.

Well, that went well.

I huff and get up, figuring I might as well go home and eat than dump money on this stuff. That's the last blind date I'm going on. Out of the entire school, Bowser somehow managed to set us up *twice*?

Me: *Did you know?*

Bowser: *Did I know what?*

Me: *That my date tonight was Felix*

Bowser: *WOT? Nah, I swear I had no idea*

I don't push because Bowser wouldn't lie about something like that. He's too direct and honest.

Bowser: *What are the fucking chances?*

Me: *Yeah, pretty damn slim*

Yet it happened anyway, and I swear for a second there, we were actually getting along. Sure, he was having fun at my expense, but I've never been someone who takes myself too seriously, so why not? I sorta liked seeing him enjoy himself.

I hold my breath when I get home and walk inside, preparing myself for another gut punch at seeing him, but he's either not here or already in his room.

Which isn't disappointing. It's not like I *wanted* another date with him. Or to see him again.

We're too different.

At this point, my only aim should be getting along with him well enough that it doesn't affect everyone else in the house. I need them to want me to stay on next year—going back to the dorms isn't an option.

6

Felix

I OPEN MY BEDROOM WINDOW THAT FACES THE ROOFTOP GARDEN outside and prop my chin on my hand, watching Darian outside as he moves through his yoga poses. The smell of coffee rises from my cup as I admire the view of his round ass, pointed skyward.

It's been our morning ritual for a year now. He gets fit and healthy, and I get a healthy eyeful.

He finishes up a few minutes later, and after drowning himself in half a bottle of water, he ambles over for the coffee I've made him.

"Thanks, Fe." He sighs as he drops onto the bench I was sitting on the other night.

I smile and take a sip from my own cup, loving being up early enough to see the sun rise.

"Got any tests today?" he asks.

"No, what about you?"

"Yeah, O'Dally loves to spring them on us."

"You can't tell me that guy doesn't moonlight as a sadist."

Darian laughs. "So don't want to think about that."

"Why not? I bet he's hot under that poorly fitting blazer."

His face contorts with a cringe, and we fall silent again. Other than our early mornings before class, I don't see Darian much. He usually trains after school and then either holes up in the library or heads to work at the hardware store. But at least I do see him occasionally, unlike Jason, who I only know still lives here because his rent is always on time.

And thank god, because if Jason moves out, it means *another* new roommate, and I'm still reeling from the last one. And by *reeling*, I mean unable to stop thinking about him.

"You met Marshall yet?" I ask.

"Yeah, the other day. He's quiet, seems like a good fit."

I hum but don't reply. Objectively, I see his point.

"What's wrong? You don't like him?"

Well, he clearly hasn't heard what happened—yet. With Bowser in the know, it won't take long to get around, and I really can't be bothered going into it now. "I think it's more what he thinks about me."

"*He* doesn't like you?"

"He ..." I shift, unsure how to put it. "He doesn't ... *not* not like me."

"If you talk in riddles like that, I'm not surprised."

"We had a date, and he turned me down."

"Yikes."

"Yeah."

"Right." Darian runs a hand through his slightly damp hair. "And ... you can't just be friends? He doesn't want that?"

"I ..." Have no fucking clue.

Darian laughs. "What? You assumed it was dating or nothing?"

"When you put it like that, it sounds incredibly idiotic."

"I'm not going to point out the obvious here."

"Much appreciated."

He gives me that indulgent look a lot of people get around me. "You're dramatic and I love it, but he's only just met you. Give him time to warm up."

To warm up to me, I'd have to actually give him a chance. "We'll see."

Darian drains the last of his coffee, and I hold out my hand for the empty mug.

"I can take it down myself, you know," he says.

"I know." I shrug. "But you have an early class today."

"And I don't rinse it properly before putting it in the dishwasher," he guesses.

"The better we look after it, the longer it will last!"

"You're such a mother hen." He passes me the cup and stretches. "It's why we love you. Marshall will too—give him time."

Darian leaves me to it, and I set both cups on my desk and grab a tin of cat food instead. Then proceed to make kissy noises that are the cry to cats everywhere.

"Butters!" I call.

While I wait, I try desperately not to remember Marshall's invitation to stay and have dinner with him Friday night. That whole conversation was strange because I'm pretty sure he was humoring me for part of it, and I'm definitely sure I didn't hate it.

He looked ... fucking delicious. Even clean-shaven, he's one of the hottest guys I've ever seen, and I'm only mildly offended that he turned up looking like that for a date with some random when he was a complete mess for the one with me.

A small meow gives warning before a scrawny, cream-colored cat jumps onto my windowsill. She looks like she was supposed to be ginger but got halfway there and ran out of energy to go any further.

"Aww, Butters."

She trills and starts to annihilate the tin of fish, and I smile as I watch her. She used to be a lot thinner than she is now, but ever since moving in, I've been feeding her every few days. She doesn't always show up, but when she does, I know it's going to be a good day.

Once she's finished eating, I let her clean her paws before I scoop her up and snuggle her to my chest. The vibration of her purrs echoes in my rib cage, and I take a minute to enjoy the hugs and comfort.

"You like me, don't you, girl?"

She answers by headbutting my sternum, and I reward her with scratches behind the ears. We hang out for a while longer before she perks up suddenly and leaps from my arms to the window. She gives a low meow, and then she's gone.

I guess it's time to start the day.

I change out of my pajamas and pack my laptop bag. At least dealing with biology means I'll be too busy to agonize over room-mates and playing nice.

But as I'm walking down the stairs from my room, I immediately notice Marshall's door is open and voices are coming from inside. I debate whether to keep walking or take my first steps toward swallowing my pride. The pride thing does *not* seem like a fun option, but I can't hold his rejection against him forever. He's not interested. No big deal. Definitely doesn't hurt to know I'm not good enough. I will be the bigger person. So against all my better life choices, I force myself to stop.

Prepared to flirt up a storm with Bowser, I swing around and lean against the doorframe ... but he's not in there. Marshall's alone, with his back to me and his phone sitting on the desk beside him. A deep voice comes through the speakers.

"I dunno, Marshmallow. If he's being a dick, just be one back. You're easily the most chill guy I know, so fuck him."

Marshall's chuckle is dark. "Shockingly, your advice isn't helpful."

"What do you want from me, bro?"

"You're the one who's good with people. How do I ... you know, not suck?"

My laugh slips out, and Marshall immediately swings around. The shock on his face makes me instantly feel bad for eavesdropping, especially when that shock makes him go red, all the way out to his ears.

The loud voice comes again. *"Maybe you should take a leaf outta my book and actually suck. Me and Brando have never gotten along better than since we started hooking up."*

Marshall hurries to grab his phone, almost dropping it on the floor in the process. His large glasses have slipped halfway down his face when he switches the phone off speaker and puts it to his ear. "I gotta go."

There's a loud response that I can barely make out.

"Seriously, Robbie, I gotta—yeah, it's him." Marshall's eyes fall closed as Robbie answers, and then he hurries to hang up. His entire face is blazing.

"Talking about me, huh?" I ask.

"Just general conversation." Marshall drops his phone in his bag, and my gaze runs down the length of his long, muscled arm.

"Did you tell him what a pain in the ass I am?"

His expression is warm, and I hate that I like it. "I did mention something like that."

"What else?"

Marshall crosses the room to drop against the door opposite me. "That was a private conversation."

"Your door was open."

"I was getting ready to leave."

"Your door is *always* open."

He fixes his glasses, gaze across the room. "I've got nothing to hide."

"Nothing except private conversations ..." I decide to push my luck. "*Marshmallow.*"

He bites his lip, and his stormy blue eyes meet mine. "That was my brother, and only he's allowed to get away with calling me that."

"Is there a reason for it, or is it because it's basically your name?"

Marshall's lips kick up at the side, and he pats his stomach like he did the other night. "Cos I'm chunky and sweet."

"Sweet?" I challenge.

"Not gonna question the chunky thing?"

I can't tell if he's actually asking or trying to be a dick. "Why? It's true. And I don't see being chunky as a bad thing." In fact, I think it's a very, *very* good thing.

Marshall's smile spreads. "Neither do I."

This close, my neck is craned back to look up at him, making me overly aware of the differences in our heights. Which is no good because my dick kinda loves it, and my brain kinda hates that my dick likes it.

This is when I really should step away. He's made it clear he doesn't want my *buffet*, and like Darian said, I need to get over myself and extend an olive branch. But Marshall hasn't broken my gaze, and it's such a huge difference from the squinting, blinking mess he was on our date.

Then it hits me.

The glasses.

He wasn't wearing them then.

This little *ding* goes off in my head that *maaaybe* he wasn't as disinterested as I'd thought that night. Still, backing down and admitting when I'm wrong isn't exactly a strength of mine, and every time I try to grasp something nice to say, I draw a blank.

I swallow, open my mouth, but before I can get a word out, the door across the hall swings open suddenly, and Bowser steps out of his room—then freezes when he catches sight of us.

Marshall straightens, and I jump back a step as though ... well, *nothing* was happening, so I'm not sure why I jolted like I had something to hide.

Bowser nods to us. "What are you blokes doing out here?"

"Talking," Marshall answers.

"Talking?" Bowser swings a finger between the two of us. "You and him?"

"I have a name," I point out.

"Course you do, sweetheart." Bowser pops some gum into his mouth. "Enjoy your ... conversation."

Marshall watches him leave, and I decide to follow while I can. Before ... well, before I'm sucked back into whatever that vortex of lust was.

"I'm off to class," I say.

He crosses his arms, still leaning against the doorframe. "I could walk to campus with you."

I quickly shake my head even though he hasn't made a move yet. I sort of wish he would, but I'll never admit that. The last thing I'll ever do is give him a chance to reject me again. "I'm meeting Brady. But I'll ..." *Nice, Felix, be nice.* "I'll catch you later, Marshmallow."

His eyes light up. "Catch you later ... Fe."

7

Marshall

"WHAT THE HELL IS THIS?"

I glance up at Felix's voice, ready to point out that *this* is the study room, and since I live here, I can use it, but my words falter when I notice what he's holding.

Hanging from one finger is a pair of my underwear.

"Ah ..."

"Oh, that was a rhetorical question, by the way." He pops his hip, and my nerves threaten to rattle me.

With the way we left things this morning, I'd hoped we could start seeing eye to eye, but every time he's around, I get so unsure of myself. How can I expect him to like me if I'm not even *me* with him?

I clear my throat and stand, relieving him of my boxer briefs. "Thanks. I ... where were these?"

"On the floor in front of the washing machine."

Fuck, I must have dropped them when I was transferring

things over to the dryer. "How do I convince you it was a total accident?"

"I'm sure it was, but fishing your manties out of the way so I could do my own washing wasn't how I pictured this day going."

"Manties." I crack a smile, starting to relax. "I thought at one point you *wanted* to see my manties."

"*Not* what I had in mind."

I chuckle as I leave him and throw these bastards in the dryer with the rest of my clothes. The last thing I want is to keep accidentally annoying Felix, but it's not like I can help dropping something without realizing it. I'd been trying to transfer the load in one go; it was an accident.

When I get back to the study room, he's sitting on the opposite side of the table to where my things are. I try not to get excited that he's here, willingly joining me.

"So how did you know they were mine?" I ask, sitting back down and trying not to stare at him.

"You're the only one who wears that brand ... and style."

He's got me there. While I dress tame overall, my underwear has always been where I let my fun side out. "You like the monkeys?" I ask.

"They were frolicking."

"Fun, right?"

He scratches his chin and doesn't answer me. Probably a good thing since I'm trying to write a paper, but it's hard to focus when this buzzing wall of tension has slammed down between us.

"What are you doing over there?" I ask.

"Studying."

One word answer, cool, cool. "Can I know what, or is it a secret?"

"I'm going over my notes on immunology."

"That's ..." I blink, surprised, and hate myself for being surprised.

"What's wrong?" he taunts. "Too smart for me?"

"I don't know you well enough to make those kinds of judgment calls."

"And yet, you did."

He's right, and I guess I deserve to be called out on it. Felix looks like your typical twink—he's on the shorter side, slight, and the curls make him look adorable—but he also acts flirty and like he doesn't take anything seriously. Except maybe sex. If I had to guess, I would have gone with a liberal arts degree, which makes me a stereotyping dick. "Sorry."

His smile is tight, but it's something.

"What's your major?" I ask.

"Biology."

"Heavy," I say.

Felix nods, then shifts to face me. "I'm smart, you know. I understand everything, but freshman year, I kinda went a bit off the rails, and I've been clawing my GPA back ever since."

"That's really admirable."

"Thank you."

Our conversation is stiff, and I'm not sure how to push past that guardedness he has toward me. I want to see the friendly Felix everyone else gets to. "Do you know what you want to be when you grow up?" I ask dryly.

"A vet. It's why I'm busting my balls to ace my classes."

"Nice."

He hesitates, tapping his pen against the table, before he glances over again. "What about you?"

"Nothing as useful as biology." I laugh, though it's not really funny. "I'm getting my degree in history, because I love it, but there are so many possibilities after that. If I can't get a scholarship for my master's, I guess statistically, I'm going to end up with a retail career." Even with the scholarships I'm currently on, my student debt won't be managed by working in a clothing store.

"And if you get your scholarship?"

"Ideally, academic research. Sure, I could minor in accountancy and go into trend analysis, but unless they're dates, numbers bore me."

"What do you like about history?"

"Studying the different civilizations and how people lived long before we were ever thought about. It's sort of comforting to think that someone like me will be looking back on our time and doing the same."

Felix pulls a face. "What you call comforting, I call depressing."

"Why?"

"Because we'll be dead."

"Everyone has to die," I say. "Every civilization has to fall. In a thousand years, the world won't look the same as it does today."

"If it exists at all."

I spread my hands like he's made my point. "And that's why thinking of people in the future looking back is comforting. It means as a race, we survived."

A shiver runs through Felix even though it's not cold. "I need to get back to this."

My gut sinks at the clear dismissal, but despite his words, Felix doesn't look away. "I can't get a read on you," he finally says.

"How so?"

"Well, sometimes you're nervous, and sometimes you're flirty, and now, you're all … philosophical."

I laugh. "I'm not allowed to be all of those things?"

"Well, yeah, but … it makes me feel like I'm meeting a new version of you every time."

I run a hand through my hair, not liking this sudden detour. Growing up, I learned to be a chameleon as a way of fitting in. Around family, I can be loud if I need to be, I can argue and roughhouse and talk smack, but it drains me. I can be laid-back at work and at attention in class, and around Felix, sure, I can be flirty. "The more I get to know a person, the easier it is to be myself."

"So, you're not yourself now?"

"I'm a version of myself, that still counts."

"Does it?" His vibrant blue eyes are narrowed in thought. "How can there be more than one Marshmallow?"

My grin is automatic. My brother gives me so much shit with that name, but I like Felix using it. It's like his way of trying to connect with me, outside of the basic hands-off shit we have going on now. "The same way there's more than one Felix. You're not the same guy now as you were on our date. Neither am I."

He cocks his head. "To be fair, I thought you were completely uninterested."

"I could tell something was up and that you didn't want to be there." Felix didn't hide his sighs or the way he was glancing around for help out of our situation. "It's why I was so fucking nervous. And surprised when you kissed me."

"It was a *really* good kiss."

A bark of a laugh leaves me. "Yeah, we can both agree on that."

His gaze shoots up to mine and holds for a second before it jerks away, and he shifts, tucking a curl behind his ear. "So ... do you have any other dates on the horizon?"

"Nah, I'm done with blind dates."

"How many have you had?"

"Just the two."

He smiles, and for maybe the first time since we've met, it's a real one. "Damn, how badly did I scar you?" he asks.

"I'm dangerously close to joining the priesthood."

"No," he moans, pressing his hands to his face. "I might not

be able to access all that"—he waves a hand in my direction—
"but don't deprive the world. That body was made to be enjoyed."

Oh, shit. My cheeks flare with heat, and Felix's sweet smile
turns evil.

"Did that embarrass you?"

"A little," I choke out.

"Why? I refuse to believe I'm the first guy to tell you that."

"You actually are. I, uh, haven't dated much?"

"Wow." He crosses his arms loosely over the table. "Now I
really do feel bad for ruining the two you've been on."

"Eh." I wave my hand. "They were an experience, at least. I
now know never to follow a guy into an alley unless I'm planning
to sleep with him, and if I'm going on a date, I need to get a name
at the very least."

"My work here is done."

It takes me a beat to realize we're smiling at each other, and
this time, I'm the one to look away. Flutters are going off in my
gut, and I wish I could get them under control because my only
focus when it comes to Felix is getting him to like me. That's it.
He's my roommate now, and things have already been awkward
enough without me sending us right back there. I'm not in a position to offer him sex, and being turned down a second time is
something we wouldn't recover from.

I want to keep the conversation going, to draw him out, but
there's no guarantee I won't screw things up. We've made good
progress; I should be happy with that much.

I have to physically bite my lip to keep quiet though, and
reluctantly, I gather my shit and stuff it into my bag.

Felix glances up in surprise. "You're going?"

"Ah, yeah. I was just finishing up when you got here."

His eyes narrow again, and I know he doesn't believe me, but
he doesn't have to. We need to make sure this little balancing act
we're working on doesn't go toppling over again.

"Catch you later?" I check so he knows I'm not totally blowing him off. Socializing like this is hard for me—the thinking through each step, stressing over each word—that I need to take some time to myself and recalibrate.

He nods, slowly, eyes still trained suspiciously on me.

Fuck, he's cute.

Nope, no more of those unhelpful thoughts.

I flee the room before I can do something dumb like tell him he's pretty and head upstairs. After dumping everything on my bed, I grab my ukulele and climb out my window onto the flat rooftop outside. There's a small square of shade at this time, so I relax back, start to play, and let myself—just for a second—think about Felix and his delicate fingers and strong personality. The way he wraps himself in defensiveness, how his curls catch the light, and that moment, just before, when I caught a glimpse of him totally unguarded.

Those little flutters hit hard, but this time, I don't shove them away.

8

Felix

"How do you know Marshall?" I ask Bowser.

We've laid a blanket out in the courtyard, and I'm sunning my legs since I've caught up on coursework. Not an easy task when I can't get one tall drink of water out of my head.

"Class together freshman year. Why?"

"No reason," I say with exactly zero conviction.

"That's a load of shite."

I snort at his word choice. "Okay, Doctor Who."

"Seriously, Fe, that's the third question you've asked about him." Bowser rolls onto his front and shifts his wide-brimmed hat further back on his head. "You like him?"

"Like a hole in the head."

"Funny, I would have thought your mouth hole was a favorite of yours."

I snigger and flip him off. "He's ... different."

"Different how?"

"Well, normally when I talk to guys, I can tell they're cataloging all the ways to get me naked."

Bowser lifts a hand. "Can honestly say that's never been a thought of mine."

I pump my eyebrows. "You don't think I'm pretty?"

"You're very pretty. Doesn't mean I've ever wanted you to take your clothes off."

"Fair enough." I roll over onto my front as well. "The thing with Marshall is that I never get that feeling with him. I know nearly nothing about him, but then the other day, we had this weirdly deep conversation about dying and the world—"

Bowser laughs. "Yeah, that's him. Skip the small talk and jump straight into the intellectual foreplay."

"Foreplay?"

"You know how some guys are a butt-guy? Or a boob-guy? Marshall's a brains-guy."

I tilt my head. "You know, that could sound really odd taken out of context."

"Just think of him as a zombie lover. *Braaains.*"

"And that's an image I could have done without."

Bowser chuckles, closing his eyes, while I gnaw on my thumbnail, unable to stop my thoughts from swirling back around to Marshall. I blame the fact that I know so little about him. He's an enigma, with a presence so large I feel him everywhere in the house, so it's not my fault that every spare brain cell I have goes toward fixating on him. "I don't understand why he can't close a goddamn cupboard." The words explode from me before I can stop them, and Bowser's eyes pop open again.

He watches me for a second before shrugging. "Haven't the foggiest. You should ask him."

"We're not friends."

"That's your loss, then."

I humph. "Why is it that meddling friends only exist in movies and books?"

"You want me to meddle?"

"I want you to open up. Talk about him. Fill me in so I know who the hell I'm living with. Is it so much to ask that you expose his every darkest secret so I don't actually need to talk to him?" I give Bowser the biggest, pleading eyes I'm able to muster.

"I'm getting mixed messages here." Bowser sits up and crosses his legs. "Do you want to talk about Marshall or not? Because if it's a yes, I'm going to assume it's because you like him."

"No," I say automatically. "*I* don't want to talk about him. I want you to do it."

"There's no way I'm monologuing over my friend."

"Not even for me?"

He laughs and swipes at my head. "Just talk to him. Fuck. He's a really great guy."

"Is that why he leaves his underwear lying around the house?"

"Name one time he's done that."

"The *other day*," I shriek.

Bowser narrows his eyes. "Why do I feel like you're leaving something out?"

"Nope, I had to pick them up myself. His underwear *and* his towels, and yesterday, he left his toothbrush on the sink."

Bowser gasps. "That monster."

"I don't appreciate your tone."

"Mate, you've gotta relax a little. You live in a house with a bunch of messy guys. If his toothbrush is the worst thing—"

"And the cupboard—"

"Sure. Cupboards. Right." He's holding back his amusement. "On a scale of one to ten, how desperately do you want to bang him?"

I sniff and look away. "I'm not answering such a stupid question."

"I left the bread out last week and bugs got into it, but you just laughed and threw it in the trash. So either you're super concerned about oral hygiene, or you're sexually frustrated and I'm the poor bastard who has to hear about it."

"Don't know what you mean."

"When was the last time you got laid?" he shoots back.

And … that's a question. I try to think. It wasn't last weekend, and I didn't when I went to the bar with Brady, or while I was away for Christmas break, *or* the weekend of our disaster date. Has it been … a month? Two? No wonder I'm so tense.

"Back to my original question," Bowser says. "One to ten."

I groan and flop facedown, the blanket muffling my words. "Hard eleven. *Hard.* Eleven. Constantly so hard."

He pats me on the back, and I'm so touch starved I lean into it.

A shadow falls over us, and I jerk my head up to find Marshall standing there.

"Hey." He's in his work polo, and his hair looks damp with sweat—a lock of his dark hair is stuck to the side of his neck.

"Just finished?" Bowser asks.

"Yep." He hesitates before dropping down to sit with us. "I walked in on something I probably shouldn't have."

That catches my attention. "Ooh, like what? Sex stuff?"

His cheeks pinken. "Think so. I got the hell out of there as fast as I could."

I can picture exactly what the big guy would have looked like, all bashful and stuttering. And where I found it annoying on our date, now I maybe, kinda, might think it's cute. "What did you say?"

"Told them I didn't want to know." He pulls at a weed peeking through the stone tile. "I'm an idiot sometimes."

I frown at the way he mutters that. "Maybe they were the idiots for hooking up at work."

"Yeah, but I didn't have to stand outside and wait for them to be done."

"Well, what else were you supposed to do?" I sit up, scowling. "I would have bashed on the door and really ruined the mood, but that's not your style."

"Not really." Marshall shifts, giving me a shy smile.

"Total marshmallow," I say.

"Chunky and sweet."

Bowser clears his throat, and my attention snaps back toward him. "You know, it's been way too long since we've had a proper Liberty Court party," he says.

I screw up my face. "We had one right before Christmas break."

"Yeah, but Marshall wasn't here then. And that was almost two months ago."

"Keenan literally drank too much last Saturday that he threw up in those bushes over there," I say.

Bowser chuckles. "Yeah, I saw the whole thing."

"Then …"

"Party! Marshall, get a night next weekend off work. We're doing this."

"That actually sounds perfect."

"Really?" I ask.

Marshall gives me that quietly confident smile. The one that pings the needy side of me. "I do like to have fun, you know?"

"And when do you manage that between buying cartoonish underwear and learning about Tutankhamun?"

"I have a schedule. Be boring ninety-five percent of the time, but reserve that other five percent for fun."

"You should have made our date fall into that five percent block."

"You're right. Why didn't I think of that?" His lips twitch, and I get all squirmy under his steady gaze.

"I am full of wisdom." My gaze flicks to Bowser and back again. "Some say I'm *extremely* clever."

"All brains," Bowser adds, then presses his lips tightly together.

I flourish my hands toward him. "See?"

"Kinda figured that out for myself."

I refuse to look at him but feel like goddamn sunshine inside. Letting my eyes fall closed, I lie back down again.

"Hey, Marshall," Bowser says. "I've got another date for you."

My entire body stiffens.

"Nope," Marshall says.

"Come on. I swear you'll love this one."

Marshall's laugh is soft. "Like I loved the others?"

"They were shitty timing," Bowser says.

And I kinda hate that. That if Marshall and I had better timing that things might have turned out differently. The idea that he's going to hit it off with another guy just because their date is more convenient for him. Picturing Marshall with a boyfriend doesn't sit right with me. How would he even manage that when he can barely get through a conversation without stuttering.

"Come on, mate," Bowser pushes. "We both know any guy would be lucky to have you. You'd treat your boyfriend like a prince."

I scoff. "Lucky him. I'd rather be treated like a filthy ho, myself."

"Hmm ..." Marshall hums.

Against all better judgment, I peek out at Marshall and find his focus running along my legs.

"Have you ever been treated like a prince?" he asks.

"No. I've never wanted to be."

"How do you know you wouldn't like it, then?"

"Calculated guess."

Marshall drags his teeth over his lip before abruptly looking away. "I'm heading inside. Things to do."

"Date," Bowser says, pointing at him. "I'll text you the details."

"Please don't."

I have no right to feel buoyed by Marshall turning down the offer, but I really fucking am. I jump to my feet. "I'm heading in too. Don't want to get this pretty face burned."

"That would be a damn shame."

I pretend to preen, and when Bowser laughs softly, I subtly flip him off behind my back. I'm a shameless flirt. So sue me. Maybe Marshall doesn't want to sleep with me, but it doesn't mean I can't indulge in a little harmless flirting. What's the worst that can happen?

We walk back into the house, and it's immediately a million degrees cooler than it was outside. At the stairs, I pause, and Marshall turns back to me.

"Not going up?"

I shake my head. "Might grab something to eat first."

He nods, gaze straying away and then back to me again. "You deserve it, you know? To be treated right."

I shift, stunned silent, which is rare for me, so I make a noncommittal noise instead. Then he surprises the shit out of me by reaching out and giving my hair a tug.

I jerk my attention back up to his.

"What are you thinking?" he murmurs.

Well, fuck me, I can't answer that. I can't tell him that when he looks at me like that, my pulse twitches. I can't tell him that I wish our dates had gone better or that I wish I was good enough for him.

Because I'm starting to suspect that the reason everything

unraveled so quickly was because my head was too far up my ass to appreciate how sexy quiet can be.

So instead, I deflect.

With a flirty grin, I reach out and lift the bottom of his shirt. "Just wondering if you're wearing the monkeys today."

I'm expecting him to blush, so when he tugs up the side of his boxer briefs to reveal the dolphin wrapped around the side, I'm caught off guard. My attention is locked on the movement, the sliver of tan skin, a dusting of hair on his lower belly.

I wet my lips and look up at him. "I approve."

"*Wow.*" He draws the word out. "I did something that gained your approval? Quick, write down the date. We need this for prosperity."

"Lucky you're such a diligent record keeper. It's not going to happen again."

He tilts his head back and forth. "We'll see."

"What makes you so confident?"

And he is. Confident. It's there in the way he's holding himself, the way he meets my eyes and refuses to look away.

"I'm starting to figure you out," he says. "And I have plenty more underwear you haven't seen yet."

9

Marshall

WHY AM I SUCH A PUSHOVER?

I look around Shenanigans, grimacing as I meet Brax's eyes again. No matter how much I try to act cool about the whole thing, knowing what he and Tyson were probably doing in the storage room is too much for me to make eye contact again so soon.

Bowser's right—maybe I *am* a prude. Sure, sex isn't something that drives me, but even when I consider being with someone like that, I know I want it to mean something. A random hookup at work is miles from my own experiences.

Maybe one day when I lose my virginity, I'll get it.

But maybe not.

I still can't believe I agreed to this date. The only things that got me out the door were Bowser promising that this was the final one and being given a name so I could social media stalk the guy.

In his favor, he's really fucking cute. Clearly has hobbies if his fishing photos are anything to go by, and he works at a clothing store on weekends. He looks friendly and motivated. Maybe fun.

But unlike the first time I saw Felix and got hit with that instant influx of nerves, this guy is more of an objective beauty. Like how I might look at art or a statue. He didn't give me that *zing*. To be fair, there aren't many people who do.

I've worked out that I have three levels. The majority of people are friends. They're fun and maybe good-looking, but they elicit nothing but companionable feelings from me. The second group—who I can probably count on my fingers—gives me an instant spark. It's like my body telling me there could be something there if I look into it further, but through a series of shitty events, there's only been one time that spark burned into lust-filled attraction. The kind that made my dick hard and my brain stupid.

I would have done anything for her, and she used it and took advantage of it. Since then, I've been wary about giving people my time.

Bonus of being demi, I guess. Cut off any attraction at the roots before it can take hold. Total control. No falling for someone that I really shouldn't be—

Felix plonks down in the booth opposite me.

I stare for a second. "Okay, I know we've been set up twice already, but I definitely got the guy's name this time."

He pouts. "I'm not here for your date."

"You're not?"

"Well, not *totally* for your date." Felix's legs are bouncing under the table.

"What's going on?"

"You can do better than stupid Lyle. He's in my class, and he goes around sleeping with guys and then tells everyone about it and never calls them back." His words are so fast they blur together.

"Isn't that what you do?"

His eyes narrow. "Just because I like to sleep with people doesn't mean I'm a dick about it. He'll fuck you and then tell all his friends everything that was wrong with it and act like he's never seen you before if you ever run into him."

Felix is coming across even more pissy than usual. I'd wonder if maybe Lyle did it to him, but from everything I've heard, Lyle is the opposite of Felix's type.

"He'll be disappointed, then," I say. "Because I have no plans to sleep with him."

"You ... don't?" Felix glances up at me, bottom lip pinned between his teeth.

"No. One-night stands aren't for me."

"Oh."

"Exactly."

He fidgets some more, and this role reversal of him being the nervous one is making me all warm.

"Well, either way, you should cancel on him," Felix says.

I cock my head. "You don't want me to have this date?"

"No."

The corner of my lips struggles against a smile. "Why?"

"Well, just ... you know ..."

"Compelling reasons." I nod.

His frown deepens, and he goes to stand up. Immediately, I go for his wrist but pull up short, remembering how much he hated that.

"Fe ..."

His back tenses under his shirt before he slowly turns back to me. The scowl is gone, but his eyes are trained on the ground. "Well, you've already had two shitty blind dates ... Not like I could let you have a third."

My heart fucking wallops the backs of my ribs. "Didn't know you cared that much."

"I don't. I simply feel partially responsible."

"Partially?"

His awkwardness melts, and he props his ass on the table right beside me before dramatically rolling his eyes. "Fine. It was all me. I'm a total, complete shit. Happy?"

"Reeling, actually. Did you admit you were wrong?"

"Don't get used to it."

"I'm adding this to my list of dates. *The day Felix Andrews swallowed his pride.*"

He gives me a flirty look. "Tastes different from what I usually swallow."

I choke on goddamn air at the picture that creates. Felix, on his knees, licking the cum from my ...

Oh, fuck.

My cock thickens along my thigh, and my face immediately fills with heat.

He blinks innocently down at me, completely unaware of the lust pumping through my bloodstream as I stare up at his angelic face. He's so close I could easily reach out and set my palm on his thigh, but I squeeze both hands firmly in my lap.

"So ..." Felix says, drawing my attention to those plump lips and reminding me of our kiss. It had been nice, passionate, but even that didn't get me hard. I'd been leaning into that little spark between us and trying to build affection where there was none.

My mouth is so dry I hurry to scoop up the glass of water and chug it down. "Ah, so what?"

"Are you going to cancel?"

"He's probably on his way here already."

Felix gives me a pitying look. "It's eight. Your date doesn't start for another half an hour, and I can guarantee it's forty-five minutes to an hour until he shows up."

Even with how confident Felix sounds over that, I waver. I hate letting people down. But then, is it worse for me to cancel or to go through with this date, knowing there's only one person I want to be spending the night with and he's currently sitting right in front of me? "What happens if I cancel?"

"What do you mean?"

"Well, if I cancel, are we both going to head home alone?" My eyes are struggling to stay on his face and not dip to take in all that leg he has on display.

His bright blue eyes widen as it clicks. "We can walk to the pier and get tacos?"

Tacos have never sounded more delicious. Still, canceling on someone goes against everything I've ever learned, and my mom would probably kick my ass if she found out.

Felix nudges my phone toward me. "At least call and see where he is."

He holds my gaze for a moment, and I'm sorely tempted to touch him. His cheek or his chin or his ear ... I dunno. My skin just wants to make contact with his skin.

"You know, a walk and dinner sounds almost date-like."

"No date, don't worry."

Disappointment creeps in and dulls the ache vibrating in my bones. It's not enough to make me tell him no though.

Then Felix drops his voice and gives me the realest side of him I've seen yet. "Seriously. I wouldn't have even come here if he was a good guy. You said I deserve someone who'll treat me right, and, well ... same goes for you."

I've never picked my phone up faster. I don't look at Felix as I call, but I'm so aware of him it takes me a moment to realize Lyle has answered.

No matter what Felix says, there's no hostility at all on his end when I tell him I need to cancel. The twist in my gut is all on me.

But when I hang up and look back at Felix, it's completely worth it.

"So, tacos?" I say, standing. Then, on a whim, I hold out my hand.

He laces his delicate fingers between mine. "One question though: hard or soft?"

"Are we still talking about food?"

Felix laughs, and I follow him out into the cool night, and instead of heading up toward the road, he leads me onto the sand. The beach is louder down here, but it's also darker and more peaceful away from the streetlights.

"Dinner and walks on the beach," I say. "It's getting suspiciously dateish around here."

He drops my hand. "We're roommates. *Maybe* even friends. We're allowed to hang out together."

And yet, I sort of wish it was a date anyway. The pull I have toward Felix isn't a common thing for me, and it's kind of terrifying. He's the type of guy to only want sex, and that's fine, but that makes him completely incompatible with me.

So of course my dumb body would make the dumb choice to want *him*.

Even with all that knowledge, when I glance over, my heart does this stupid little squirm, and I have to acknowledge I'm well and truly fucked.

Where I take this from here is on me though.

I've already had one person completely mess with my feelings, and I don't know Felix well enough yet to trust he won't be the same.

Smart Marshall, the one who's obsessed with history and finding patterns, would yeet my ass as far from Felix as it could get. I'm overly conscious that Felix has a lot of parallels to my high school crush. She liked the attention too.

But she was also manipulative and picked that I was interested in her right away. Instead of letting me down easy, she strung me along. Doing her schoolwork, driving her and her friends places, free entry to the movie theater where I worked part-time.

The final straw was when she wanted tickets for her *and* her date. It upset me so much I'd actually told Robbie everything about her, and that night, he and Banjo snuck into the henhouse and disappeared for a few hours.

Dad was confused why there were no eggs the next morning.

Felix might like attention, but he's his own person who's happy being single and overly picky on dates.

It's just my luck that I find someone I could genuinely see myself starting something with, and once again, they're not interested.

I'm going to be a virgin forever.

And the status itself isn't something I care about, but … I *want* to experience sex. Mind-blowing sex. I want to know what the big deal is, and I want to be close enough to someone to want them that badly.

And right now, I want Felix.

There are no guarantees I'm ever going to be sexually attracted to someone again, and for all my talk about wanting to lose my virginity to someone special, I've never defined *what* special means to me.

I don't have to be dating them. I don't have to even be friends, I guess.

All I need is that explosive attraction, the kind of chemistry that will take me to a high I've only ever reached with my hand before.

Felix has made it clear so many times that he's interested. Would it really be so bad if I took him up on the offer?

Another wave of heat passes over me as I think about our kiss and picture doing it again. My hands in his hair, on his back, grabbing his ass …

This could be a very, very big mistake. If it goes south and shit is awkward, I'll have to move out because I don't want to create an unbearable living situation for everyone in the house. But if it goes well …

Shit, I have to try.

I can find another room. I can't find another Felix.

My hand finds his before I've even made a conscious decision, and when he turns around, confusion pulls at his features. My gut is a riot of nerves as I look down at him, trying to talk myself out of this, trying to remind myself of all the reasons why it's dumb.

But I want to be dumb.

Before he has a chance to ask me what I'm doing, I lean in and kiss him.

10

Felix

MARSHALL'S MOUTH ON MINE BRINGS A SURPRISED SQUEAK TO MY throat that I swallow down again. I'm caught totally off guard with what's happening, but I'm not about to break the kiss and say something stupid because that's what sent our last one spiraling south.

He cups my face, and my lips part, allowing his tongue to press forward. The kiss isn't as slow and patient as our last one; it's messier, needier, and I push up onto my tiptoes to get closer. My hands close over his smooth, broad shoulders, and a moan vibrates from me.

Marshall laughs, a soft chuckle that hits my lips and gets swallowed by my mouth. I'm not letting him stop to think because thinking means this ending, and *fuck*, there's something about the way he kisses that I can't get enough of.

His big hands slide from my jaw to my neck, anchoring me as his fingers tangle in my hair. "Fe …" His mouth leaves mine to trail slow, hard kisses along my jaw, kisses that feel desperate and like he's trying to hold back. I don't want him to hold back though. I want him to consume me.

Because as much as I might pretend Marshall irritates me, in reality, everything about him turns me on.

His panting breaths sound right next to my ear. "You are so pretty."

I know I need to be careful about scaring him off again, but I can't help the words that slip out. "I'm tasty too."

A deep hum leaves him. "I don't doubt it."

"As much as I'm going to kick myself for asking this," I say as his lips make a shivery path down my throat, "what ... what's happening here?"

"I'm kissing you."

"Yeah, but what do you want? Just this or ..."

"You." He pulls back, warm blue eyes meeting mine. "I want you."

Me. Not a blow job or a quick fuck. He wants me, and the way he's looking at me—pupils blown out, lips wet and swollen —makes it impossible to dispute that. I grip his shoulders and jump, legs wrapping around his waist, and thankfully, Marshall stays upright. The strength makes my cock throb, and my head spins a little as all my blood rushes south. Our chests are pressed together, the warmth from that dumb black shirt soaking through my own.

"What's changed?" I asked.

"I know you now."

I have no idea what he means by that, but I don't question it. "How far do you want to go?"

His lips press to the corner of mine. "Don't care. I'll take whatever scraps you'll give me."

"Would you fuck me?" My gut tightens as I wait for his response, hoping I haven't taken it a step too far.

Marshall pulls back, eyes searching mine for a moment before he swallows roughly and nods. "Yeah, I … I think I'd like that."

I smirk. "You'll more than like it. I'm going to be the best you've ever had." I'm determined to be.

He opens his mouth, and I'm worried he's going to talk himself out of it, so I lean in. Our mouths meet, and it only takes a brief moment for him to relax and kiss me back. The longer we kiss, the more he gets into it. Tiny gasps, bites to my bottom lip, and arms wrapping tighter around me.

"There's no one here," I grunt between kisses.

"What?"

"On the beach. There's no one around. We can do it here."

"Won't you get sand in your crack?"

My grin is wide as I kiss him again. "There are plenty of ways around that."

"I …"

I laugh and wriggle out of his arms, jogging over to where a mound of sand blocks us from the road. We're far enough away from Shenanigans that no one there will see us, and from this point, we'll notice anyone before they catch sight of us.

"I'm not sure …"

"About fucking me or doing it here?"

"Definitely want to fuck you, but what if we're caught?"

I simmer down my horniness enough to check in with him. "We can go back home if you want? You can come up to my room …"

His tongue swipes his lips as he looks me over, and then he does something that challenges my resolve. He reaches a big hand down and squeezes his cock. And if that outline is anything to go by, I'm going to feel him for days. "I … I don't know …"

"Well, you better decide fast because if you keep touching yourself, I'm going to come in my pants."

He lets out a quiet laugh, glances around, and then, "Fuck it. How are we doing this?"

"Take off your shirt, and lay it down." I pull out my wallet and grab a packet of lube and a condom. I toss the condom to him, which he catches easily. "Put that on. I'll sort myself out."

I undo my shorts and push them and my briefs under my ass as I tear open the foil with my teeth. My eyes greedily drink in every inch of Marshall's body as it's revealed to me, and that sexy image has my cock raging while I prep myself.

His shirt meets the sand, and then he undoes the front of his jeans, shoving down the tiger-stripe boxer briefs, and *hello*.

My suspicions were correct.

He's long and thick and simply mouthwatering. *Holy shit*. My fingers work harder, and when he rolls the condom on and glances up at me, his hesitance is completely gone. His stare drops to my cock, and he gives himself a long, slow stroke.

"You're going to split me in half," I whisper in awe.

His forehead creases. "Is … I mean … can we still …"

"Can and will. I can't wait for you to be inside me." I don't need much prep since I have bottoming down to an art form. As soon as I'm ready, I kick off my shorts and drop onto his shirt on my hands and knees, tilting my ass up toward him.

The groan he lets out is so sexy my cock twitches.

"Fuck," he says, taking a step or two closer, then sinking onto his knees behind me. "Holy fuck."

"Yeah, less admiring, more pounding. Let's go."

"Felix, I—"

I cut off whatever he's about to say with a laugh. "I don't need sonnets or fancy words. It's okay for you to just use me."

I've been here and done this more times than I can count. But where I'm expecting a perfunctory hand on my hip while he guides himself inside, what I get instead catches me off guard.

A kiss. Right behind my ear. Soft hands sliding up under my shirt. A stuttered exhale.

"You might not need them, but I want to give them to you anyway. You're beautiful, Fe. And there are no words for how much I want you."

11

Marshall

I'm about to lose my virginity on a beach.

With a guy I've only known a few weeks.

And sure, said guy doesn't think very highly of himself, but I do. Plus, beach quickie or not, I'm determined to make this special. I've waited literally my whole life for this.

My brothers have told me one too many stories about their sexual exploits, and I wouldn't be surprised if many a beach was a hookup location, but this is so much more than a future anecdote. I lean in and kiss behind Felix's ear again, then linger. I love the smell of his shampoo, the feel of his soft skin, his smaller body slotted against my own.

My hands run all the way up his sides before traveling down again to settle on his hips. My cock is *raging*, wanting to get inside him already, and every second I spend touching him is a second closer to the premature end we're rocketing toward.

Because while this might be special to me, I have no doubts

it's going to be memorable for Felix as well. Just maybe not in the way I want it to be.

"Come on," he says in that flirty voice of his while he wriggles back, ass nudging my cock. It catches me off guard, and I almost nut there and then, but I'm goddamn determined to at least be inside him when that happens.

I quickly close my hands around his waist to hold him still. "No cheating."

"I need you."

"Pout all you like. I'm enjoying myself." And I am. Completely in the moment, no idea if anyone else is around, because as far as I'm concerned, there's only me and Felix in this whole damn world.

"Please, Marshmallow." The way he purrs the name makes me groan and commit to telling Robbie he can never use it again.

"Begging, huh?"

"You're packing an anaconda. I want that thing inside me."

I chuckle as my lips drag over his neck. This happiness is building in my gut, drawing out each second between us. I want this to last. I want to fuck him so good he'll never think of another guy again.

But for a first time, that's probably too ambitious, so I'll settle for any adjective north of *decent*.

A shaky exhale leaves me and skirts over his skin as I realize I can't put this off any longer. Felix is squirming, and my cock is leaking into the condom, madly wanting some action. The only thing holding me back is my head. My *actual* head. The one giving this moment way more weight than is called for.

Nerves skitter down my spine as I reach for my cock and press it against his hole. "T-this okay?"

He hums. "It'd be better if you were inside me."

Inside. Right. *Here I go.*

I hold myself steady and press forward, a strangled, aborted noise catching in my throat as his ass yields to my cock. *Holy shit*. This is everything I'd hoped it would be and more. Warm, tight, like a goddamn hug for my dick, and the way his ass is *pulling* me in is driving me crazy.

"This okay?" I ask, embarrassed by how breathless I sound.

Felix's back is arched, head dropped low, and when he answers, he sounds as wrecked as I do. "Don't stop now."

I want to tell him *never*, but with the pressure building in my balls, I'm not sure I can go around making those kinds of promises. My hips press against his ass, and the feeling is so indescribable, I literally have no words. I lean forward again, wrapping one arm around his waist as my lips find his neck again. If I move now, it'll be all over, and even though my cock is in heaven right now, holding Felix like this fills my chest with warmth.

He shifts, and pleasure shoots from my cock to my spine and back again. "You're more affectionate than I thought you'd be," he says.

"Is that a bad thing?"

"No, just … I dunno."

I run my tongue along the hinge of his jaw. "Want me to stop?"

Felix doesn't answer right away. "I … no, I …" He clears his throat and wriggles his ass again. "I wasn't lying before. I'm really fine with you giving me a pounding. You don't need … all this …"

"If it's making you uncomfortable—"

"It's not—"

"Then good. Because you taste incredible, and if it's all the same to you, the pounding can wait." I run my free hand over his abs, loving the feel of the hard muscle under my fingers, and as he twitches, the angle of his ass changes, sucking me in deeper.

My eyes fall closed, and I press my forehead to his curls.

"You're gonna kill me." The words slip out before I can stop them.

"Why?"

Because once isn't going to be enough. "We should have gone home. To your bed. Then I could have touched you all night."

"Fuck."

"I want to kiss you all over, drive you crazy, then fuck your brains out." Every word is true, and while I might not manage it this time, maybe ... maybe if he gives me a second go. I have no idea how he feels about repeats, but even though we've barely started, I can safely say I want more of this.

Felix gives a raspy moan. "You're confident when you're horny."

Finally feeling like I can control myself, I pull out a little and press back in. "Do you like it?"

"I love it. There's nothing hotter than a guy who takes control."

Oh, really? "That what you like in a guy?"

"Big. Sexy. Confident." He does this weird swirl thing with his hips that's way too hot. "A cock that could tear me in half. You're my ultimate fantasy."

It lights me up to hear that, and if confident is what Felix wants, it's what he's going to get. I slide the arm I have around his waist up higher, wrapping it over his chest, and when I shift upright, I pull him up so his back is flush with my front.

Maybe I haven't done this before, and maybe I'm inexperienced, but so far, all I've done is what feels good, and it's working out okay.

"Wish you'd taken this shirt off," I murmur against his ear. "It's keeping too much of you hidden."

"Oh, yeah?"

An appreciative moan comes from me, and my gaze drops to where I can make out his cock standing hard and at attention.

Saliva immediately floods my mouth, and I swallow it down, my hips giving an unconscious thrust.

Felix's head drops back on my shoulder, exposing his throat as an invitation. I lick and suck the skin, somehow drowning in him and needing more all at once.

"Now who's killing who?" he whines. "Please ..."

The last thing I want is for him to have to beg. I want to make him feel incredible. To make him crave sex with me again because it's how I'm going to feel about him. My hand on his chest spreads wide, fingers skimming his collarbone as my other dips south. Over his hip. Across the bottom of his abs.

My heart is thumping so hard I can hear it.

Come on, Marshall, just an inch lower. I swallow back my nerves and wrap my hand around his cock.

We both moan at the same time. Goddamn, he feels so good in my palm. Different to me, but the same. Hot and full, silky skin, but thinner, curved at a different angle. My cock pulses, letting me know that we need to get on with this, or the whole situation will be out of my hands.

I roll my hips, long and deep, keeping Felix flush against me. His soft *oh yes* spurs me on. It's a challenge to stroke him and thrust at the same time, but it doesn't take long for Felix to start pushing back against me, and even though I love the feel of him close, I wish I could see the way his ass is taking me over and over.

My brain is fuzzing, my whole body drawing tighter. Sparks are shooting off in my balls, building the intensity higher and higher. Felix's gasps and curses are right by my ear, and I turn my face to bury in his curls.

Everything about this moment feels perfect, precious, like it could disintegrate in a second. I'm trying to last not only because it feels incredible but because I don't want this to end. I don't want to have to let him go. I don't want to slip from his body or not have him pressed against me. I want him closer, I want to crawl in-fucking-side him, and the need is so deep my skin feels tight, hot, that frantic desperation vibrating anxiously through me.

God, I want this to last.

But too soon, that familiar ache pools in my balls. It's begging me to let go, to fall over the edge and experience the most mind-blowing orgasm of my life, but I scramble to hold on.

I jerk Felix off faster, pounding into him so hard we'd both go toppling over if my knees hadn't made divots in the sand.

"Please come," I grunt. "Please. Now."

"I'm close," he says.

"I promise I'm closer, so you might want to hurry up, sweetheart."

He shudders against me, impaling himself on my cock so hard I almost let go, but then a second later, his ass clamps around me as his whole body stiffens. He comes, dick pulsing with his release.

I try to stroke him through it, to give him everything he needs, but fucking him through the kind of grip he has on my cock is nearly impossible. Shock waves ripple along my spine, drawing out a full-body shudder. It's too much. Too soon. I don't want this to end.

My hips snap forward one last time, and I bury my cock inside him as deep as I can before letting go. I come so hard my brain blacks out.

When the high ebbs, I'm still holding Felix against me. His chest is rising and falling as he catches his breath, and the sweat prickling my skin has turned cold in the mild night air.

I'm clueless on the post-sex etiquette, but my brain is in full-on jelly mode, and I can't stop kissing him. He does taste good. Addictive. I'm still kicking myself over doing this here because if we were back in his bed, I'd be able to do it all night.

"You okay?" I finally ask, lips pressed against the hinge of his jaw.

"Very, very okay." He pulls forward off my cock with a hiss, then hurries to tug up his pants. "That was ... ah, thanks."

I chuckle, wondering where this awkwardness has come from.

Instead of the obvious distance he's trying to put between us, I snap off the condom and tie it up, then drop it on the sand, pull up my pants, and fall back onto my shirt.

Felix eyes me as I hold out my hand to him. "What are you doing?"

"Night's not over yet," I point out. I sit up to close my hand around his and give a little tug.

He hesitates, glancing back up at the road and then down to me again. Slowly, he lowers to his knees.

Not close enough.

I haul him against me, falling back in the sand so his body blankets mine.

"Hey, gorgeous."

His lips twitch. "Ah, hey."

"Will you kiss me?"

Felix's bright blue eyes drop to my lips, linger, then flick back up to meet my stare.

I'm about to tell him he doesn't have to when he moves. He throws his arms over my shoulders, body hitting mine, as he claims my mouth in a hungry, searing kiss.

12

Felix

I WAKE UP FEELING A LITTLE TENDER AND A LOT CONTENT. LAST night was ... well, unexpected is the first word that comes to mind, along with a lot of other sappy, dreamy words that follow it. Not only did Marshall give me the dicking out I'd been craving, but we'd lain on that beach, sand everywhere, making out like we were in junior high.

One thing is for certain: I've never had sex like that before.

My loose-morals year aside, the guys I hook up with are always cool and hot but are there for one reason. Normally, that's the same for me. Sex is about scratching an itch. It's not rocket science—anyone can do it.

Only, Marshall's scratched that itch I had for him, and instead of soothing the area, it's spread. I'm itching for him *everywhere*.

Those big, gentle hands roaming over my body. That fucking *mouth* that never stops kissing and licking and tasting. I can only imagine the damage it would do to my cock.

A shiver slips deliciously over me as I climb out of bed. I feed Butters and spend a few minutes snuggling with her before she takes off to wherever she's been going lately, and then I'm faced with the ginormous task of picking out an outfit.

Something sexy, obviously, because I want Marshall to notice me, but also, if this was a onetime thing—and the beard burn covering my face is begging me to believe otherwise—then I don't want to look like I'm trying too hard.

I settle on a tie-dye tank top with gaping arm holes that show off my sides and a pair of cutoff denim shorts. Then I pull my curls up into a half bun and all but bounce from the room.

We only got back a few hours ago, so my excitement doesn't make sense when it's entirely possible that Marshall's still in bed, but I'm vibrating with my need to see him. Hell, maybe I'll climb into bed beside him? But when I reach his door and find it open and the room empty, I'm grateful I don't need to do something so desperate.

The whole way downstairs, I try to remind myself that I'm the king of playing-it-cool, no-strings-attached sex. If that's what Marshall wants, it's what he'll get … but then I picture those strong arms wrapped around me, and head kisses, and his low rumble of *sweetheart*, and my chest pinches, just a bit.

I really do want a boyfriend. Someone who's there for me, all mine. Someone who thinks I'm pretty and gives me his time without me needing to beg for it. Someone who wants me as much as I want him.

Which is why, when I get downstairs and follow the sound of conversation, I push all that daydreaming aside to give Marshall a chance to make the first move. If he's not interested, I'll move on, simple as that.

I'm attacked with nerves as I approach, and Bowser's voice reaches into the hall.

"Finally! Are you serious?"

Marshall's chuckle follows. "Would you keep it down, idiot?"

"Dude, you finally, *finally* lost your virginity. I wanna shout that shit from the rooftops."

His ... *what?*

The floaty, happy feelings that have crowded me since last night immediately turn on edge.

"Stop being a dick," Marshall says. "Virginity is all a construct anyway."

"Construct or not, you got your dick wet. It's only taken me bugging you all through college for that to happen." Bowser sounds like he's bouncing off the walls.

"Well, now you don't have to worry about me hitting you up to do the job," Marshall answers, tone dry.

"As much as I love you, that was never happening. Now, details. I need them."

"Nope."

Bowser snorts. "I know you think you're being a gentleman or whatever, but that's not the case. Now, spill. Guy? Girl? Hand jobs? Blow jobs? Or did you go for straight up fucking?"

"Guy." Marshall laughs. "And we fucked, but that's all you're finding out."

"Not even a name?"

My gut clenches at Bowser's question, and I silently beg that Marshall doesn't say mine. A few minutes ago, I would have claimed last night myself, but now ... being someone's first comes with too much expectation. I don't know that I'm ready for that.

"No way," Marshall says.

"Is it because you don't know it?" Bowser teases. "You took my advice, didn't you? Found yourself someone easy. Got it over and done with." My heart sinks as the words register. "Good move because now you won't be so anxious next time when you're with someone you actually want to impress."

When no answer immediately comes, my jaw drops, and I spin on my heel.

What.

The.

Fuck.

Steam could be shooting from my ears and I wouldn't be surprised. The ache in my ass that had been so comforting a few minutes ago is like a slap in the face with every step.

Someone *easy*?

I can't deny I am, but how dare *he* look at me that way? Is that where his sudden change of mind came from? He just wanted to stick his dick in anyone to get it out of the way? Now he's ready for a *real* relationship? A *real* partner who's worth his time?

I'm powerless against the tears pushing at my eyes and text Brady that he better be home because I'm on my way over.

As soon as I storm inside the place he shares with his brother, I can't hold my venting back anymore.

I'm ranting before I've even reached the kitchen, where Brady and Peyton are both hanging out.

"Honestly, how *dare* he? That scummy scumbag thinking he can fuck me like he means it when all I am is a hole for him to stick it in. Like, *really*. Who the hell is a virgin these days? *Who*? And why wouldn't you disclose that kind of information so the person you're about to totally, *epically* screw over knows what they're getting themselves into? Am I a joke? A big, stupid joke for all the queer guys on campus to play with and toss aside?" I pause, partway through jabbing my finger at the counter for a third time, and glance over at my best friend. He's got his arms crossed, leaning against the island across from where his brother, Peyton, is sitting. They both look completely confused.

The fight drains out of me, and I drape myself over the island, utterly dejected. "I want a refund on today."

"What are you doing?" Brady asks.

"I'm wallowing in my disappointment."

"On the counter that we eat off of."

"Well, I didn't think Peyton would appreciate it if I used his lap."

"You know," Brady says, and I perk up, thinking something useful might be about to come out of his mouth. I should have known better. "It took you a whole two minutes to hit on my brother. That's never happened before. Should I be worried?"

"Yes, very. I demand you defend my honor." Then I turn a flirty look on Peyton. "You'd never treat me wrong, would you, handsome?"

He gives me his heartbreaking football-star smile. "If I volunteer to be the one to defend your honor, can I get out of answering that question?"

"Why do you insist on playing coy when we're going to get married one day?"

He holds up both hands. "Sorry, Fe. You know I tried the guy thing and it wasn't for me."

I bat my lashes, glad for the temporary distraction. "You know, if you ever want to double-check, *just* to be sure, I'm here for you, boo."

"Thanks for reminding me. I might have forgotten the fifty other offers you've thrown my way."

I laugh because while I joke around with him—and think he's insanely gorgeous along with most of campus—it's all talk. He might be straight and turn me down every time, but Peyton Miller knows he's hot stuff and doesn't mind the attention. As long as it's the right kind of attention. Praise him for being a football king and sex on legs? Good. Praise him for being his dads' protégé? You're gonna get a ball to the face. And not the good kind.

"I should leave you guys to it," he says, getting up and stepping closer. He gives my shoulder a squeeze. "You gonna be okay?"

I nod. "Brady will fix it."

"This is one of those don't ask because you don't want to know type of situations, isn't it?"

"Just your run-of-the-mill testicle removal," I say innocently.

Peyton cringes and grabs his junk. "And I'm out. Good luck, brother."

Brady gives him the cool-guy flick of the hand wave before his attention settles on me. "Sounds like you've got a story."

I sigh and drop into the barstool Peyton vacated. "You have no idea." I fill Brady in on the whole conversation I overheard this morning. "And this came after we spent hours, *hours* just … just *kissing* last night."

"Just kissing?" he asks skeptically.

"Well, *after* we fucked."

Brady frowns. "After?"

"Exactly!" I throw my hands up. "He was all sweet and … and … well, I thought his hesitance was cute, but turns out he had no clue what he was doing. So he got it out of the way with me."

If anything, Brady's frown deepens. "*After* you fucked, he spent time kissing you?"

"Not just time. I'm not being dramatic when I say hours. We were on that beach until 2:00 a.m."

"Fuck me."

I give him a dry look. "I've tried that, remember? Because I'm easy."

He snaps his fingers sharply. "Nope. Not going there."

"I …" I look down at my hands, not wanting to see the judgment on his face when I reveal the most embarrassing thought to ever cross my mind. I suck in a sharp breath and then just say it. "I thought maybe he actually liked me. Really liked me. But turns out he was high from using a hole for the first time." I do a mock military salute. "Glad to be of service to the men of Franklin U."

Brady tilts his head. "I'm going to ask this for no reason whatsoever and definitely *not* because it's a personality trait, but … is it possible you're being a bit dramatic here?"

I gasp, jaw sinking through the floor at the *audacity*. "I'm not disputing your point," I say, because yes, it's fair. "All I'm saying is how do you take it when one person says, 'Oh, so you found an easy hole to stick it in,' and then the guy who used said hole … says nothing?"

"You're right, that doesn't sound good."

"Thank you!"

Brady rubs his stubbled jaw. "So what are you going to do?"

I give him a winning smile. "I'm going to hide out here. I'll build myself a bed in the bath. You'll never notice I'm around."

"Well, there's no way that's possible."

"Because I'm so pretty? Aww, thanks. Flattery is just what I need."

"Sure. Pretty. And definitely not loud and annoying."

"Thank you."

The humor on his face melts away to pity. "You can't avoid him forever. Maybe you need to tell him what you overheard?"

My laugh comes out slightly hysterical. "And have him think I'm clingy and pathetic? No, thank you."

"He might as well get to know the real you now."

"I hate you," I say, with the blankest look I can muster. Then, my dumb eyes start to blur. "I thought he was different."

"Aww, Fe …" Brady rounds the counter and wraps his strong arms around me. "He's a dick."

"He is. A really, really big one."

Brady pulls back a little. "When you say big …"

I indicate with my fingers, and Brady's eyebrows shoot up. "Wow. If all he wanted was a hole, I would have volunteered."

I glower, and Brady hurries to lift his hands.

"Sorry, sorry. Bad trouser-snake man. What a giant, enormous, soul-wrecking dick. I completely understand now why you're so devastated."

"Thank you." I'll go along with his smart-assery if it means steering clear of the real reason I'm feeling so shitty.

I've *never* been boyfriend material. I've never been someone guys see themselves with for more than a night, and it's not something that's ever worried me because I've always known the score. No one makes it out to be more than it is.

Until now.

Until Marshall and his sweet words and soft hands. The slow, reverent way he started off inside me before he lost control. The way he'd told me I was beautiful.

For a moment this morning, I'd allowed myself to break all my defenses down and imagine the look on Marshall's face when he saw me again. Soft eyes, affectionate smile, all for me.

It might have only been my imagination, but losing that hurts more than I'll ever say. Especially because I'm starting to think I'll never find my person.

13

Marshall

I GIVE BOWSER THE DRIEST LOOK I CAN MANAGE.

"What?" He laughs, holding his hands up. "I know you didn't fuck Lyle because he said you canceled, so my only assumption is that you met someone and went for it."

If only he knew it doesn't work like that with me. "I'll never tell."

"You're such a dick." He collapses into the chair across from me. "How do you feel?"

"No different." Which is a total lie. It's not that losing my virginity had any effect on me outside of the mind-blowing orgasm, but being with Felix, so close, so intimate, and then spending the time together after has made me dangerously fond of him.

I'm anxiously waiting for him to wake up so I can figure out where we stand. I know casual is something he likes, but would it be a terrible thing for us to semi-regularly casually hook up? I know I won't be able to do it on my end without some feelings becoming involved, but that's my problem.

Hell, I think my feelings are already involved.

I was up way too early, not able to sleep, thinking about how it felt to hold him. Small, hard, warm. The way he straddled my lap and smiled against each kiss.

"Was it worth it?" Bowser asks, snapping me out of my memories.

"Sleeping with him?"

He shakes his head. "That part is always worth it. Was it worth holding out for so long?"

There's no one I could have imagined a better first experience with than him. "Yeah, it was."

"So much for saving it for someone special."

My lips twitch. "Who says I didn't?"

"Damn, Marshall. You're really keeping it a secret?"

"I really am."

"Killjoy."

My grin widens. "He was *really* good too."

"Dick …"

And so was his dick.

I wait as long as I can for Felix to show before I need to work. As I pull my Shenanigans polo on, I hope more than anything that he's still sleeping and not that he's avoiding me, because if that's the case, I can only assume one thing.

He regrets what happened. And I don't think I could handle it if that was the case. I'm bothered by the thought for the whole walk to work and only manage to rid it from my mind when I walk into Shenanigans to an onslaught of noise. The lunch rush is well underway, and once it finishes up, we'll get the sporting teams and fans in here either celebrating or commiserating their loss.

I duck around the crowds to slip through the employees-only door and find Brax and Ty in the hall.

I send a smirk their way. "Gentlemen."

Brax flips me off, but Ty hurries to straighten. I have no idea what they were talking about, but given what I almost walked in on with them, I'm happier to play naive.

I never would have picked Ty as Brax's type, but even I've noticed the way his stare follows as Ty clears off the tables.

"You on the afternoon shift?" Brax asks.

"Yup. Here until closing. You guys too?"

"*I* am. But Lacrosse"—he throws a thumb toward Ty—"dropped in to see my pretty face. I can't blame him. I'm basically a good-luck charm, and let's face it, he's going to need it for his game today."

"Fuck you. I can run circles around the other team. Which you'd know if you ever came to a game."

"Considering I'm always working, I don't see how that's possible. What a shame. I'm so devastated."

I slowly back away at the overt flirtation going on. That whole thing is a hot mess, and considering my own relationship confusion, I'm currently a good judge of it.

I clock in, then check the storeroom, having to bite my tongue at the mess I find. Through the week, the room is kept the way the other barbacks and I keep it, but over the weekends, Oscar has hired some casual guys who don't know how things work.

Down one aisle of shelving is everything for the bar area, and down the other is everything for the kitchen that doesn't need to be kept refrigerated. I'm not sure what went on in here this morning, but there's a whole packet of Styrofoam containers strewn across the floor, pots and pans everywhere, and what looks like maple syrup dripping down the wall.

Motherfucker.

I remind myself I'm being paid for this and get to work.

Given my mom and dad pay for my food and expenses when needed and I scored a few small scholarships, this job does well to cover my room. Plus, Oscar doesn't expect much more from me than to keep the operational side of things running smoothly.

I spend some time cleaning up, then cart out boxes before refilling all the empty spaces with supplies from the basement stores. Thankfully, only Oscar and the other barbacks have access down there, so it's always kept in order.

I'm busy for a few hours, organizing stock and jotting down a list of things Oscar's running low on, and then … I have a whole afternoon of walking things back and forth from the storeroom to the bar or kitchen. It's menial work, completely mindless, leaving my brain free to fixate on other things. Like Felix.

I'm determined not to jump to conclusions until I've talked to him, but that's getting harder and harder to do as the day wears on. By late afternoon, I know he has to be awake, but his name doesn't light up my phone, and I try not to let it get to me.

Sure, I could message him, and I pull out my phone to do it a couple of times, but what if all I do is make it weird?

I don't have experience here. I don't know what I'm doing. I'm relying on him to take the lead, but if what he's said is any indication, his lead is "been there, done that," and I really should focus on moving on.

But how am I supposed to move on when what we shared was so incredible?

Maybe this is virgin goggles.

Maybe this is what Bowser meant when he said to get it out of the way.

There's no denying if I wanted to hook up and move on, Felix would be the perfect guy to do it with, but … I don't want to move on.

I want a repeat.

More than one, if I'm honest with myself.

Everything about Felix has me buzzing, and the complete radio silence is really playing on my self-confidence.

Was I terrible?

I know I enjoyed myself, but I'd be mortified if it was all one-sided. What if he's avoiding me because he's worried I'll ask how it was, and he doesn't want to have to tell me I get an A plus for effort at least.

I rake a hand through my hair, trying not to panic.

Felix has no issues being up-front about things. I might not know him inside out, but I know that, at least. If it was shit, he'll let me know.

Hell, maybe he'll even offer to coach me. That wouldn't be the worst thing in the world. Actually, that would be kind of perfect …

If he doesn't want a relationship, fine. But sex? Surely that's something I could talk him into.

But if I really was shit, do I want to know?

I cringe as I grab two bottles of bourbon to take out front. The solid answer to that is no.

Okay. So no asking how it was.

No asking if he wants more.

Which leaves me with … nothing. If Felix doesn't want more with me, I somehow have to figure out how to do this friends thing with him when I really just want more.

Again, not something I can tell him.

I'm screwed. Why him? Out of all the guys I know, why did it have to be him I fixated on? Shit, *Bowser* would be a safer option.

But then I think of Felix's pretty curls, and how we kissed, and the way he fit against me, and I can't stop the little bursts going off in my chest.

Maybe it was dumb of me, but I can't regret it.

I refuse to.

So now I have two options. Give in completely and let him

pretend like it was one and done, like it never happened. Or …
well, Felix *is* a flirt. And if what I witnessed between Brax and Ty
tells me anything, it's that when it comes to relationships, there's
no telling what could happen.

So I'm going to shoot my shot.

If Felix likes to flirt, I'll give it right back. I'll be friendly and
… sexy? If that's even something I can manage. But my brother
Robbie has never had an issue picking up, and people say we look
similar all the time.

I can totally do this.

Make Felix fall for me.

Yep. Easy.

And the thought of putting myself out there and being rejected
doesn't make me feel sick at all.

14

Felix

I COULD BE A NINJA. OR AT LEAST DESERVE A GOLD STAR IN avoidance. Somehow, I manage to duck in and out of the house for clothes and things for class, to feed Butters and even shower, without running into Marshall once. Brady says I'm a pain in the ass, but I catch him and Peyton throwing concerned looks my way sometimes, and it makes me more determined than ever to keep my chin up and my personality bubbly.

No guy is going to get me down.

Even if I get the feeling that maybe I'm not as great at avoidance as I think I am and that it's more a case of him avoiding me too. Which doesn't hurt. Nope. Not at all. I love being used and discarded so easily.

Three days later, though, and my no-Marshall streak comes to an end. I tiptoe into the house, and before I can make it to the stairs, he appears in the doorway to the study room.

His grin is immediate, and he shoves his hands in his pockets as he leans against the doorframe. The large, bashful guy I'm used to is gone, and his eyes steadily meet mine.

"I was beginning to think I'd imagined you," he says.

"What do you mean?"

"You haven't been around."

I shrug. "I'm in very high demand. Super busy. Got a lot on, so ..."

His confusion lasts for a fraction of a second before his expression clears. "What are you doing right now?"

"About to get ready for work, actually." I only go into the vet's once a week, but I love the time I spend there. Especially when it takes me away from the awkwardness with him.

"Pity. I thought we could hang out." Then he not so subtly looks me over, stare burning every inch of me.

I'm speechless, wondering what's changed, and then I get it. *Hang out* is about as subtle a euphemism as him checking me out. Apparently, now that he's had a taste, he wants another. I brace myself against the disappointment. "You'll have to get in line, cutie."

Then he surprises the shit out of me by stepping forward, right into my space. "What if I want to go straight to the front?"

A growl echoes in my mind that makes it harder than ever to pretend. "No one ever taught you patience?"

"I've been more patient than you know."

Well, true, considering *virgin*. "I need to get ready for work."

Something crosses his face that I can't read before quickly being replaced by a smile. "Armadillos."

"What?"

He reaches to lift the bottom of his T-shirt, and there on his underwear are armadillos in various poses. Along with a good sliver of skin that takes me a second to pull my eyes away from. "Thought you'd want to know." Then he tugs one of my curls and disappears into the study room.

And I have no idea what that was.

It wasn't Marshall's usual, that's for sure, and I hate how

much I loved it. My feet stumble up the stairs, and I shower, then get changed and put out food for Butters in case she shows up today. Before I step away from my window, I catch the soft, calming music coming from outside. Not a guitar, but something I've heard before and can't put my finger on.

I linger even though I'm cutting it close to being late.

Work passes quickly. I spend way too much time playing with the puppies we had dumped on us a week ago, give some vaccinations, and sit in on a neutering. I really love this and could easily see myself doing it for the rest of my life. Is that how Marshall feels about his research? History? Damn, I couldn't think of anything more boring, but when he talks about it … I dunno. He makes me want to listen.

Which isn't helpful for anyone.

I want to read into his request to hang out as something more than it is, but how do I do that when he's always been open? Truthful? If he wanted more, I'm sure he would have said it rather than cryptic, uncommitted requests that don't tell me anything.

And don't I deserve someone who doesn't play games? Is that really too much to ask?

I text Brady to meet me after work, and we walk back to Liberty Court together. It's a nice day out, and as expected, the courtyard is full of people enjoying their afternoon. Almost all the hammocks are full, the grills are in use, and the lacrosse guys have the music pumping in their house.

The smell of weed sits heavily over everything, and even though I rarely smoke it, I breathe in deep. It's not the nicest smell, but it always reminds me of summer days and relaxed vibes. Laughter and cacti and sun.

"We should grab some drinks and hang out here," Brady suggests.

"Where?" I point to the picnic tables. "All the seating is full."

"Get a blanket, and we'll park our asses on the ground," he says like a rational human being, which my best friend never is.

"Why can't we have drinks at your place?"

"Because I just cleaned the damn thing, and I have no interest in it turning into a party and then having to spend tomorrow doing the exact same thing."

"You? Cleaning?"

He doesn't meet my eyes. "Might have visitors over later."

Code word for a hookup.

"But what if Marshall—"

Brady cuts me off. "Dude, you need to get over him."

"I *am*. Well, as much as I can get over someone who means absolutely nothing to me."

"Mhmm."

"Don't give me that tone."

"There was no tone."

I give him a stern look. "You're not fooling anyone."

"All I'm saying is that I've never seen you like this."

"Like what?" I go for disinterest, but my voice is a pitch too high.

"Hiding out, for a start. Talking about him nonstop. Sulking and bitching about what a mean person he is and refusing to confront him even though I've seen you tear a guy a new one in the middle of Shenanigans before flipping his carton of fries over the top of him."

"Okay, but I was drunk then. And I'd just found out he used me to cheat on his girlfriend. Not cool."

"Hey, I'm not saying he didn't deserve it. Only that you never have an issue addressing shitty behavior, and for some reason, you're avoiding it with him."

He's right. Skirting around the issue isn't something I'm used to, but calling Marshall out on using me as a cheap trick will get him offside and could end the small amount of contact we have.

Which shouldn't be an issue. I shouldn't want contact with someone like that. But a small, tender part of me wishes I could be good enough for him, could be the kind of guy he's holding out for.

"There's Ty," Brady says, nodding in the direction of the lacrosse king himself. They exchange a dude-bro head jerk *hey*, and I have to hold back a laugh. Peyton and Tyson have a friendly rivalry, both being sporting royalty of the FU Kings, and Brady always makes it clear he's firmly on Peyton's side. As if there was ever any doubt.

I am too, but that doesn't stop me flirting with Tyson. Or any of the other guys on the lacrosse team.

But as we pass by them to grab what we need from inside, I can't even manage to blow Ty a kiss. I'm … empty. The flirting that used to be so fun and a total mood boost now seems childish. I feel exactly as cheap as Marshall sees me. So I duck my head instead and keep walking.

Brady grabs a blanket, I grab the tequila, and then we set up outside. After two shots, he nudges me.

"You really aren't yourself, Fe. You know that all that stuff you heard was bullshit, right?"

"It isn't though. That's the problem."

"Why? Because you like to have sex? That has nothing to do with your worth. If he's judging you for it or using you for it, that says more about him than you."

On some level, I know that Brady is right, but knowing that and believing it are two different things.

15

Marshall

By the time I get back to Liberty Court, I'm drained and still have a Monday test to study for. It's not even senior year and I'm tired. Not of the coursework—that, I love—but of trying to find a balance between school and work while somehow managing to sleep *and* have a social life.

I'd hoped to get out of work early enough tonight to catch up with Felix because my flirting plan doesn't work very well when he isn't around to flirt with. I know he's avoiding me, and it sucks, but at the same time, I'm not giving up on him. If there's any chance to convince him to give me another shot, I'm going to take it.

I'm halfway across the courtyard, dodging drunken college students, when my gaze catches on something that makes me freeze.

Felix. And that same guy I caught him on a date with. They're on a picnic blanket with a couple of others, including Bowser, and Felix is lying down with his head on the guy's lap.

My gut twists painfully. I watch as Felix tells some story, hands gesturing wildly, and the guy absentmindedly strokes his curls.

My curls.

The curls I can't get out of my fucking head. The ones I want to touch and stroke and pull tight as I kiss him, and that asshole has his paws all over them.

Is this date number two, then? Or ... more?

Is that why Felix has been avoiding me? Are he and this guy ... dating? Before I even got a chance to show Felix how perfect we could be together?

Before I know what I'm doing, I lift myself up to full height and head over there. "This looks fun." As annoyed as I am, somehow, my voice comes out light. Like I'm not being fake as shit.

Immediately, Felix scowls. "Well, it *was*."

"*Hey*." Lap guy taps Felix's shoulder, and Felix tilts his head back to pin the guy in his glare.

"What?" Felix asks. "It *was* fun."

"Get up and make room for your friend."

The glare lands back on me. "He doesn't want to join us."

And somehow, I get a boost of the Harrows confidence because I stare right back and say, "Sure I do. Make room, Fe."

He reluctantly sits up, swaying slightly before folding his lean legs under himself.

I take the vacated spot, and for a second, his glower dims. I manage to throw out a *hi* at Charlie Martin, who I've had a few classes with, and the other guy in the circle looks familiar, but I can't place his name. Neither of them holds my attention when Felix is *right there*.

"So how do you two know each other?" I ask, waving a finger

between Felix and the guy who's very possibly bigger than me. He's certainly more *muscular*.

"Brady," the guy says, sending me a quick half wave. His assessing gaze runs from my head down.

"Marshall." I eye him as well.

Bowser snorts. "You don't know Brady Talon?"

"*Talon*?" Okay, that name I know. Not because I want to, but because Robbie has been obsessed with football for our entire lives and rambles about the greats all the time.

This is just perfect. How am I supposed to be any competition to someone with famous fathers? My gut sinks as I realize I'm completely screwed here.

"Big fan?" Brady asks dryly.

"Ah, no. Actually, my brother. He loves football and …" I trail off at the look on Brady's face. Completely closed off.

Felix laughs and drops his head against Brady's shoulder. "Then surely even you'd know who Peyton Miller is."

My whole face is heating up, and just as I could really use some of that Harrows confidence, it completely abandons me. "Yeah. Heard of him." My brother couldn't get over the fact I'd be going to college with the son of the greatest quarterback to ever live. He'd tried to pay me to find Peyton and befriend him, but my idiot brother is even more strapped for cash than I am.

"Dude," the guy I kinda recognize says. "It's *Peyton*. He's the greatest around here."

Brady throws a bottle lid at the guy. "Shut the fuck up, Cobey. It sounds like you're sucking up my brother's ass."

Cobey looks perplexed, and it's then I realize he must be another football player. "I'm not sucking up. It's a fact."

"How was work?" Bowser asks, trying to interrupt the derailing conversation.

I fill him in on what was thankfully an uneventful shift, until a whole party came in before closing time and some chick vomited over a table.

Guess what loser got stuck with cleaning that up? I've never gagged so hard in my life.

Every time I glance across the group at Felix and Brady though, a bolt of nasty pain shoots through me. They're constantly chatting and flirty, sitting too close, clearly comfortable with each other.

I want that with Felix. I want to reach across, grab his ankle, and haul him to me. To touch and laugh and sneak kisses while we sit around with our friends.

"Marshall?"

I jolt out of my thoughts and turn back to Bowser. "Huh?"

"I *said* I finally got my hands on some Emerald Idol."

"That's great!" And the news briefly distracts me. It's not my area of expertise, but apparently, Bowser has been after this rare cactus since he started at this school. He works in the FU greenhouse and is studying to be a horticulturist so he can work with repopulating some of the endangered flora or whatever.

I don't understand much about plants, but I understand preservation.

"Innit?" He stretches, eyes on some girl a few feet away. "Damn, she's fit."

"'Fit,'" I tease. But he's right. She *is* good-looking. Tall, brunette, nice ass. And not one part of me wants to touch it. I find her as nice to look at as an ancient Egyptian artifact. Though there's no way in hell I'd ever tell her she's as appealing as a five-thousand-year-old mummy. Maybe even less so.

She's definitely not as fascinating.

But Felix …

My gaze strays back to him, and we lock eyes for a second before he turns up his cute nose and whips back around to Brady. I swear my molars crack I grind them so hard.

The thing is, I was totally prepared for Felix to blow me off and treat me like any other person. To maybe flirt with me but not be interested in a repeat.

But to be blatantly hostile toward me has me confused. The glaring? The low-key anger? Where the hell is it coming from?

And why does it have to hurt so much?

Felix suddenly pushes to his feet and sways for a moment. "Oh, that Chris Delaney is looking so fine tonight. I wonder if he'll bend me over and have his filthy way with me."

I'm stunned as Felix stumbles away from our group toward a tall, lean guy with dirty-blond hair that flops around his chin. I recognize him as one of the guys who lives in Stormer house.

What the hell was that?

My gaze pings back to Brady, who looks as stunned as I feel. I'm not sure what their deal is now, but I'm also not so sure Felix is in any state to be making decisions with the way he can barely walk straight.

"How much has he had to drink?" I snap.

Bowser shrugs. "Dunno. We've all been passing around the bottle."

I glance at Charlie and Cobey, who are both as big as Brady and Bowser. "You all do realize he's half your size, right?"

"We're not responsible for him," Charlie says, sounding unsure.

I jump to my feet at the same time as Brady. "I've got this," I snap at him.

"Fuck off. You're not going near him like this."

"Me?" I step up to him. "*You're* the one I don't know. How do I know you can be trusted with him?"

Bowser stands and pulls me back. "They're best friends. It's fine."

Best … friends? "No, they're not. I saw them on a date together."

Bowser laughs. "There's no way."

"We weren't on a date," Brady says.

"But—"

"He said it to make you jealous, moron."

Jealous? I blink at Brady for a second, face completely slack. "But ... why?"

"I'm not going to spell it out for you. Now, excuse me, I need to check on him."

This weird overt possessiveness takes over me. "I *said* I'll do it."

Before he can argue back, I turn on my heel and approach Felix. Chris is eyeing him, more with amusement than true interest, but when Chris catches sight of me, he sends *help me* eyes in my direction.

"Hey, man. Felix is heading to bed."

Felix grunts dramatically. "It's my keeper," he stage-whispers, throwing his arm around Chris. "Quick, run away with me now." His words are coming out slurred.

"If I thought you could run, I'd do it in a heartbeat," Chris says, prying Felix off him.

Felix stumbles over his feet, and I catch him before his ass hits the ground.

"Come on, Fe, time for bed."

"I don't wanna."

"You're really drunk." I brush that one wayward curl off his forehead and force him to meet my eyes. "And it's late. Plenty of time for parties another night."

"You're not my boyfriend," he sneers.

Ouch, thanks for pointing that out. "No, I'm your friend. And friends don't let their friends do dumb shit while they're drunk."

Chris sniggers. "Am I 'dumb shit'?"

"Sorry, didn't come out right."

He waves my concern away.

"*Friends,*" Felix mimics. "I'm so happy I have *a friend.*"

"You have a lot of friends."

"Well, snaps for me." He starts to snap his fingers, but it's weak, and his whole body sways with the movement.

"What's going on with you?"

"You're a *dick* and a *virgin* and I hate you."

My jaw drops.

Chris sniggers beside me, but he clearly thinks Felix is drunk rambling. I'd think so too if he wasn't uncomfortably close to the truth.

Felix chuckles, then tugs me down to whisper in my ear, "I *know* ..."

I don't ask how. I don't ask why it matters. I don't ask a single fucking thing because my heart is beating faster, and I don't want to have this conversation around other people. Being a virgin means nothing—especially since we're both well aware I'm not anymore—but I have a feeling that it might mean something to *him.*

Then his tongue runs along the shell of my ear and makes me shiver. "I know you want to fuck me. Cheap Felix. Easy Felix. Might as well use me until I'm useless to you."

The pain in his words hurts me. I draw back, hands planted on his shoulders. Chris has disappeared somewhere, and I don't bother looking over at the people we were with.

When I look at Felix, cheap and easy are the furthest things from what I see. But I'm not going to tell him that while he's so wasted.

I swallow my objections down. "Let's make a deal."

"What?" He narrows his pretty eyes.

"I'll let you yell at me for as long as you like in the morning —you can say anything you need to get off your chest, and I won't interrupt—*if* you let me take you inside."

"To do what?"

"To put you to bed. Alone."

"Well, that doesn't sound like fun." When he pouts, I can't help smiling. He's so fucking adorable.

"I'll even tuck you in," I promise.

Something in his stare sharpens. "Fine." And without warning, Felix launches himself into my arms.

"*Oomph.*" I grab him in time to stop the both of us from crashing to the ground. His legs wrap around my waist. "What are you doing?"

"You said you want to take me inside. So take me." His face buries into my shirt, and even though I should probably argue, he feels way too good there. Those ridiculous flutters are back.

I carry him inside and head all the way up to his room. I've never been in here, but it smells like him, and all the bright, happy colors are everything that reminds me of Felix.

We reach his bed, and I lean down to drop him on the mattress, but he holds tight. "You gotta let go, Fe."

He *hmphs* and clings on harder.

I hate how much I love it. My teeth dig into my bottom lip as I try to figure out what the fuck comes next. The last thing I'm going to do is to take advantage while he's drunk, but if Felix doesn't want me to let go, I'm in no hurry to.

Resigned, I drop down onto the edge of the mattress and hug Felix against me. "You know, you can sit like this tomorrow when you yell at me. All day if you have to. But you need sleep, and you can't get it like this."

"Wanna bet?" comes his muffled reply. Felix scrambles closer to my body, face pressed into my neck, and just like the other night, my heart feels too big.

I groan, hands tightening on his back. "You're *really* testing me here …"

Finally, he eases up, just the smallest amount but enough so he can see my face. "Why?"

"Because I don't want to let you go either. But you *do* need sleep."

He watches me, blinking and clearly trying to bring me into focus as he slides a hand from behind my neck and down to my chest. "Marshmallow …"

A throat clears from the doorway, and I jump at finding Brady watching us.

Felix grunts and buries himself in my chest again.

Dammit. "He won't let go," I explain.

Brady's suspicion melts away to be replaced with something that looks like concern as he approaches us. He sets a large hand on Felix's back. "Dude, you're not an octopus. You need to let go."

"Don't wanna."

"I'll remember you said that tomorrow when I'm teasing you nonstop about this. You're going to be *so* embarrassed."

Felix stiffens and then slowly crawls from my lap to flop onto the bed. "We will never speak of this again."

"Can't make any promises," Brady says, pulling off Felix's shoes and tossing them into the corner.

I watch them together for a moment, that same obvious familiarity between them, but I can't detect anything sexual no matter how much I try.

"Want Marshall to tuck me in," Felix mutters.

Brady shoots me a *please get out* look. "Not a good idea, boo."

I back toward the door, and before I can leave, Felix whines, "I just want someone to snuggle with."

Brady's sigh is so loud I catch it from the hall. "I know, Fe. I know."

16

Felix

THE SPRAY OF COLD LIQUID IN MY FACE MAKES MY EYES SNAP open as I jackknife off the bed.

"The fuck?" I gasp at the familiar sound of my best friend's laughter.

"Oops?"

I swipe the water from my eyes so I can properly send a glare his way, but the room is too bright, and my head is *pounding.* "I'm going to assume by your presence that I didn't get laid last night."

"Not for your lack of trying." He stretches out across the other side of my bed.

"How bad was it?" I ask.

"Not bad."

Oh, thank god. The haze in my mind is making it impossible to even think.

"If you class 'not bad' as getting so drunk you couldn't walk straight, throwing yourself at Chris, and then making the guy you apparently hate carry you up here and refusing to let him go."

My dramatic sob is long and drawn out.

"But, hey. You didn't shit yourself, so ..."

"I'd almost prefer that."

"Imagine if you'd shat yourself *while* he carried you."

My jaw drops. "Why would you put that out there?"

"It'd be hilarious for me, to be fair."

"I need new friends."

"Cute you think anyone else would stand you for as long as I have."

My laugh cuts off on a groan. "Can you please be nice? I'm tender. And mortified."

"For good reason."

"Not helping."

"I know, but I figured I'd warm you up to this conversation because I doubt you're going to like what I have to say next either."

"Oh no, I really did shit my pants, didn't I?"

"No." He glances at me with what I've come to think of as his big-brother look, and I realize it's worse than I thought. "Have you actually spoken with him about what you heard?"

"Who?"

"Are we really going to do the play dumb thing? Because Peyton's my brother—I can do this all day."

I scratch my ear. "I ... no. I haven't. Well, not about ... you know."

"You should. Sure, I only spoke to him for about a second, but the guy was ready to take me on. *Me.* Just to protect your honor."

The words fill me with unexpected—and unwelcome—hope. I stamp it down. "You're wrong."

"It's like you don't know me at all. I'm never wrong."

I eye him, but he seems to be telling the truth. "You know that would make a really cruel joke, right?"

"Yup."

"Then why are you saying all this?"

"Because despite being prepared to hate him on principle, I saw how he looked at you. That isn't how someone looks at a cheap hookup." Brady leans over and kisses my forehead. Then he puts on an exaggerated baby voice. "And I know how much you wanna snuggle with him."

"Get out."

He climbs over me, setting down the empty glass he used to dribble water over me. I watch as he pulls on his clothes. As much as I tease Brady and Peyton about being my type, they're cut to shit with muscle, and I … well, apparently, I want someone softer.

"Okay, I'm leaving!" Brady shouts obnoxiously loudly.

"What are you—"

He throws the door open wide and leaves it that way. "Text you later," he calls. Then he's gone.

Leaving me either to fall back into a crappy sleep where anyone—okay, only Darian—can walk by and see or haul my whining ass out of bed.

I half sob and flop dramatically back onto my pillows. I don't like either of those choices.

A soft knock on the door has my eyes snap open *again*, and my heart immediately does a flip-flop at seeing Marshall standing there.

"Thought I'd bring you these," he says, holding up a glass of water and some Tylenol.

I blink at him, mouth parched and suddenly unable to find words. The gesture is so … considerate. Is it the kind of thing someone does for the guy he fucked and wants another turn with? Or is it … sweet?

I sink back into my pillows. "My hero." The flirty words don't hold the conviction they normally do.

"Hero? Well, I *did* have to stop a runaway train before coming up here. On my way to foil a jewel heist next."

"Busy man."

"And yet, not too busy to do a quick drop-off." He doesn't wait for me to answer before he walks in and sets the water and drugs on my bedside table.

"Don't tell me you were hanging around waiting for Brady to leave," I say, scooping up the glass.

"I, uh, might have already been up with some water."

My stare finds the empty glass. "So, you supplied him with his weapon."

"Weapon?"

I nod toward the one in question. "Let's just say my wake-up was *refreshing*."

He laughs, and I point to him.

"No taking Brady's side."

"I wouldn't dream of it." His smile has crinkled his eyes behind his glasses, and he looks so sweet, I almost wish I was drunk and uninhibited again so I could blurt everything out all over him.

"So," Marshall says. "Ready to yell at me next? Or do you need the painkillers first?"

"Painkillers. But … why am I yelling at you?"

His eyebrows lift. "You tell me. You were pissed off last night. Did I do something wrong?"

The tone makes me want to tell him no, even though that would be a total lie. "Did you?"

"I …" Marshall nudges up his glasses and rubs at his face with one hand. "I'm not sure how you found out, but I'm sorry I didn't tell you I was a virgin. It's not something I've ever cared that much about, but clearly you do, and if it's something that upset you …"

I hate how adorable I find his rambling. "I don't care," I hurry to say, because I *shouldn't*. "It's just … why *didn't* you tell me?"

"Would it have made a difference?"

"Maybe."

Marshall drops down onto the side of my mattress. "That's why I didn't say anything. Being a virgin meant sweet fuck all to me. It's not like anything magically changed because we had sex."

"You mean it's not like the *Princess and the Frog*, but instead of kissing, it's fucking, and instead of a frog, it'd be, like, a unicorn or something fun?"

Marshall screws up his face. "There is way too much to unpack in that sentence, so how about we skip over it? You're not mad about the virgin thing, so …"

My mood drops as I suddenly remember the real reason why I've been so intent on avoiding him. Being around him makes pesky little things like being used for sex irrelevant.

"Oh, *wait*." He hands me the Tylenol, and then once I've taken it, he shifts back to rest against the headboard and holds his arms out.

"W-what are you doing?"

"I told you that you could cling to me while you yell at me. So, come on, then."

"You want me to …"

"Get comfortable." He pats his belly. "You said you want someone to snuggle with, and there's a lot of me to do just that."

I gape at him. "Am I still drunk?"

A laugh sounds in his chest. "I'm trying to be a good friend here."

"Are we friends?"

"Well, I already told my brother we were, so if not, that means

I lied. Don't make me a liar, Fe. He'll never let me hear the end of it."

The first real smile I've had around him in a long time breaks free. "You want to snuggle with me?"

"I do. Now get your scrawny butt over here."

I'm still not really sure what's happening, but I'm not about to argue with him. If this is all a ploy to get sex, I'll text Brady to come and kick his ass. My friend's not a fighter, but he *is* likely to show up with the entire football team to intimidate the hell out of someone.

I scooch back on the bed until I'm sitting beside Marshall, then kinda … lean over. It's awkward. Where do I touch him? Where do my arms go? My head doesn't sit properly on his shoulder.

Then his giant arms wrap around me, and he pulls me in close.

His shirt smells like sunshine and soap, and I want to bury my face into his chest and live there forever. Instead, I settle my head over his left pec and relax into him.

"This is weird," I grumble. And it is. So, so, so weird that I don't find it weird at all.

He clearly does, though, because his arms are stiff, and he's sitting up way too straight to be comfortable. "Little bit."

"Hold me like you mean it."

At first, I don't think he's heard me. Then his entire body softens. "Is it time for you to yell at me now?"

"Suddenly don't want to."

"You were angry over *something* last night."

"Nope, not at all." As if I'm going to tell the guy I like that I overheard him calling me trash. Kinda. Shit, Brady's right. I've never gotten like this over a guy before. "I was drunk. Drunk people are dumb and say stuff. In fact, *you* were probably drunk too and are totally misremembering the whole night."

"I didn't drink."

"High, then. All those fumes aren't good for you."

"Is that why you tried to hook up with Chris?" His tone is completely flat.

I smile. "Why? Jealous, Marshmallow?"

"You're a right little shit sometimes."

"'Right little shit.' You sound like Bowser."

His chuckle rumbles through his chest to my ear. "Fine. You're a pain in the ass."

"Does that make you not want to be friends with me?"

He doesn't answer at first, but his chest falls on a long exhale. "Actually, it makes me want to be friends with you more."

"That's psychotic. Should I be worried?"

"No," he chokes through a laugh. "It's just … I come from a family of pains in the ass. You kinda remind me of them."

I shift. "Really?"

"Well, not physically." He doesn't offer any more, but I want details.

"What are they like?"

"My brothers are all like me, but only in looks. I'm the *quiet* one. It's not my favorite thing to be known as, if I'm honest."

"Why?"

"Because when people think quiet, they think boring." He shrugs. "Maybe I am. But I like me. I like the things I'm interested in."

"Considering they're your interests, that makes total sense," I say dryly.

"Yeah, you've already given me your thoughts on my interests."

And now I feel shitty. Because I don't remember the exact conversation, but I wouldn't be surprised if I told him history was the most boring thing ever. "Tell me stuff."

"Like …"

"What's your favorite part of history to study?"

He shifts awkwardly. "You don't have to—"

"Tell me." I snuggle into him more and this time take a chance to wrap my arm around his waist and pull my knees up to rest on his thighs.

"Let me guess," Marshall says. "You had a big night and you're tired and now you want something to put you to sleep?"

I actually really just want him to talk some more. His voice is all rumbly under my head. "That's exactly it."

He sighs, but there's a smile in his voice when he speaks again. "Fine. It's the Renaissance era. Arguably one of the biggest changes in modern civilization. Where there was a huge shift from people surviving the world to actively enjoying it."

That's even deeper than I was prepared for, but then, Marshall isn't exactly the kind to dumb things down. And I like that. That there's a point where people can go from struggling to enjoying. "Some people are still just surviving though."

"They are." His arms tighten around me. "But they deserve so much more."

17

Marshall

A LOT OF THE TENSION BETWEEN ME AND FELIX STARTS TO EASE up, and I'm grateful. It means I don't have to find excuses to run into him or start up a conversation, and the guy I get to see is the one he is for everyone else. It's nice to know the barriers between us are gone.

Especially during times like last night where he plonked down beside me on the couch and watched TV practically attached to my side. If Felix has a love language, I've found it. Between how he is with Brady normally and how he's been with me the past few days, he loves to be touched.

And I'm only too happy to touch him.

But that's all I'll let myself do. Surprisingly, Felix hasn't mentioned sex again or even tried to hit on me, and I'm glad for it. I want him, so fucking badly, but I'm also not going to go for it when sex isn't *all* I want. I'm worried if we cross that line again before I get a chance to show him how I feel that he might close off like he did last time.

I've seen what he thinks of himself, and I don't want a part in validating those thoughts. Not when he's so goddamn incredible to me.

When the door to the vet's opens and Felix steps out, my whole being lights up. It takes him a second to notice me, and I use that entire second to drink him in, from his copper curls to his strong jaw that he hasn't shaved today to his long, lean arms that lead down to slender wrists, ringed by beaded bracelets.

"Hey," he says, approaching. His work shirt is pale blue and matches his eyes.

"Hi." I hold out his smoothie. "It's watermelon."

"My favorite."

"I know."

He eyes me, smile struggling to break free. "Someone looks proud of himself."

"Someone pays attention."

"Hmm." His stare is shrewd as he takes a long sip, then starts us on our walk home.

My gaze rests on his pink lips. The way they wrap around the straw and how his tongue gently swipes them once he's done.

I'm not used to this kind of lust. The kind where I know what he tastes like. Am dying for it again. Can't stop wondering what that watermelon flavor would taste like on his lips. My cock makes its presence known at the thought, but I'm determined to be good.

Ignore it.

Which is way, way harder than I thought it'd be, given I've managed to go twenty-one years without.

I force my attention away, and it lands on the bracelets again.

"Those are nice," I say, reaching over to brush my fingers against the beads. "Where'd you get them?"

"My dad. He likes building stuff and making things out of wood."

"That's really cool."

He hums and shakes his wrist out. "I thought so. He could have bought them, but he chose to make them instead. I liked that."

"It makes them more special."

"Exactly." His face lights up with a smile. "The big one he carved with the letters of our first names." Felix pauses and twists the bracelet so I can see. *F, P, G, H.*

"What do they stand for?"

"Well, *F* is mine, obviously. *P* for my mom, Poppy. *G* for Griff, my dad. Then *H* for Uncle Heath."

"Your dad's brother?"

"His husband."

My jaw drops. "He … uh … married your uncle? What?"

Felix peels over with laughter. "I will never get tired of doing that."

"I'm glad you're amused, but I'm still lost."

His laughter subsides, and he tugs me to keep walking. "Dad and Heath have been best friends since high school. Growing up, he was my uncle. Godfather too. And then when Mom and Dad split after I started college, those two got together."

"And got married?"

"Yup."

"And now you tell people your dad and uncle tied the knot?"

He blinks up at me angelically. "It's basically the truth."

"Yeah, except for one major part." My voice drips with exasperation, but it's all fake. "And you wonder why I called you a pain in the ass."

"I don't wonder that at all." He steps in and bumps my side. "But you also said it's why you like me."

I grin down at him, and this close, his head is tilted back a bit so he can see me. "It's one of many, many reasons."

It might be my imagination, but I swear his face gets flushed before he hurriedly looks away.

"You didn't get one?" Felix asks, giving his drink a shake.

"I did, but I finished it while I was waiting for you."

"And why *were* you waiting?"

"I was——"

"Don't say in the area," he hurries to cut me off. "I know you didn't have to work today."

"I wasn't going to say that," I lie through my teeth. "I wanted to hang out."

"Oh, *really*?"

"Isn't that what friends do?"

It's the wrong thing to say because his face falls and he looks away. "Of course. But real question …"

I hold my breath, bracing for whatever he's about to hit me with, only when he glances my way again, he's smiling. "What's your smoothie flavor?"

"Nah, I'm a milkshake boy. It's vanilla all the way."

He smirks. "Like your sex life."

I almost choke on air. "Fuck you very much. I'll have you know I had sex on a beach once."

"*Once*? Ohh, you rebel."

My insides practically dance at the teasing. "Single hottest moment of my life."

He tugs his bottom lip between his teeth before his eyes dart to me and away again. "And the others …"

"Other what?"

"Hot moments. I mean, beach guy would be hard to beat, of course, but I'll bet you've tried."

Is he … I think he's asking if I've had sex with anyone since him. I almost laugh, the idea is so ridiculous to me, but

I'm not interested in getting into the *why's* with him, so I go vague.

"Nah, that memory will keep me going for a while."

"... Really?"

Then I give him more than I was planning to. "Yup. I don't sleep with just anyone." It's hard not to ask him the same question, but somehow, I keep it to myself. Do I like the idea of Felix having sex with someone else? Not at all. But it's less of a jealousy thing and more that I don't want him to keep playing into those feelings that it's all he's good at. If he loved having random sex, that's one thing, but it doesn't seem to be the case with him. Maybe it was once, but it isn't anymore.

I can't imagine sex without feelings attached.

I want to show him what it's like to be consumed completely, inside and out. To make him feel what I felt when we were together. Even walking beside him makes me want to reach out and wrap my arm around him. To press my nose to his curls and tease him about how short he is. I'm pretty sure he'd let me do it, but he's had enough men touch him purely because they want to, so I'm leaving everything up to him.

Striving to give him what *he* needs instead of what I need.

Which is why I keep my distance and will my cock to behave itself.

We get back to Liberty Court, and I nod at a few people we pass before heading into the house. Felix crosses the tiled entryway to head upstairs, when he suddenly stops and spins to face me.

"I almost forgot."

I cock my head for him to go on when he stalks closer again and reaches for my shirt. The material is too soft over my sensitive stomach as he drags it up, inch by teasing inch, and then his gaze drops.

"Hmm ... I can't make them out." His fingers lightly brush

my skin, sending goose bumps crawling over it, before he reaches for the waistband of my boxer briefs. His fingertips dip into the crease of my hip, dangerously close to my groin, and I swear I stop breathing. Slowly, he pulls the material up. "Pokémon, huh?" His stare is heated when it meets mine. "Who's your favorite?"

"Pikachu. The OG."

"You are such a nerd." Then he surprises me by pushing onto his toes, fingers still heating the area way too close to my junk, and tilts his mouth to my ear. "It's one of the many, many reasons why I like *you*."

Then he steps away and turns to jog up the stairs while I beg my feet not to follow him. My nerves are swimming, blood pumping hard and cock like a magnet pulling me up those stairs to his room to ask him how many ways he likes me.

I force in a stuttered breath. Refusing to move. Willing my hormones to take the back seat they've ridden on my entire life.

"So that was interesting."

I jump and whirl around to find Bowser leaning in the doorway to the study room. "What was?"

He gestures vaguely. "Whatever the hell I just witnessed. I'm proper confused."

"You and me both."

"I thought you guys didn't like each other."

Shivers of addictive nerves hit my gut. "Clearly, I'm growing on him."

"More than that. You better be careful, dude. From what I saw, he wants to shag you. Bad."

"Nah, we're friends …" For now.

18

Felix

I HAVE A TOWEL LAID OUT OVER THE GRASS IN THE GARDEN outside my room, ankles crossed as I lie on my stomach and go over notes for class. Spring isn't far away, and there's something in the garden that must be in bloom right now because it smells amazing. The calming music I hear every now and then is being played, and the sun is hot on my hair and legs.

It's so fucking relaxing, I could drift off.

Butters lets out a trill as she jumps up onto the garden wall and then drops down beside me. I've already fed her this morning, and twice in one day is unusual but not unwelcome—even when she climbs onto my back and kneads me with her claws.

Must make human into comfy pillow.

Comfy pillows make me think of Marshmallow, and I have to tuck my smile into my arms. I've been pushing my luck lately by cuddling up against him more and more, but he never says a thing, and to my annoyance, he hasn't mentioned wanting to sleep with me again. All he does when I invade his personal space is either lean into me too or, if we're alone, wrap an arm around me. Which makes me swoon harder than a '50s-era Hollywood starlet.

I don't want to fall for him, but he's making it impossible not to.

Which is why I'm doing my coursework here instead of in the study room where I know he is, because if I go down there, I'll be too distracted trying to get his attention and won't get anything done.

"Hey, Fe," Bowser says, walking out carrying a bunch of gardening supplies.

"Morning."

"I think it's more like lunchtime by now."

I've been out here for a while, then—and got next to nothing done anyway. Apparently, Marshall has the ability to distract me no matter where he is.

"You studying?" Bowser asks.

I close my laptop. "I was trying to. Some days I think I'm too dumb for this course."

"Uh-huh. Which is why you're top of the class."

I'd deny it, but it's technically true. I don't have the best grades because I'm smart though; it's more that I'm really interested in the work and put in the effort to learn it. With Marshall constantly popping up in my brain, watch how quickly that goes downhill.

"I can't concentrate," I complain.

"Need me to go back in?"

I cross my arms and prop my chin on them. "Won't help."

"Why's that?"

"Because I couldn't concentrate *before* you came out here."

His deep laugh comes from behind a group of cacti. "What's on your mind, then?"

Bowser is easy to talk to, and normally I don't hold much

back from him, but he's also Marshall's best friend. I haven't even told Brady that I'm catching actual feelings, even though I'm ninety percent sure he knows, given those self-satisfied looks he keeps throwing my way.

On second thought, I'll probably deny Brady's suspicions even when he's giving my best-man toast—anything to stop him from being right.

"I don't think I should tell you," I say.

"What?" His head pops back into view. "Why?"

"Because you're a gossip."

"*You're* a gossip. I believe in freedom of information."

I lift my eyebrows, and he laughs.

"Us redheads have to stick together," I remind him.

He lifts his hat. "*This* is red. My hair is everything yours wishes it was. Your hair looks like unicorn vomit."

"You're so great for my confidence."

"Anytime, babe." He throws a look my way and turns to inspect some harsh-looking plant. "If I guess what's on your mind, will you tell me?"

"Maybe."

"Well, that's a wuss's answer."

"You take that back." I sit up suddenly, forgetting about Butters, whose claws clamp into my back before she lets out an annoyed hiss and takes off. "*Argh.*"

Bowser chuckles. "That hurt?"

"A little." I try to reach the sting in my back, but she got me good.

"I'm going to assume that's the universe's way of toughening you up."

"I'm plenty tough."

"Sure. Which is why you're out here daydreaming about Marshall's dick and don't want to talk about it."

My jaw drops. "How did you know?"

"I didn't, but I do now. Damn, it's a hardship being the smartest guy in the room."

"You pronounced smart-ass wrong."

"Maybe, but can you pronounce *right*? Because I was that too."

I give him the most unimpressed look I can manage. "Technically, I wasn't thinking about his dick."

"Yeah, okay. Mhmm. Your reaction definitely said otherwise though."

"That's because you were partially right, and I wasn't expecting it."

"So you were thinking about Marshall … but not his dick?" he clarifies.

"Exactly."

"I didn't know you could do that."

"Oh-ho." I pretend to be offended. "Are you slut shaming me?"

"Dude, we probably have the same amount of sex—the only difference is I can talk about chicks without mentioning their racks."

"I talk about plenty of guys without objectifying them." Now I'm *actually* starting to get annoyed.

Bowser must pick up on it because he holds out a hand. "Most guys, sure. But someone who's your type? Never happened. As soon as you see a big dude, your first thought is how quickly you'll be able to sleep with him."

Well, that's an exaggeration. There was … okay, not Brady because I *did* hit on him. Bowser too. And sure, I never actually mean it with Peyton, and it's become more of a running joke than anything, but originally, I definitely meant it a little. I hit on Cobey Green before he even said a word to me …

So.

It appears Bowser has a point.

"I'm a horrible human."

"Fuck off. That's so not the point here," Bowser says.

"Wait, you had a point?"

He lets out a *ha* and roughly chops the leaves off … something. "Kinda. Maybe?"

"With how clear you're being, I have no idea how I missed it."

He stands there thinking, tapping the scissor things against his chin. "I dunno what to say."

"That's not like you. You always know what to say, and even when you don't, you say whatever shit comes to mind anyway."

"Fine, then. This is me saying whatever shit comes to mind and hoping I don't offend you. Please back off Marshall."

"W-what?"

He shifts. "For the record, this is probably the most uncomfortable conversation I've ever had, but … you guys aren't a good fit. I thought the date would be a fun way for you both to let off some steam, but I was wrong. He's all about love and romance, whereas that's not you. And *no*, that isn't a bad thing—all I'm saying is you're yin, he's yang. You're day, he's night. There's a reason your date didn't go well, and I've been watching you this past week …"

I'm glaring at him so evilly I can barely see.

He points at me. "Don't give me that look."

"Why? You're confirming all the thoughts I've already had about how I'll never measure up and I'll never be good enough—"

"Fe, come on, now. I never said you weren't good enough. You know I adore you. And Marshall's my best mate. I'm trying to look out for you both. He can't give you what you want, and you can't give him what he wants."

"And what are you so sure we both want?"

"You want someone casual, someone to fuck around with."

He holds up his hand again before I can interrupt. "And there's nothing wrong with that because we're in college, and I'm totally doing the same. But Marshall wants his forever. And he's a picky bastard and won't give up the ass to just anyone. He's—" Bowser shakes his head. "Just trust me on this."

"You're wrong."

"Fe …"

I can't correct him about the sex thing because Marshall clearly hasn't told him for a reason, and I'll respect that, even if it drives home the cheap hookup thing in a very real way. But I can correct him about me. "I don't *only* want sex anymore."

He stares at me like he's trying to put the words together. "What are you saying?"

"I'm saying I want a boyfriend." I can't look at him as I force the words out. "It's why I was so open to you setting me up in the first place. It wasn't to find another guy to casually hook up with. I … I want my person." My throat gets worryingly thick, so I don't bother saying more than that.

When I look at Bowser again, his lips are parted, and he's staring at his gardening stuff like he doesn't actually see it. "Sorry. I … I didn't know."

"Well, obviously. I never told you before now."

"And what does that mean? You like Marshall, or …"

I twist my hands, thumbnail driving into the other palm. "I think so. And I know you believe in"—I make air quotes—"'freedom of information,' but you can't tell him. Please. I've already put myself out there once, so I'm leaving it up to him."

"Probably not the smartest choice."

"Why not?"

"Because Marshall will never put himself out there," Bowser says. "It's not what he does."

He did when he kissed me. My lips still ache to feel his against them again. "Maybe," I hedge.

"Seriously, Fe, if you do want him—and I mean the full thing: college boyfriends, happily ever after type shit—then you'll have to make the move. If you can't give him that—"

"Then don't bother. Got it."

He hangs his head back on a groan. "I hate this whole conversation. Every part of it. I don't want to tell you what to do. I just really don't want either of you to get hurt."

"Naw, look at you being all caring."

His face goes red. "Marshall has a big heart, and he'd treat you like you were worth the whole world. He's the kind of guy whose affection would smother you if you weren't ready for it. You'd never have to worry about there being someone else for him, and he deserves the same right back."

Well, that's one thing Bowser and I can both agree on. Marshall really would be like that in a relationship. We're not even together and I've already had a taste of what dating him could be like, and I want it all. I want to be smothered. To selfishly be the center of his world because I could easily give him it all back.

I'm already trying to do the right thing by him, which is why I haven't asked for sex again. Letting him take the lead is my way of showing that I respect him, and if he gave me the slightest hint that he wanted more and wasn't sure how to ask, I'd fix that for him too.

"I know," I finally whisper.

I'm not sure what my face is saying, but Bowser's expression softens. "You really like him, huh?"

"You're not allowed to tell him."

"Swear it." He mimes locking his lips. Then a grin splits his face. "I've never seen you like this before."

"Yeah, I'm an embarrassment."

"Maybe." He turns back to his plants and starts cutting again. "But it suits you."

19

Marshall

CALIFORNIA IS THE BEST. SATURDAYS ARE THE BEST. MOVING OUT of the dorms is the best. I'm sitting on the rooftop outside my room, enjoying the sunset and messing around on my ukulele. I picked up an extra shift through the week, so I don't have to work tonight—and thank god since those lacrosse guys sounded rowdy earlier today, which will likely mean a big night at the bar—and my coursework is more or less caught up on.

I have no idea what any of the other guys in the house are up to, and I'm trying to work up the courage to text Felix to see if he has plans tonight. The problem is that this late on a Saturday, it's unlikely he's sitting around. He's probably with Brady. Drinking. Getting ready to go out.

It's what's making me hold off. I don't really need to know if he's planning to hook up; I can just be the pathetic roommate waiting here to offer him aspirin and make him coffee after doing the walk of shame tomorrow morning. Yep. That will be me. The guy ready to be his *friend*.

Suddenly, Saturdays don't feel so great. Is it too late for Oscar to let me work?

I stay outside playing the ukulele until the sun disappears over the water, then figure I should head inside and see if anyone is around. If not, maybe I'll go for a walk or see if anyone I know is hanging out in the courtyard.

My room is a lot colder than it was earlier, so I pull on some sweats and a clean T-shirt, then head downstairs.

And pull up short when I find Felix in the kitchen.

His curls are half pinned up, and he's wearing pajama shorts and a shirt that says "small & feisty" in swirly letters.

"You're not going out?" I ask, trying to play it cool and completely missing the mark.

He lifts a delicate shoulder. "Brady had plans, and … everyone needs a night off now and then."

"So, you *don't* have plans?"

He laughs, and his smile tugs something deep in my gut. "No. You really think I'd be going out looking like this?" He waves a hand over himself, and I take the invitation to check him out.

"If you did, you'd never keep the guys off you."

His face lights up. "Tell me more."

"Do I start with how your ass is obscene in those thin shorts? Or mention that teasing flash of skin." I pinch his side on my way past, right where his shirt is slightly too short to cover him.

"Like you can talk. I don't know how you stayed celibate all these years."

Yikes. There's the question again. Maybe I need to put it out there and tell him I'm demi before this thing goes further. It feels like too much pressure to put on someone who does casual though. *Yeah, hi, it's because you're the only guy I've ever actually wanted to touch like that, and there's no guarantee I'll ever find someone else again.* Terrifying thought. Either he feels an obligation to keep pity-screwing me, or he runs hard and fast in the other direction.

Besides, when I think of it like that, it sounds as though I'm only interested in him for sex, which is what I'm actively working against.

I check the cupboard without replying at all, and when I don't see anything that interests me there, I move on to the fridge.

Felix clears his throat, and I glance over to find him giving me a pointed look.

"What?"

He crosses to the cupboard and closes it with his hip. "What do you have against closed doors?"

"You mean the cupboard thing?"

"*Yes.* It takes no extra effort whatsoever, and I'm constantly having to close them for you."

"Ah. Well." I run a hand over my hair. "It's probably stupid, but it's sort of a habit now. I guess. I just … I don't really notice it."

His lips twitch. "So where did this habit come from?"

"Everyone in my house is loud. Like, *really* loud. They always want to talk and be around, and for a couple of years there, no matter which of my brothers I ran into, they'd attack. Wrestling was a big thing in my house. I hated it. My brothers found it hilarious. So I started sneaking around and being as quiet as I could to avoid attracting attention. Between the ages of eleven and fifteen, my parents basically forgot I existed."

He gasps. "That's horrible."

"I'm exaggerating." I chuckle. "They love me, but my brothers are a handful. And …" I throw a thumb back toward the cupboard. "Our kitchen doors at home were loud when they shut."

Felix crosses his arms and leans into the counter. "Huh. I'm understanding you a whole lot more now. And the bedroom door?"

"What about it?"

"It's *always* open."

I let out a short, self-deprecating laugh-sigh type of noise. "My bedroom was at the end of the house, right next to my parents, and whenever my door was open, Mom would always stick her head in to say hi."

He's staring at me like that's the most pathetic thing he's ever heard.

"No." I nudge him. "No judging. I have a great family—there's just a lot of us, and I wouldn't have it any other way. One of my brothers is basically my best friend. He's on the opposite side of the country, so it's a bit harder to keep in touch, but we've always had each other's backs."

"Even when he was attacking yours?" Felix asks dryly.

"Exactly. My family has a different way of showing love, but they always *do* show it. Like, when we were younger, Dad had this thing where when we did something that impressed him, he'd lock us in the henhouse. It happened to all of my brothers, and I was stupidly jealous … until the day he did it to me." And while everything I've told him does smack of desperation and loneliness, I don't want him to picture it that way. Those things were only a small part of my childhood.

"I'll never understand the competition between siblings."

"Only child?" I ask.

He gasps, hand covering his heart as though I've greatly offended him. "Are you calling me spoiled and self-centered?"

"What would give you that idea?"

"Your only child assumption, for one …"

"Are you denying it?"

"Oh, no, I definitely am. I'm also very spoiled and self-centered. I wanted you to deny it, and you failed."

"One thing you never have to worry about is me lying to you, Fe. Also, you forgot to mention how you're particular and that you like things done your own way."

His jaw drops. "I have no idea what you mean."

I cock my eyebrow, then reach out and pop the cupboard door, leaving it closed but not all the way.

His jaw flexes, eyes on me as though he hasn't noticed.

I mimic his stance and cross my arms too. It's like I can see the thoughts racing through his mind, see his struggle as he tries to leave it, and I keep my mouth closed because it would probably be a bad time to point out he looks adorable fighting something that is so ingrained in him.

"*Ergh*, you win," he says, pushing the door closed again. "So maybe I like things in order."

"Maybe." I snort.

"Now who's the pain in the ass?"

"Definitely still you."

Felix's expression melts into a soft smile, and he steps forward. "So—"

"There you two are," Bowser calls.

I have never wanted to hit my best friend more. Somehow, I manage to *not* grab Felix, jump behind the fridge door, and call out, "There's no one here," but it's a close call.

"It's so hard having everyone want me," Felix says as Bowser walks in.

"Yeah, you look like you're really struggling there. Any-hoo. Dinnertime. Darian and I cooked for everyone."

I blink at Felix, who looks equally surprised. "Were you going to tell us that?"

"I am now. Geez. What do you want from me?"

"What if we had plans?"

He shrugs. "More food for me. I'm just grabbing drinks. It's all set up in the dining room."

The dining room that we never use?

"I'll help," I offer, hoping to catch Bowser alone and ask where this has come from.

He waves me away. "No need. I'll only be a second."

Felix and I exchange glances, but it's not like we can argue—or *want* to argue, because who doesn't like having dinner handed to them?

But when we get in there, it's clear *cooked* is a stretch. And there are only two table settings.

"What's—"

I turn in time to see Brady framed by the double doors. He flicks us a wave, then pulls them both closed. There's a rattle and then—

"I know you didn't lock that door, Brady Talon!" Felix yells, crossing to try them. They don't budge.

"I didn't even know they locked," I say.

"They don't," Brady calls back. "We had to improvise."

"Enjoy your dinner," Bowser adds.

Then footsteps retreat along the hall.

Felix slaps the door. "This is a safety hazard!"

"I think they're gone."

He slumps. "They're cut off. The both of them."

"Should I text them the devastating news now?"

"No need." He gestures to the window on the opposite side of the room. "We can climb out there."

"Or …" I say, pulling out a chair and sitting. "We could have dinner. Since they want us to, and we need to do that anyway." I'm trying not to be offended over the fact I've lit up like I've just been handed a gift while Felix is trying everything he can to get away from me.

His eyes narrow slightly, and he creeps forward like a scared kitten. "You want to have dinner with me?"

"Sure."

"But you are aware that they're obviously planning for this to be a date, right?"

His voice catches on the word, but I don't call him on it because I'm nervous too. I just somehow hide it better. "Is that what the candles are for?"

I have to say they went overboard with them. And they're those nasty bug-repellent smelly ones, which probably isn't giving the ambiance they were going for.

"There are also flower petals on the tables."

"Bowser's all about the cliché." Felix still hasn't moved, so I pull out the chair beside me and grab the plate from the other side of the table. "The way I see it is we're eating pizza, drinking—" My eyes almost bulge out of my head when I see the only thing on the table is tequila. "Ah, *this*, and we didn't have to pay for any of it. They might have wanted it to be a date, but that part is up to us. We're two friends eating together."

He smiles lightly as he takes the seat I offered, looking more reserved than I've seen him.

"But, look," Felix says. "We have pudding cups for dessert. How are we supposed to ignore that kind of romance?"

"It'll be a hardship, but I think we'll be okay."

"Fine." Felix reaches for the tequila. "But you're having a drink with me first. Trust me when I say it's the only way you're going to get through a night alone with me."

I know he's joking, but I hate it. I'd been enjoying our conversation in the kitchen before Bowser came in. So before he can get the bottle open, I cover his hand with mine.

"I don't want one."

He eyes me suspiciously. "You did hear what I said, right?"

"I did. Which is why I don't want any. I'm confident I can handle you sober."

Those pretty blue eyes blink up at me before he sets the bottle down again. "Okay, but don't say I didn't warn you."

20

Felix

I WILL NOT JUMP MARSHALL. I WILL NOT JUMP MARSHALL.

It's getting harder and harder to keep my resolve and follow his lead when he's so fucking perfect. Even without the tequila, our conversation hasn't stopped once.

"… somehow, Robbie's hand was broken, Kynan took the skin off his leg from ankle to knee, and Banjo looked like he'd stuck his finger in a power socket."

I narrow my eyes. "And this all happened in the space of time you glanced down at your book and back up again."

"I'm telling you; my brothers are crazy."

"I don't believe you."

He shrugs, and I eye his big shoulders.

"Maybe you'll see for yourself someday," he says.

That snaps me out of it. "Naw." I bat my lashes. "You want me to meet your family already? You really are a romantic."

His laugh is deep and loud. "You don't need to run scared. I only mean if they come to visit, or … well, if you don't go home for spring break, you could probably tag along. Bowser does every year rather than fly home to Florida."

"To … your place."

"Yeah."

"With your big family?"

"It's not as noisy anymore." He smiles. "Most of my brothers have moved out, except Banjo, who's stayed to help my parents look after my grandparents."

As much as I want to bounce up and down and say *yes, pick me pick me*, I'm also not going to get too excited over a throw-away invitation. "I'll keep it in mind."

"Cool. So, what's it like where you're from? I've never been to the East Coast before, but my brother Robbie is at college in Connecticut."

"What's he like? You talk about him all the time."

"Well … like I said, we're the closest. He's the one you heard me on the phone to."

"Is he like you?"

"No. When I said I'm different, I meant it. We look very similar, but he skipped needing the glasses. He also plays football and is part of a fraternity, which he takes *very* seriously."

I amuse myself for a moment, trying to picture Marshall as a frat boy. Franklin U has an active Greek life, but I couldn't see him fitting in with any of them. "He's not a DIK, is he?" I ask, referencing the largest frat on campus. Apparently when it came to naming things, the Franklin U Kings didn't give a FUK.

"No, they're Sigma Beta Psis. Which I only know because he wears the merch everywhere at home."

"He sounds cool."

"He is. He's never had an issue making friends." There's a wistful note to Marshall's tone that I want to make go away.

"From the looks of things, you don't have that issue either."

"Yeah?" His expression is hopeful, and it warms me from the inside out.

I lightly tap his forearm. "Don't fish for validation. We both know you have plenty of friends." And he does. He mightn't know everyone like me, but that's not a bad thing. Especially when most people only know *of* me, and not all the rumors are pretty.

"Friends like you," he says.

I force myself to smile and nod. "Exactly."

"I'm glad."

The words, his warm tone, the steady eye contact ... it makes me feel more than the simple sentence should. So I do what I do best and make things weird. "And I'm glad I took your virginity."

He bursts out laughing. "Yeah, umm ... I'm glad you did too."

I try to get a read on him. To work out if there's any regret, or if he wants to go again, or if I really was a means to an end. He doesn't give anything away. "It was good."

"Yeah, it was."

I'd do it again. I want to say the words so badly, it hurts to hold them back.

Instead, I grab the tequila. "Now that you've proved you can get through a dinner with me sober, I don't see any harm in doing a shot together."

"Oh, really?"

"Just one shot." And hopefully, it's enough to loosen up some of these worries I've got.

"Fine."

I pour them out, and we do them quickly. Marshall grimaces the whole way through his while I try not to gag. Tequila is nasty. "One more?"

He opens his mouth, and I'm sure he's about to say no when his gaze flicks to me and away again. "Go on. Just one though."

I pour them out, and we shoot them. Then I replace the lid to stop from being tempted again.

"So …" I turn in my chair to face him, and Marshall does the same. We're so close one of my legs is between his, and one of his knees is dangerously close to my groin. Feeling emboldened by the alcohol I know will be hitting me soon, I carefully rest my hand on his thigh, like it's a totally casual move that doesn't have my heart drumming against my ribs. "Have you had any dates since Lyle?"

His attention flicks up from my hand to my face. "I didn't have a date *with* Lyle."

Urg. It's hard to work out if he's being oblivious on purpose or not. "Fine, then … have you had any dates since … me?"

His stormy gaze holds steady. "No."

"No one?"

"My lack of a love life really shouldn't be making you so happy."

Even him saying that can't stop me from smiling. "Do you want to know how many I've had?"

"No."

Annnd there goes my good mood. I snatch my hand away and straighten, trying to shove down the dirty, gross feelings bombarding me.

Then Marshall shocks me stupid by leaning right into my space, hand closing over my bare knee and fingers skimming the inside of my thigh. "I don't need to ask you because whatever you do while you're single is up to you."

My head doesn't like that answer, but my body is too distracted by him touching me. It's completely PG, and yet the skin running from my knee to my cock is alive and aching for more. "You wouldn't care if I fucked someone?"

"That's your business."

"I didn't ask whose business it was," I say, leaning forward too. "I asked if you would care."

He swallows roughly.

"Would you care, Marshmallow, if I went out right now and bounced on some other guy's cock?"

His grip on me tightens, and I love the way his features shift, his jaw tightens. "Of course I'd care."

I light up inside. "Why?"

"Because I want you here with me." His voice is rough, and when I glance down, there's no mistaking the monster bulge in his sweats. I'm hard too and not even trying to hide it. I want him, and there's no point in making a secret out of it.

I wrap my hands around his neck and climb into his lap. "Would you be jealous?" I tilt my lips to his ear. "Tell me that you'd break anyone who touched me."

"I would." His hands run up my thighs to grasp my hips. "You deserve the world."

"Do I deserve *you*?"

"No." The word makes me pull back. "You deserve so much more."

That's all I need.

I sink to my knees.

"What are you doing?" he gasps.

"I want to make you feel good." I stick out my bottom lip. "Please?"

His mouth is hanging open, glasses slipped down his nose, and brown hair a chaotic mess. Damn, I want him so bad. I want to make him feel amazing and show him how good we could be together. I want to be good enough for him. I want to be the only one he needs.

"What if they come back?" he asks.

"We'll be quick."

He finally cracks a small smile. "*Quick* won't be a problem."

"Then …" I run my hands up his beefy thighs, getting closer to his straining cock. His gray sweats have a spot of precum seeping through the thin material, and my mouth is watering over the thought of tasting him. "Please …"

He stares at me for the longest time before stroking my cheek. "You know I don't need you to do this, right?"

Irritation flickers through me. "Do you at least *want* me to?"

"More than I've ever wanted anything. And that's saying something. But that wasn't my question."

"I know you don't need this." I lean in and nuzzle his groin, and his shaky inhale is music to my ears. "Yet." Because by the time I'm done, I want him to need this. To need me. Over and over. "Can I?"

"I feel like I should say no, but I really want to say yes."

"So say yes."

He's torn, and I'm trying not to let it get to me. Maybe I was supposed to be an easy out, someone easy to move on from, but fuck him. If I have to suck his cock every day for the rest of the year to get him as addicted to me as I am to him, I will.

"O-okay."

"Lift your hips."

He does as I say, and I tug his sweats down his thighs. He's going commando, which turns me on more, and I finally have my first proper look at that glorious cock. The quick glimpse of it in the moonlight didn't prepare me for it full frontal and in my face. He's proportionate to his body. Long, thick, and the perfectly smooth head is glossy with precum and an angry purply red.

"No funderwear?" I tease.

He shakes his head. "I didn't think I'd see you tonight."

"So you only wear them for me, do you?"

"They're a conversation starter." He groans, and his giant hand cups my face. "I really need you to get started."

"Make me."

"Fe …"

I lean in and swipe my tongue over the tip. "I want you to make me."

"I've never done this before."

It shouldn't turn me on that much to know that no one else has ever tasted him. Sucked him. Seen his cock like this. This whole experience is all mine. "I know." I brush a kiss over his thigh. "It's okay. Just … do what feels right. Anything."

He swallows and nods. "Can you open your mouth? Please?"

"Such a gentleman," I purr. But I drop my jaw and let my tongue slip out. I don't move forward though, just wait to see what he does.

And what he does do is completely surprise me. The pad of his thumb strokes over my tongue, once, twice, before he presses down in the center and triggers my gag reflex.

"Fuck, that's hot," he gasps.

I wrap my lips around his thumb and suck.

"*Ngh.* Shit, so is that."

Wait until it's your dick. I run my tongue from the center of his palm to the top of his thumb before releasing him. "Just a little preview. I'm ready for the main event when you are."

"Okay. Yeah." He grips my hair and guides me toward his cock, but before I can get a taste, he says, "Wait."

My heart sinks. "What—"

He cuts me off when he yanks me up toward him and brushes his lips over mine. The kiss is another of those sweet ones of his. Soft and slow, and then his tongue pushes in deep and strokes over mine. "Sorry," he says when he pulls back. "I needed to do that first."

"I'm never going to complain about you kissing me like that."

He huffs a laugh. "In that case, be prepared for a lot more of them tonight … you know, in approximately five seconds after you've sucked my cock."

I snigger and ease his thighs open as far as his sweats will allow, then sit back on my heels. "You lie back. I've got this."

And maybe being so easy all my life has its perks because I know exactly what to do now. There's no way Marshall is getting away with only letting me have his cock for five seconds.

I spit into my hand, getting it nice and slick before I lightly stroke him up and down. Precum mixes with my saliva, and when his shaft is practically throbbing, I dip my hand and roll his balls in my palm.

Marshall's thighs twitch. "Oh … wow."

I've barely gotten started.

I know how badly he wants my mouth, but I take my time, stroking him, tugging his balls, letting my fingers graze over his taint. He keeps licking his lips, gaze trained on my hand, and I keep careful watch of his face. I take note of what gets his eyelids fluttering, what makes his jaw clench or his lips part on a sudden breath. His expressions are so open, it's turning me on more than if he was the one touching me.

"God, I'm already close."

I immediately let him go.

He grunts and goes to grab himself, but I bat his hand away. "No coming yet."

"But—"

"No."

"They could be back any second."

"And if they are, they're going to see you getting the best blow job of your life."

"Can we claim best when it's the only one and it hasn't even started yet?"

I push up onto my knees. "If I have anything to say about it, it'll be the best. No matter how many other guys suck your dick, they'll never compare to me."

His smile is shaky. "Might I suggest actually sucking it, then?"

"Patience. Let the master work."

I go back to teasing him, but this time, I throw in a few tighter strokes amongst the loose ones. My tongue flicks over his slit and traces slow patterns over his balls. Marshall's breathing has picked up a notch, and I can tell he's desperate for more. His hips keep tilting forward whenever my mouth gets close to him, and every time I sense he's close and pull away, he lets out something between a curse and a sob.

"Wow, you're leaking," I say, then swirl my tongue around his tip to gather it all up. I hum. "Tastes so good."

"Shit, Fe."

"I can't wait to taste it all."

"Me neither. Please …"

I give him an innocent look as I run my lips up his shaft, the kind that says *I have no idea what you could possibly want.*

"Fe …"

His balls are tight and swollen, his cock an angry red, and I can only imagine how good and bad he feels right now. *I'm* horny as fuck, and I'm the one doing the teasing.

His hand tightens in my hair as his thighs flex powerfully. "I need you."

And if I want to blow him, I'm going to have to do it now because my teasing has done what it was supposed to and drawn this out, but soon he's not going to be able to hold it back.

I work his balls down before wrapping my fingers tightly around their base.

Then I lean in and swallow him whole.

"Holy *shit*," he cries, and I really hope Brady and Bowser don't have their ears pressed to the door, or they're going to be getting a full-on porn soundtrack. Marshall's mouth has hit fast forward on a string of praises that range from how good this feels to calling me beautiful again.

I bob up and down, working my tongue over his shaft, circling his head, and using my hand to jerk him off at the same time. I'm aggressive and making a mess with my spit, and I'm so consumed by what I'm doing that I don't even bother reaching for my cock. This is all about making Marshall feel good. Making Marshall need me. And when I glance up and find him greedily watching, our eyes lock, and I'm hit with this shocking certainty that I'll never get enough of him looking at me like that.

Then his head falls back, his hand tightens, and he starts to fuck my face.

His cock jams the back of my throat, and that, combined with him gasping my name over and over, makes me so high I never want this to end. This is the control and power I crave.

But almost as soon as I have that thought, his cock swells, and the first salty spurt hits my tongue.

I lap up every drop, sucking him until he's done. I'm about to reach down and make quick work of my own dick, but Marshall doesn't let me get that far.

He hauls me to my feet, yanks down the front of my shorts, and wraps his mouth around my cock.

Seeing the big guy, leaning forward, trying to ram as much of my length into his mouth as possible, gets me to the edge fast. He's clearly had no experience, but seeing him blissed-out, sucking and moaning as he gives me his all, is hotter than anything I've ever experienced. His mouth is warm, and the suction is perfect, and all it takes is one gag before the feel of his throat contracting sets me off. My orgasm hits hard, and I ride out the feel of it, barely conscious of Marshall struggling to take it all.

He pulls off, cum pooling in his scruffy stubble, and gives me a cocky grin. "Not bad for a first time, huh? I think you came faster than I did."

I laugh, then lean down and clean his chin with my tongue before pulling him into the type of filthy kiss we've never shared before.

His pupils are still shot to hell, and when I pull back, I'm only half-convinced he isn't about to maul me again. "That was amazing."

"Why, thank you." I pretend to dust off my shoulder, and he wraps his big arms around me and pulls me into his lap.

Then he does what he promised: he kisses me. The same worshipful kisses that reach from my toes to my scalp, the ones that make me warm and fuzzy and so happy, I push my luck.

"We can do that again, you know." I pull his lip between my teeth. "Whenever you want."

He makes a noncommittal noise and keeps kissing me. And while his kisses are as sweet as ever, that happy feeling ebbs.

Because his lack of answer says more than he probably wants it to.

Friends.

I've never hated the word more.

21

Marshall

"You'll never guess. I'm going to a"—I pretend to gag— "frat party."

Robbie's booming laugh comes down the line. "Bro my god, is little Marshmallow growing up?"

"Being forced against my will, more like it."

"Bowser taking you?"

"He is."

"Good." Robbie pauses. "I like him. He fits right in with the family …" Robbie's doing that thing again that I've noticed recently. Hinting at something between me and Bowser despite the fact none of our family knows I'm bi. Robbie's only just started to figure it out about himself, and I'm happy for him, but it also feels like if I say anything now that I'll be encroaching on his *thing*, and as far as I know, all our other brothers are straight.

"He does get along well with everyone," I agree.

"Yup. He visiting home for spring break again?"

"Of course." He's come the last two years. "I think Mom would send out a search party for him if he didn't." I hesitate before adding, "And I invited another friend with us too."

There's a pause. "What kind of friend?"

"Just a friend," I say quickly.

"Right. But your voice did that thing."

"I have no idea what you're talking about."

Robbie scoffs. "You totally know, and you're totally avoiding it. So spill. Girl … guy?"

"*His* name is Felix." My cheeks are burning, and I'm glad this conversation is over the phone. "And he's a friend. Relax." At least, he is for now. The blow job the other night was out of this world, and as desperately as I've wanted to ask him for more, knowing the answer will be yes, I can't bring myself to say the words.

I'm so worried about screwing this up.

"It's okay if he's not just a friend," Robbie says, sounding more serious than he normally does. And just when I'm considering saying more, he comes out with one of his usual Robbie-isms. "I mean, brojobs are fucking incredible."

"And this is where I leave you."

"Fine, but don't forget the fanny pack. Stock up on mints … snacks … fentanyl test strips …"

"I've told you I don't do drugs."

"It's not for you but your bros as well. Test everything. Pot is legal there, but you don't always know where it comes from, so every time someone wants to light up, bam! Marshmallow is there with the assist."

I chuckle. "All I'm picturing is you coasting through a party, sprinkling testing strips over people like glitter."

"Damn straight, little bro." He sighs. "Damn, I wish I was a DIK—but don't tell my brothers I said that."

"You just want to be able to go around saying, *hey, wanna see my DIK*, and then showing them your frat sweaters."

"I was thinking more along the lines of *this is my brother's DIK* and then showing one of *their* sweaters."

I crack up laughing. "You have issues."

"You know it."

We hang up as Bowser raps on my door. "Ready to go?"

Ready for a frat party? Never. I could think of a hundred and one other things I'd rather be doing on a Wednesday night. Like spending more time with Felix. Not that *more* time is going to be easy since he's basically been my shadow the past few days. He sits next to me to study, we walked down to the pier to finally get tacos last night, and he spent the whole time playing a game of "remember that time you fucked me on the beach?" then he practically climbed me and asked me to carry him home.

Fuck knows I wasn't complaining.

I wish I could get a read on him. Could figure out if he's interested in more than sex. I want to believe there's more—I ache for it—and nights like last night, when I'm holding him close and feeling warm inside, it's easy to believe it might be the case. But then Bowser or Brady or Darian stop by, and he gets all touchy and flirty with them, which leaves me more confused than ever.

"How do I look?" I ask Bowser, not committed to it. The party theme is DIKs Around the World, and I panicked and ended up going as an Oktoberfest stereotype.

"Love the lederhosen." He sniggers. "All I can picture is you yodeling."

"That's exactly the imagery I was going for." I cringe and glance down. The knee-high socks and checkered shirt probably don't help matters. And since it's rented and they didn't have my size, the whole costume is *snug*. "What are you?"

Bowser is dressed head to toe in khaki and is wearing a cowboy hat. "I'm Australian, aye?"

"Sounds Canadian to me."

"Fuck off. This is Aussie, innit?"

"I don't think you know *what* you are."

"I'm an Irwin."

I pat his shoulder as I pass. "At least I can be assured I won't be the dumbest-looking person there."

We walk a few blocks to where the Delta Iota Kappa house is, and even if I'd never been there before, it would be impossible to miss. College kids are everywhere, the music is loud, and I can make out pulsing lights coming from inside. Here we go. A night of college memories that I'll attempt to wash from my brain with vodka. Can't wait.

The first person I see when I walk inside is Charlie Martin dressed as the Statue of Liberty, then the frat king of the DIKs himself, Cory Ingram, along with his best friend, Will. They're dressed as Mario and Luigi, with cardboard go-karts hung over their shoulders, and are racing up and down the halls, knocking people out of their way.

"Already off to a great start," I say, setting the girl who'd bumped into me back on her feet.

"No one's hurt. Calm your farm, mate," Bowser says.

"That accent is going to get old fast."

"Throw another bloody shrimp on the barbie."

"Shoot me now."

Bowser drags me through to the kitchen, where a makeshift bar has been set up. "Here. Maybe this will help you loosen up." He pours out a generous helping of vodka and Coke into a red Solo cup. "Bottoms up, my man."

We cheers, and I drink it down—anything to make this party more bearable. The humidity of a hundred bodies, the laughing and conversation all mixed together, the thumping bass from a few rooms away … I mix another drink and slam that one back too.

Bowser slaps my back. "There we go."

"I'm gonna need way more than that."

"Your wish is my command." Bowser fixes the next drinks, hands mine over, and then motions for me to follow him. I'm already starting to sweat through my shirt, and when we step out into the backyard, even the warm night air feels like relief on my skin.

Bowser makes a beeline for some of his friends, and I look around for anyone I know. Felix hadn't been quite right in saying I had a lot of friends. I'm friendly and can chat with anyone, but actual friends are few and far between. There's me and Bowser, a handful of guys I know on campus, and then … everyone else.

If only I wasn't so quiet and boring.

"Gah." I shake off the thought and drain my cup. Three drinks in quick succession probably isn't smart, but it's not like I ever get to go out and have fun, so I might as well give it a go. I head back inside, make myself another drink, and throw back a shot while I'm at it. I don't think I've ever consciously made the choice to get messy before, but fucked-up, here I come! Where better to get shitfaced than at a frat party?

How's this for boring?

High-pitched squeals hit my ears, and I turn toward the sound. "No way," a pretty girl shrieks. She's dressed like a— "I'm a beer wench!"

"I can see that."

"We match."

"We do." Her shirt is even a similar blue to mine.

"What are you drinking?" she asks.

I vaguely gesture toward the drinks on display. "Anything and everything."

"I like your style."

And okay, I might be inexperienced, but I know she's definitely flirting with me. She's cute and nice, but I got nothing. No zap. No spark of interest. "You having something?"

"Why don't you surprise me?" she suggests.

Well, that's not smart. "You really should mix your own drinks," I point out. "You can't trust someone you just met."

She looks me over like *I'm* the odd one. "Okay ..."

"Just looking out for you."

Her smile immediately comes back. "That's very sweet." She tips way too much Bacardi into a cup, then steps closer. "Cute *and* sweet. Tell me you dance and you're a triple threat."

"I don't dance."

"Damn, I knew there had to be *something*." She bats her lashes, and it's nowhere near as cute as when Felix does it. "Maybe you'll make an exception for me?"

And as though thinking of him summons him from nowhere, Felix—dressed like a mime in black hot pants, a black-and-white striped crop top, and a red neck scarf—appears at my side. "He *is* a triple threat. Cute, sweet, and chunky." He grins up at me and lightly pats my stomach.

"Well, *that's* rude," the girl says. "You can't just call people fat."

Felix turns a glare on her that's so icy it makes even me think twice about crossing him. "Fat isn't a bad word. And neither is chunky. And *no*, he won't make an exception for you because he's making one for me. Thank you, *byyye*."

Then Felix's fingers link through mine, and he drags me away. We're barely out of the room when he turns and backs me into the hallway wall. He presses between my legs and rests his hands on my chest, turning an adorable pout up at me. His bottom lip is pink and shiny and sticking out, and I want to tug it down and kiss him.

Instead, I'm trying not to laugh at him very obviously

marking his territory back there. I'm supposed to hate it, I guess, but I just don't.

"She was flirting with you," he says.

"Yeah, I know."

"Did you like it?"

I shrug, because how do I tell him I'm neither here nor there. "Didn't really bother me."

He *hmphs*. "She wanted you to fuck her."

"Probably."

"Did you want to?"

"No."

Finally, his pouting settles down. "Is there anyone at the party you *do* want to sleep with?"

My eyes lock onto his, and slowly, I reach up to rest my hands on the bare skin at his sides. "Yes."

His smile is breathtaking. "Good." Felix presses up onto his toes and drops a kiss on my cheek. He lingers there for a moment, body pressed to mine, and it's taking serious willpower on my end to keep from flipping our positions and kissing him. "Maybe I'll see you later."

Felix very purposely brushes my cock as he turns and bounces away.

This whole being friends thing is going to be harder than I thought. All I know is I better slow down on the alcohol because Felix being here is dangerous. If I want sex, I know he'll willingly give it to me, but until I'm sure of his feelings, I need to protect mine.

Maybe that means Felix goes home with someone else, and if that's the case, I'll have to suck it up and deal with it.

It'll hurt, but not as much as blowing my chance at having him properly.

22

Felix

I GRIND MY ASS AGAINST BRADY AS HE JUMPS AROUND WITH HIS arms raised like the rest of the frat guys surrounding us. He's a chameleon, can fit in anywhere, and he's had just about every patriotic jackass at the party high-five him for his Uncle Sam costume. I'd judge him, but the metallic silver booty shorts are hot as hell.

I do worry he's taking his SEAL obsession a little too far, but who am I to judge? I'm trying to seduce my confusing teddy bear roommate, who's still not biting even with me practically throwing myself at him every day. I'm determined to get him back into bed again tonight.

"Four o'clock!" Brady shouts in my ear.

"I don't know what that means!"

He turns my chin toward the door, where I see Charlie Martin chatting with *my* Marshall. Charlie is a player. A careless one too. I've heard a bunch of rumors about him dating people and moving on without even telling them, which is a huge change from when I dated him freshman year. We were together a few weeks, and he didn't put the moves on me once.

I don't have time for that kind of negativity in my life.

Charlie and I are still the kinds of friends who chat at parties and stuff, but if he tries anything with Marshall, he's going to become my enemy real fast.

My jaw tenses so hard it hurts.

Brady's laugh sounds over the music. "You look stabby."

"If I had a knife, I would be."

"Wanna go over there?"

"No …" My answer is so small there's no way he's heard it, but he obviously catches the way my lips move.

"Fine! Stay and dance. Let's see how long it takes Charlie to put the moves on your man!"

Like hell he will.

I'm trashed, but I manage to walk in a straight line toward them. I think. Objectively, I don't blame Charlie for approaching Marshall. His costume is tight in all the perfect places, and that monster cock imprint is like a homing beacon for thirsty-ass queer men.

But emotionally? I want to rip his gorgeous face off.

Once I reach where Marshall is sitting, I don't hesitate to drop into his lap and loop my hands around his neck. "Hey, Marshmallow."

"Hey, Felix the cat."

"I used to love that show!" Charlie exclaims with all of his golden retriever energy. It does nothing but get on my nerves.

I ignore him, my attention fixed on Marshall. "Whatcha doing?"

"Talking to Lady Liberty." He nods toward Charlie, and there goes my plan of pretending he doesn't exist. I reluctantly turn side-on and give him my attention.

"Yes," Charlie cries. "I've had to tell people to call me that all night. Don't they know that isn't in the spirit of a costume party?" He holds out his fist to Marshall for a fist bump, and to my complete surprise, Marshall returns it.

"You two look *cozy*." I don't bother to cover the bite in my tone.

Marshall laughs, and his big hand rests on my hip, giving it a squeeze. Happiness explodes behind my ribs, and I get comfortable leaning against his chest.

A long *awww* comes from Charlie. "Are you guys together? I love that! Felix is the sweetest little dude, Marsh. I'm happy for you guys." His words are so sincere, I realize I *may* have misread the situation.

"So you two *weren't* flirting, then?"

Charlie looks confused. "With Marshall? No way. Ah, I mean, you're hot, of course, but I ... well, I—"

"We had class together last year," Marshall says. "Charlie took notes for me the week I was off sick and dropped in every day to check if I needed anything."

And as much as I want to be jealous about that ... it sounds like Charlie. He's always gone above and beyond for people—except in the sex department, at least with me—which is probably why he dates around so much.

With that crisis averted, I let them chat and glance around for Brady. He's found Peyton, and they're doing shots. Peyton's idea of dressing up was to borrow the sombrero Brady got at some party ... and then spent the night throwing up in. I'm not sure Brady shared that anecdote with his brother.

Bow down to Franklin U's football king and lord of the puke.

I'm about to get up and join them when Marshall's hand absently moves to my lower back, and he rubs circles into my bare skin. It's shivery, comforting goodness, and I decide that relaxing here for a little longer can't hurt.

Sure, I'm apparently overly possessive of him, but even at a party like this, I wouldn't expect to be glued together even if we were dating. I've always been a firm believer that partners should have their own lives outside of each other, but considering we're *not* partners—or anything, if I'm going to get technical about it— I can't help being clingy.

It doesn't help that he's really, really snuggly.

Bowser shows up and steals Charlie's attention.

"I should probably go find Brady," I say.

Marshall's hands clamp down on my waist. "Yeah, not right now you're not."

"Why?" I turn so I can see him and nudge something under me that doesn't require further explanation. "Oh, I see. Someone has a big problem."

He chuckles. "It's your fault. Can those be called shorts?" His voice hitches. "They don't even cover your ass."

And because I want him to talk more about my ass, I stand and lean forward, hands on my knees, and twerk slightly. "These shorts?"

"Fuck, Felix." He pulls me down on top of him again. "I didn't think it was possible in these ball restrictors, but you're gonna make me come in my pants."

I grin at him over my shoulder. "Sounds like a challenge to me."

"Please be nice." His voice squeaks.

"Fine. You're no fun."

His voice is warm at my ear. "You sure about that? I would have said we've had *lots* of fun."

I pretend to swoon back against him, head dropping onto his shoulder. "It's such a turn-on when you talk about us having sex."

"I'll keep that in mind."

"It's even more of a turn-on when we do it."

"Fe …" He rests his head against mine. "Sex is great, but it's not everything."

I swear my jaw drops. It's not everything, but it's a big thing. At least to me. And if he doesn't feel the same way, does that mean I've completely failed at initiating him into the wonders of how good sex can be?

I shrink in on myself, feeling completely rejected and unwanted.

Even as Marshall wraps an arm around my waist and holds me close, I'm confused. He's sweet and affectionate. Showers me with attention. But when it comes to anything more than this, he hasn't made a move, and there are only so many times I can throw myself at him without coming across as completely fucking desperate.

Sure. Because I haven't already reached that point ten times over.

"You coming, Fe?"

I glance over at Bowser with no clue what the hell they're talking about, but I did pick up on one word. "Coming? You offering?"

"If I was queer, you'd be the one for me." Bowser blows me a kiss, and I pretend to catch it and tuck it in my pocket. Marshall's arm tightens.

Interesting.

"You'd have to go through Marshmallow first." I accidentally-on-purpose wriggle in his lap, and a strangled noise catches in his throat. "Isn't that right?"

"I know what you're doing."

I smile at him angelically. "Making sure everyone knows how smitten you are with me?"

He laughs and rolls his eyes while I try not to huff at the lack of an answer. He turns back to Charlie and Bowser. "Bowser always comes back to Arizona with me," he explains.

I reluctantly join the conversation again.

"Sure do," Bowser agrees. "His brothers are a lark."

"Sounds fun."

"That's what I was asking before. Marshall mentioned that he invited you—you going to come with?"

"You were really inviting me?" I ask.

Marshall shifts under me. "Well, yeah. If you don't have plans."

"Is it a pity invite, or do you actually want me to come?"

He turns his head to see me. "Course I want you to come. We're friends. Friends hang out together, don't they?"

Friends. That fucking word again. All right, Marshall, messaged received like a smack to the face.

I force a smile at Bowser. "Oh, I'll be there. I can't wait. Three friends hitting the road together. The three musketeers. The Kardashian sisters but young and without all that work done. Maybe I should buy a headscarf and oversized sunglasses for the occasion, and you can both call me Audrey and ..." I'm rambling, and no one stops me. "We'll all have fun and be such good friends who are friendly."

Charlie and Bowser are giving me concerned looks, and I'm sure Marshall is probably doing the same behind me.

"Well," Bowser says. "That was a lot of words used to say a whole lot of nothing."

"And you didn't think to stop me?"

Bowser shrugs. "I figured the more you said, the more likely something useful would come out eventually. It didn't."

He and Charlie laugh, but all it does is cement the shitty feelings churning inside me. The alcohol hasn't sat well, and knowing that they—and probably Marshall—all view me as some pathetic joke is hard to swallow. How is it fair that the guy who's treating me better than anyone before him is only doing it as a friend? Only *wants* to be doing it as a friend.

My stupid heart feels like it's stupid shattering at the idea that I'll never have Marshall the way I want. That one day someone else will, and he'll smother them with affection, in Bowser's words.

I stand up long enough to turn and straddle Marshall's lap, then wrap my arms around him and bury my face in his neck. He smells like body spray and something else that's completely him. "I want to go home."

"Now?"

"Suddenly not feeling it."

"Okay, then." His hand runs down my back. "Want me to carry you?"

I hate the way that simple question lights me the hell up inside. On some level, I'd known he'd offer. I'd known that if I wanted out, he'd be only too happy to leave as well, but hearing him roll with it, no hesitation, is cementing this infatuation to dangerous levels. "You don't have to leave." And he doesn't. The fact he *would* is what's important.

His chest moves with his laughter, and then his arms wrap around me tightly as he stands.

I immediately close my legs around his waist to take my weight.

"We're gonna head," he says to the others.

"Oh, I bet you are," Bowser sniggers.

"Not like that." The sigh comes through loud in his words. "Fe's drunk and needs to go to bed."

"Marshall's going to tuck me in."

He pats my back. "I am."

I hug him tighter to me.

The others say goodbye, and we leave, me clinging to him and Marshall carrying my weight easily. His strength is such a turn-on, and I'm sure he can feel how hard I am against his stomach, but he doesn't say a thing.

Just carries me home, talking and joking with me the whole way. He takes me right up to my room, but when he drops onto the side of my bed, I don't release him. I pull back enough to see his expression in the moonlight coming through the window.

"Stay," I beg him.

His face tightens. "You're drunk."

"Not for that. Just ..." I don't want to say it. Don't want to admit how desperately I'm craving the closeness.

Maybe he reads it off my face, and maybe he doesn't, but next thing I hear is his shoes hitting the floor. "Let me go change out of this fucked-up costume, and I'll be right back."

I climb off his lap, and while he's gone, I strip off. I didn't bother with underwear tonight, so out of respect for Marshall, I cross to my drawers and pull on a pair of briefs.

Then I climb under my covers, and a moment later, I hear Marshall come back.

"Fe ..." he whispers.

I throw back the covers, and Marshall closes my door before climbing in behind me.

"Just to sleep," he says.

And as his warmth engulfs me and I roll over to snuggle into his chest, a satisfied exhale leaves me. "I'll take whatever I can get."

23

Marshall

I'VE NEVER BEEN HAPPIER IN MY LIFE. THE MORE TIME I SPEND with Felix, the more I want him. Not only physically, though definitely that too, but everything. I want to be able to call him mine.

Waking with him sleeping quietly on my chest gives me a solid whack to the heart, and I lie there and watch him until he wakes. It's an addictive feeling, made even better by the slow, genuine smile that stretches over his face.

"You're still here." His voice is slow and husky from sleep.

"Did you want me to go?"

He folds his arms over my chest before resting his head on them. "No." His eyes drift closed, but his soft smile lingers. "It's been a long time since I slept with a teddy bear."

"A teddy bear, huh?" I chuckle. "Is that all I am to you?"

"Pretty much." He slowly opens his eyes again. "What am I to you?"

Everything.

You're every single thought, decision, and daydream I have. Every single day.

But if I say that, guaranteed I'll scare him off for good. It's a hard question to answer because everything he is to me are things I can't tell him. I can't mention how I look at him and see my hopes for more. Or that his opinions mean more to me than anyone's. That he's the reason I'm happy half the time and the reason I'm exasperated and sexually frustrated the other half. Telling him that I'm on edge until I see him each day, and when I do it's like something inside of me relaxes, sounds like some stalker-level bullshit.

But every second that passes without an answer is taking his smile with it.

"You're … *wonderful.*"

I think he's just as surprised as I am by that word coming out of my mouth. He blinks his pretty blue eyes at me in confusion, and he swallows obviously before his lips part.

"I am?"

The clear need for validation has me brushing the curls from his forehead and meeting his eyes. "Everything about you."

He ducks his head, pressing his face to my chest, but I don't miss that his smile is back. He's happy, and it makes me so sickeningly proud to be the one who made that happen.

"You never did tell me about your family," I say to lighten the mood. To have a reason to stay lying here with him.

It works because he launches into a damn monologue. Everything from growing up in a small town, knowing he was different, to his parents' divorce, to seeing them both with new partners now. It's nice the way he talks about them—all of them—like he considers his parents' new partners as much a part of his life as his mom and dad. He talks about his dad's husband a lot and how he was the only out person Felix really knew until he moved here.

"I couldn't imagine having all those brothers," he says. "I was my parents' sole focus for so long, and now …" He forces what I'm sure is supposed to be a light laugh. "I'm no one's. Being a grown-up sucks."

"Well, I've *never* been the sole focus, so I know what you're feeling and can promise you it's not that bad."

"Maybe, but … you deserve to be, you know? You're pretty wonderful yourself." His gaze dips away from me. "One day, we'll be someone's number one."

Ouch. Guess I need to work a little harder, then. "You already are."

He scowls. "My parents don't count."

It's amazing. How can he be so oblivious to how I feel about him? I wear my worship on my chest, but he obviously needs something more than that. Something tangible. Inarguable. And that's how I'll do it. That's how I'll prove to him that what we have is stronger and more important than anything he's had before.

Any guy can give him sex.

I want to give him what he deserves. To show him that I have actual feelings and intend to follow through on them.

I just … don't know how.

What I do know is I want him to be my boyfriend. No games. No doubts. I want him to know exactly what he means to me.

Luckily, I've heard about someone on campus who can help me.

Bowser's used a guy called Mr. Romance before to help him plan a date with a girl he liked last year. It was apparently epic and something he couldn't stop talking about. It must have worked too because they dated for four months before Bowser decided he wanted to live his college life to the fullest, i.e. fuck around.

The guy has a website set up where I punch in some details and then hope like hell he gets back to me fast. I've got all these feelings trying to get out, and maybe I should tell Felix how I feel with no bullshit, but I *want* to do the bullshit. I want to make him feel special.

What I don't want is to string him along so long that he loses interest, though I suppose if all it takes to do that is a couple of days, it was never going to last anyway.

Thankfully, by the end of my second class, I have a message waiting.

Hey, thanks for reaching out. I've emailed you a questionnaire to fill out, but I'm going away for spring break next week so if you want something before then we really should meet up in the next day or two. Let me know what works for you.

The next day or two? I can do that.

I text Mr. Romance straight back to let him know I'm available whenever because I'd rather get this over with done with before we go away as well.

My shift at Shenanigans passes that night in a blur of Brax and Ty flirting, one of the kitchen guys burning himself on a fryer, and Gwen catching a freshman trying to buy underaged beer. I'm beat by the time I get home, shower, and go to climb into bed.

But my bed is nowhere near as cozy without Felix here with me.

BEAN NECESSITIES IS JUST OFF CAMPUS AND ONE OF THE BUSIER cafes near Franklin U. I tend to avoid it because I don't like waiting forever, and they always seem to be short-staffed, but everyone is nice and my coffee is great, but most importantly, this is where Liam asked to meet.

If he's going to give me the ideas I need to sweep Felix off his feet, I'll do anything he wants.

I make my way to a table in the back and find ... well, someone who doesn't look anything like what I was expecting.

He's around my age, with floppy brown hair, and while he's not exactly attractive, there's something interesting about his face that makes me want to keep looking.

He offers me a friendly smile and then actually holds out his hand. "Liam."

"Ah, Marshall." I give his hand a quick shake before taking the seat across from him. "Thanks for meeting with me."

"That's okay. You actually got lucky—I had someone cancel, and we leave tomorrow, so I was able to squeeze you in."

"I really appreciate it. I have no idea what to do."

"Well, why don't you start by telling me who the person is that you want to romance and what the problem is."

I launch into the whole story of Felix's and my rocky start, about how I think he's incredible, but he doesn't see himself the same way. "So I want to do something extra. Show him that I think he's special instead of saying it and hoping he believes me."

Liam nods, eyes going unfocused for a second before he lights up. "I actually just saw ... hold on a minute." He grabs his phone and searches for something. "You've probably already seen this since it's all over campus. I've watched it a hundred times, I swear." He lets out a self-deprecating laugh. "I'm not sure if this is how big you want to go, but all I know is that if a guy did this for me ... well, okay, maybe not *exactly* this because I'd be embarrassed as hell at how public it is, but *something* like this, I'd —" He abruptly cuts off. "You know what, this isn't about me. Here."

He hands over the phone and hits Play.

At first, it's just an empty street with a guy standing in the middle, and then when the shot gets closer—

"Holy shit, *Robbie*."

"You know him?"

I groan. "It's my brother." I can only watch in shocked morti-
fication as Robbie completely embarrasses himself while having
the absolute time of his life. He's got a full-on movie moment
going, and seeing him sing to Queen, backed up by a marching
band and just about the whole street of fraternities, makes me
want to die of secondhand embarrassment.

I'm fucking horrified.

But the guy he's singing to, Brandon, is smiling at my idiot
brother like he's the greatest thing on the planet.

The knot of anxiousness loosens at his reaction.

"That," I say, jabbing a finger at where Brandon's face is on
the screen. "That's how I want Felix to look at me."

"Well, your brother had the right idea. Find something that fits
the two of you. Any chance you'd want to—"

"Nope." I hand the phone back. "I'm the introvert of the
family. No amount of feelings for the guy could get me to do
that."

"Okay, good to know where you're at. Sometimes, people
push themselves into big public things like that, but it comes
across as awkward and uncomfortable because it's not who they
are. We need to play to *your* strengths. Now, with that being the
extreme, where are you at with the public scale?"

"Restaurants or whatever are fine." Apparently, so is sex on
the beach. "But I think I'd rather it be only me and him."

"Okay, good. That narrows it down a lot. What does he like?"

Way to hit me with all the hard questions here, Liam. "Um …
I'm guessing sex isn't the right answer here."

Liam sniggers. "Try again."

"Fine, he … he likes attention. And comfort. He likes being
close, and when he feels important, he just … lights up. I love
seeing it."

"How can you make him feel important?"

"Isn't that what you're supposed to tell me?"

Liam shakes his head, but he's smiling. "I'm here to help get the ideas out of you. Sure, I'll plan the hell out of your date, but we need to nail down what you want first."

"That's what I was afraid of."

"Okay, let's forget about him for a second. What about you?"

Well, if there was an even more uncomfortable conversation than my feelings, we've found it. "I'm … boring."

"Trust me when I say that's never the case. What do you do?"

"Ah … go to school and work, hang out with my friend Bowser."

Liam's dark eyebrows bunch together. "And what do you study?"

"History."

He hums, and I can just imagine *Boring! Boring!* flashing through his mind. "Hobbies?"

"Video games." I laugh because that sounds pathetic. "Fuck around on my ukulele, read, cook, help Bowser with his plants …"

"Ukulele?" Liam perks up. "How good are you at it?"

I shrug, self-consciousness sinking in. "I'd say okay. I've never had professional lessons and usually play by ear. Most of the time, I make it up as I go along."

"Right." He claps his hands together. "We have two options here. You can cook him a dinner, which is an oldie but a goodie, and tell him how you feel. It shows you cared enough to put in the effort. *Or*—wait, you don't sing like your brother, do you?"

"No one sings like my brother." The dying cat vocals are all him. "I'm actually kinda decent."

"Then … my other idea is that you find somewhere private that either has significance or a view or …"

"The roof outside my window."

"What?"

"Yeah, it's got a view of the beach and looks amazing at sunset."

Liam sits up straight. "Oh my god, *yesss*." He flicks open his laptop and starts to type away, and I swear he's even more excited for this than I am.

By the time my coffee is finished, he's got the entire thing worked out.

I read over it and nod, nerves in full force. "That's ... perfect. And terrifying."

He stares at his screen with hearts in his eyes. "I'd kill for someone to do all this for me."

I'm lost for words, but thankfully, he shakes himself out of it before I get a chance to reply.

"Right. We can do this after spring break. Does that work for you?"

That's still over a week away. "It'll be hard, but I should be able to put it off until then."

"Sorry." And he sounds it. "But think, this could be the start of your forever. Isn't that worth waiting for?"

And even though I'm not dumb enough to think one perfect date could make a college relationship last forever ... that doesn't stop me from hoping it gives it a fighting chance.

24

Felix

Bowser drives the entire way to Arizona, which is probably a good thing because even though I don't get motion sickness, I *am* feeling queasy over the thought of meeting Marshall's family.

I'm not an idiot—I know I'm an acquired taste. Spoiled and selfish are two things I'm working harder to distance myself from, but I fall back into habits too easily. And if his family don't like me, I can kiss goodbye any hopes of something real happening between us.

Marshall's childhood might make me sad, but it's clear he loves his family a lot. Thankfully, it's only his parents and one brother there for the next few days, so I have fewer people I need to impress.

My stomach clenches again because apparently that thought isn't anywhere near as comforting as it should be.

"Nearly there," Bowser calls happily from up front. Marshall's riding shotgun, despite offering the seat to me about a billion times, but there was no way I'd force him to squish those long legs into the back seat of a Honda Civic. So I'm stuck with the bags, where I miss half of the shit they're talking about up there, and a couple of times during the drive, I swear they forget I'm here at all.

Which doesn't help my anxiety over meeting the family. Even if it's as nothing more than a friend.

I'm not sure how to play it—overly friendly or polite and laid-back—and the thought of having to tone myself down makes this whole thing harder. I think I'm getting a headache.

Camp Verde is not what I was expecting. I grew up in a small town, so they're familiar to me, but this place is tiny. Where Kilborough has a constant buzz of energy about it, Camp Verde is relaxed, quiet, the kind of place you come to get away from the world.

Bowser pulls into a long driveway, gravel crunching under the tires, and I get my first look at the property. The house down the end is a yellowy cream color with dark red painted trim, and an actual barn sits beside it. Behind that is all dry earth until it meets the trees at the other end of the property.

"This place is huge," I say.

I spot a basketball hoop beside the garage and can picture Marshall, with four other look-alikes, playing in the afternoons.

"It is, but I still had to share a room with Robbie until I was twelve, when Banjo went off to college. Now he's built himself a loft above the barn."

Bowser pulls up, and my nerves double as I climb out into the hot sun. It smells like dirt and animals—probably the horses I can see in the back paddock—and when a large man in a cowboy hat steps out from beside the house, it's like I've been transported back in time.

"Dad," Marshall says, moving forward to pull him into a hug.

"Hey, boy." He looks him over. "What're you eating at that college of yours? You're getting too thin."

Thin? Marshall's a solid ten, thank you very much.

He laughs his dad's comment off and nods in my direction. "Dad, this is—"

But before he can introduce me, his dad cuts him off.

"Bowser? Good to see you." He hauls him into a hug. "I say, if you hadn't come this year, Tracy would be pissed at missing you."

"As if I could stay away. It's been a good couple of months since I've been forced into manual labor and been elbows-deep in horse shit."

Marshall's dad claps him on the back. "Come on in. I'm sure she's been baking for her boys."

"*Dad.*"

His dad glances back at Marshall like he'd forgotten he was there, and Marshall walks over to stand by me.

"This is Felix. Felix, this is my dad, Earl."

Earl looks genuinely surprised to see me standing here, but I know for a fact Marshall told them I was coming. He's got a tiny line between his eyebrows as he looks me over, and I don't think I've ever felt more self-conscious.

He tips his hat. "Nice to meet you, son."

"Nice to meet you too." Meek and polite it is, then.

Earl clears his throat roughly. "Right. Well, we better get in. Robbie's waiting with some news he wants to tell us."

"Robbie's here?" Marshall asks, and the excitement in his voice makes me smile.

"Yup. Brought a friend with him."

Dread twists my insides. Parents and older brothers are one thing, but the brother he's closest to? The one he talks about more than the others? Fuck me, I'm not prepared for this. But then

Marshall rests his hand on my lower back as Bowser follows his dad inside, and it helps loosen the knot in my gut.

"I can't wait for him to meet you. I only spoke to him last week, and he said I wouldn't see him until the summer."

"I can't wait to meet him too."

And when Marshall said he and Robbie looked the same, he wasn't kidding. Robbie doesn't have glasses and has more muscle and shorter hair, but everything else is the same.

Except his personality, apparently, because as soon as he sees Bowser, he jumps up and almost tackles him into the wall. "Broser! How you doing, man? And my little Marshmallow!" He releases Bowser to wrap a beefy arm around Marshall's neck and proceeds to give him a noogie. They jostle each other a couple of times, and I can't believe Marshall is actually laughing and rough-housing. It's ... eye-opening. And fucking adorable.

The other brother who's older than them is chatting with Bowser, and their mom is fussing over him, and I'm just left hovering awkwardly in the doorway, trying not to resent Bowser and how much they all love him.

Marshall catches my eyes and breaks away from Robbie. "Hey, come here." His warm hand closes around mine, and he tugs me into the room. "Gang, this is Felix. He's my ... room-mate. He lives with me and Bowser too."

There's a beat of awkward silence before his mom steps forward with open arms. "Welcome, honey. Are you a hugger? I'm totally a hugger."

Marshall snorts. "I think he's even more cuddly than you, Mom."

She swamps me in a mom-hug—and I mean *swamps*, because she'd have to be at least six foot—then starts pestering Bowser and me about what we've had to eat before hurrying out of the room to grab food. She's been baking something sweet because the whole house smells like it.

"Hey, dude," Banjo says, giving me a nod. He's wearing a similar hat to Earl's. "Good to meet you."

"Wait … you're the roommate who hates him." Robbie starts to laugh. "But you're so *little*."

My mouth drops, and now I know what the odd looks I've been getting are about. The room is full of giants compared to me.

"I have a big personality, and that's what counts."

"Hell yes, it does." He holds out a giant fist for me to bump, and I follow through because *dammit*, I need him to like me. "And anyway," Robbie says, giving me a cheeky smile. "I like bite-sized things. Don't I, Brando?"

A sigh comes from behind Robbie, and a guy I didn't notice before pushes off the wall. At least *he's* kinda regular-sized. "Stop scaring Marshall's friend …" He trails off, and we both eye each other. "You look familiar," he says.

"Yeah … do I know you from somewhere?"

Bowser leans in with a stage whisper. "Tell me you haven't fucked Marshall's brother's friend because talk about *awkward*."

I backhand him. "You don't live in Kilborough, do you?"

He snaps his fingers. "Felix Andrews."

"Brandon Blakely." Just having a small reminder of home makes this so much easier. "Well, this is random."

"You know each other?" Marshall asks.

"Okay, I was joking before, but my question stands," Bowser says.

Brandon laughs. "Nah, we went to high school together. He was a year or two behind me."

"Small world." Marshall squeezes my hand, and I realize he hasn't dropped it yet. "Dad said you have news?"

Robbie nods to the table, where Earl and Banjo are already sitting. "Yeah, but you already know it."

I glance over at Marshall to find his smile huge. He lets go of

my hand to pull his brother into a hug and says something too low
for me to hear.

"Okay, help yourself," Tracy says, coming into the room and
dropping a huge tray of food down. "Aw, we're hugging? What's
happening? Robbie, you didn't tell them your news before me,
did you?"

"Of course not." He clears his throat dramatically. "Parentals,
bros, and … bros' *friends* …" He shares a look with Brandon that
makes Brandon snigger. "I want y'all to meet my boyfriend."

Tracy squeals and claps her hands over her mouth while Earl
sits there looking stunned. And apparently, Robbie doesn't give a
shit about either of their opinions because he wraps an arm
around Brandon, tugs him close, and smacks a kiss on his lips.

"Better get used to having a sixth son because he ain't going
anywhere."

And I'm taking it from this whole conversation that Robbie
isn't out, which makes me wonder … is Marshall? From what I
can tell, he's never had an issue being seen on dates with men in
public, but Earl still hasn't said anything, and my anxiety is going
through the roof.

Then he suddenly smiles. "Course you had to be different
from your brothers, didn't you, Robert?"

"I'm not following after some fucking geeds."

Banjo flips him off, and when they start to talk shit, I turn
slightly toward Marshall, cutting off my line of sight to his family,
and lower my voice.

"Are you … not …"

He shakes his head. "It's … a long story."

"I won't say anything."

"I know." He looks down at me in a way that makes me all
fluttery inside. "But …" He takes a deep breath and walks over to
Robbie. "Sorry to tell you this, *bro*, but you're not as unique as
you think."

Silence falls for the second time since we've walked in here, and already I can tell how unnatural it is. Banjo and Earl exchange a look. Tracy seems confused, and Bowser's giving Marshall a shit-eating grin.

"I knew it!" Robbie slaps his hands down on Marshall's shoulders. "The little bro likes the big D too!"

"Dear god," Marshall mutters, dropping his face into his hand as an explosion of noise breaks out.

"Oh, sweetie, thank you for telling us," Tracy says.

"Does that mean …" Banjo points at Bowser. "Are you our seventh brother?"

Earl turns toward him. "We've always loved you like one of us, anyway."

And as they all make a fuss over Bowser, this gross jealous feeling takes over. I fold my arms tight to stop from saying anything and to hold myself back from walking over there and climbing into Marshall's arms. But not one of them considered that it could be me, and that *hurts*.

"No," Marshall says. "No boyfriend … *or* girlfriend. I like both, but I'm, uh, still single."

"Oh." Tracy looks crestfallen.

Bowser lifts a hand. "And still single, but if I could love a dude, Marshall would be my man."

"I thought you said I'd be your man," I correct playfully.

"You both would. We'd be one big poly playhouse."

Marshall groans. "Definitely not that."

And even though I still feel a bit shitty over the Bowser assumption, I laugh along with the others.

"I'm, uh, actually demi. Umm, demisexual?" he says.

Tracy's face creases with confusion. "I don't think I've heard that one."

She might not have, but I know exactly what it means. It means that Marshall doesn't feel sexual attraction … unless he has an emotional connection first. And suddenly, every single thing between us makes sense. Him not wanting to go further that first night, him being sweet and cuddly and trying to connect through conversation instead of cum.

I see sex as a way to show how I feel, but he's the opposite. He needs to feel *before* the sex works for him. No wonder me trying to win him over that way didn't work. But now that I know … that man is going to be mine.

Suddenly, his family fawning over Bowser means absolutely nothing to me because *we* have a connection. I didn't know at the time, but he was showing me that every time we had sex. Now I just need to turn that connection into more.

Until I catch Robbie watching me. He's wearing a shrewd look that only deepens when his smile stretches over his face.

"While you give Marshall all of your attention, I'm going to grab the bags from the car, and Felix is going to help me," he announces way too loudly. Then he all but drags me from the room.

"I thought Marshall was overexaggerating when he said you Harrows aren't known for your subtlety," I say when we step outside.

Robbie laughs, then says in a singsong voice, "You're in love with my brother …"

"The only L-word here is *like*."

"Uh-huh."

"I don't care if you don't believe me."

He snorts. "And I don't care if you wanna play the denial game. I tried it with Brando too and failed. I love the shit outta him, and I'll tell anybody. Love's the best word ever. Well, except *bro*."

I get the feeling that ignoring him won't work. "What gave me away?"

"The fact you looked like you wanted to go Django on all our asses when we thought Bowser was his boy." Robbie pops the trunk and hauls out a bag before passing me a smaller one. "Here, little bro-ite."

"Little bro-ite?"

"Yeah. You're my little bro now … *lite*. Because you're teeny. Get it?"

"Jokes really aren't funny if you have to explain them."

"Is it my fault you don't have the smarts to keep up with me?"

"Oh, my mistake." I pull the backpack on while Robbie gets the rest. "I wasn't prepared for the amount of mental gymnastics it would take to decode that."

"You're forgiven this time, but you gotta be quicker than that if you want to keep up with the Harrows."

"I'll keep that in mind." I glance at Robbie. "I'm going to make him mine, you know."

"How do you know he isn't already?"

"Your brother's confusing."

Robbie frowns. "Bro … ther?"

I roll my eyes. "Your *little bro*."

"That's better." He wraps an arm around my shoulders and gives me a shake. "You're gonna fit in around here just fine, bro-ite."

"I'm stuck with that now, aren't I?"

"Sure are. Congrats, we already have our own inside joke. There's no getting rid of me now."

"If that's all it took, Marshmallow and I would be married by now."

"Marshall's a special kinda guy. I didn't know about the demi thing, but I don't think he's ever dated before, so he's probably a bit unsure."

I purse my lips. "That can't be right. We met when we were set up on a blind date."

"I dunno. I'm just saying we tell each other everything, and if he had dated someone, he would have said."

"He didn't tell you he was bi …"

"True, but I don't think it was because he was scared or anything. We've talked about me a lot. I have a feeling that he didn't think it was worth getting into. And now, for some *completely unknown reason*, it is." He gives me a pointed look as he holds open the door.

"Let's hope you're right," I say.

"I am. *You're* not the one who gave the two of you away."

"What do you mean?" I ask it even though I have a fair idea of what he's saying; I just don't want to hope.

"I'm saying that the way my brother looks at you … he's never looked at anybody like that before."

25

Marshall

I LOVE BEING HOME. IT'S LOUD AND CHAOTIC, AND DAD MAKES me, Robbie, and Bowser get up at the asscrack of dawn to help him with the horses, but it's a nice break from college and constant studying.

I head upstairs dirty and sweaty, wanting a shower, but the sound of Felix talking on the phone makes me pause outside of my room.

"I dunno, Dad … he's …" Felix doesn't finish that thought, and I glance around the doorframe to see him sitting cross-legged on my bed, playing with the bedsheets. He hums at something his dad says. "I know, I just … I really, *really* like him."

Happiness explodes in my gut. This tingly, consuming, mind-buzzing happiness. Felix *could* be talking about anyone, but I'm not an idiot. He's been actively trying to get me into bed, and while I didn't want to assume feelings were involved when relationships have never been on his radar, this confirms it, right? *Right*?

Whatever's said next makes Felix sigh. "I know you're right, but I don't have to be happy about it." His voice lightens. "Okay, thanks. Love you both too."

I quickly sneak back over to the stairs and approach my room, louder this time. "Hey, Fe." I'm trying to keep the sheer fucking elation out of my voice, but when he looks up at me, I'm blown away by how gorgeous he is.

"How was playing farm boy?"

"This isn't a farm. We just have some horses, chickens, a few sheep, two cows …"

He gives me a pointed look. "Well, I'm convinced."

"*Not* a farm."

His amusement fades, giving way to a cute pout. "Your dad doesn't ask me to help."

"Because you're a guest."

"So is Bowser."

"He's been here too many times to be a guest."

But that doesn't make Felix look any happier. "He thinks I'm too weak."

I rest against the doorframe and don't deny it. The thing is, Dad probably does think that. It's nothing against Felix person-ally, but not only is Felix small, he's *pretty*. Shiny and breakable. I know that isn't the case, but it's what Dad's been raised to see. "He likes you," I assure him. "He thinks you're funny."

"Mm. Funny and weak. Exactly what I want Papa Bear thinking of me."

I chuckle and cross toward him so I can ruffle his curls. "Does that make you Goldilocks?"

"The three bears eat her in some versions of the story."

"Well, that's dark."

He rests a hand on my stomach. "There's one bear I wouldn't mind eating me."

Oh, fuck. I laugh because if I don't, I might do something dumb like take him up on the offer. My cock tries to thicken, but I will it down. "You *do* taste delicious."

Felix stands, pressing close and looking up at me through his lashes. My heart thumps in my ears, and the spike of my pulse rate has me wanting to be reckless. He *likes* me. This beautiful, fun, feisty man *likes* me, and I'm dying to kiss him, but I'm on that tightrope again of do I go with it and hope things go well or wait and follow the plan I have with Liam?

Patience, Marshall.

Sex is great, but the connection for me is most important. I want to fall in love, and I want him falling right alongside me.

"I wanna do something today," I murmur. "Just us."

"What about Bowser?"

"He can look after himself. He's practically family."

Felix scowls. "I've noticed."

"You jealous, Fe?"

"Madly."

"Don't be." My smile is out of control. "With him distracting them, I get you all to myself."

His expression softens. "Yeah?"

"Yeah."

"And you *don't* wish Bowser wasn't straight so he could fit nicely into your family?"

I shake my head. "Nah, I have my sights set on someone else." I slap his ass. "Now, get changed while I shower. Put on jeans."

"Where are we going?"

"You'll see."

"I'm sorry, we're going *where*?" Felix asks. He's sitting behind me on Chomps, holding on for dear life.

"Wet Beaver Creek," I say again, managing to keep a straight face. We've ridden off my property all the way to the trail. Since California and Arizona have spring break at different times, it's not busy down here. If we'd come two weeks ago, we wouldn't have had any privacy.

As it is, we trot out of the trees to gleaming, still water.

"Fe, welcome to the Crack."

"The Crack?"

"Yep. The Crack of Wet Beaver Creek."

He swears under his breath as I jump down from Chomps and tie her to a tree.

"You have to be making these up," he says, leaning forward to hold on to me as I help him down. His waist is warm in my hands, and I hold on a fraction longer than I need to.

"Nope. It's actually called that."

"The Crack?"

"Yes."

"And Wet Pussy?"

I snort with laughter. "Beaver."

"I don't have one of those either." He turns and wanders onto the rock overhanging the water and dramatically grabs his ass. "I have a bussy though."

"Please don't call it that."

"Why?" He arches his back and pushes his ass right out. "I thought you liked it."

"I love it. But not when you call it a bussy."

"*You're* the one talking about wet beavers. You're making me jealous." But unlike the true jealousy from earlier, he's using his teasing tone.

I sit down on the edge of the rock, feet dangling about a foot above the water. Then I pat the place beside me. He sits, pressed flush against me, and I realize how much I've missed something as simple as sitting together. It hasn't occurred to me that he's kept his distance the past few days until now. "Do you like it here?" I get the balls to ask.

"I do. It's peaceful, and I feel like I know you better."

"Sorry my dad is—"

"He's fine. Really. He's been nice and super welcoming, but it sucks that he doesn't think I'm capable of doing the things you guys do."

"I know. I'm sorry."

"Stop that." He thumps my chest gently and looks up at me. "Unlike him, you make me feel capable of anything."

"Because you are."

He leans in, closer … closer … My breath catches as he gets closer because if he kisses me, I'm not going to stop it. I bend down, until our lips are almost touching, and Felix's breath hits my mouth as he says, "Including skinny-dipping?"

"What?"

"Well, I'm capable of anything, right?" His warmth is suddenly gone as he jumps to his feet and strips out of his T-shirt. "You coming?"

Am I? But as my gaze drops to greedily drink in all that lean muscle, I decide that fuck it. Yes, yes I am. I pull my shirt over my head before standing and unbuttoning my jeans. Felix pushes his down and steps out of them, and I'm just behind him. Then we're both standing there in our briefs, and my cock is already at half-mast, wanting to see more.

"Crocodiles. Cute." Felix's lips hitch on one side as he links his thumbs in the waistband of his underwear and slowly pushes them down. We keep eye contact the entire time, and it's nearly impossible to stop myself from looking, from seeing him completely naked for the first time.

"Your turn," he says.

I swallow and shove my briefs off in one quick movement. Unlike me, Felix has no issues shamelessly checking me out.

A strangled noise leaves him. "Hello, big boy. I've missed you."

"Are you ..." I tilt my head. "Are you talking to my dick?"

"*Maybe ...*"

I laugh, take a quick, greedy look, then before he can say anything else, I take two running steps, pick him up, and throw him in the water.

I cannonball right beside him, and when I resurface, he's coughing and brushing water from his eyes.

"Why do you hate me?"

"Hey, you're the one who wanted to go skinny-dipping."

Water drips from his curls, and his lashes are all clumped together. I really didn't think this through because the only thing sexier than Felix is a *wet* Felix. Before I can stop myself, I wrap an arm around his waist and drag him to me.

He sucks in a shaky breath as his arms snake around my neck. "Hey ..."

"Legs," I rasp.

They immediately lock around me, and I tread water with him practically sitting in my lap. "There. That's better, isn't it?"

His hard cock nudges my belly, and he keeps dragging his teeth over his bottom lip, gaze darting down to my mouth and back up again. All that warm, wet skin pressed against me is pure temptation, and my cock is aching as it brushes his asscheek.

"Is that all you want?" he asks.

"No." I get us over to a place where I can reach the bottom, because I need him so badly it hurts. I dig my free hand into his hair and tug his mouth to mine.

Warm lips, a strong tongue, moans that I try to taste like a physical thing. I hold him close and practically devour his mouth, and even though I told myself I wouldn't, I can't hold back. I might not have said the words, but I haven't hidden how I feel about him, and if everything goes to plan, I want to show him every day. I want to wake up pressed against him like this. I want to kiss him like this each morning and night. And the more we kiss, the more I want, until my cock is aching.

I break away from his lips to nip at his jaw. I lick and taste and bite my way along to his ear. "Touch me," I beg.

"W-we don't have to have sex," he says, breathless.

"You don't want to?"

"I think that's physically impossible when it comes to you, but I just … I get it. I didn't before, but you never told me."

"Shit." I duck my face. "Sorry. I—it's kind of hard to talk about. I didn't want you to feel stuck with me or worried I wouldn't want you, or—"

Felix's hand closes over my mouth. "Promise me one thing."

I frown but nod, and he eases his hand away.

"Don't have sex with me because you think *I* want it."

"What part of our first date gives you the impression I'd ever do that?" I lower my mouth to his neck and place a line of kisses up to his ear. "I want you. So much. Now can you *please* touch me?"

Felix whimpers, and instead of just wrapping his hand around me, he wriggles down and closes his fist around us both.

"Oh, fuck," I gasp, giving a little thrust. "Shit, that feels so good."

"Tell me how much you want me."

"Want?" I shake my head. "Need you, Fe."

He shudders and strokes us, tight and firm. His cock is hard and flush with mine, and it feels incredible rubbing against me as he works us both over. Felix's legs tense and relax around my waist as he rolls his hips, fucking forward, giving me the delicious friction I crave.

I pull him into another kiss, hungrier this time. Hungry for him, for his cock, for feeling like this with him always. Objectively I know it's too soon to be talking about forever, but my heart doesn't care. It's chosen this flirty little firecracker, and I never want to change my mind.

All I can hope is that he grows to feel the same.

I drop both my hands to cup his full ass, coaxing him to move faster. The water makes him slide deliciously against me, and I get that feeling again, that full, addictive feeling that I'll never be close enough to him.

"God, I wanna fuck you so bad," I groan against his mouth.

"So do it."

I shake my head. "No supplies."

"You really think I'd go anywhere with you without being prepared?"

I take a second to process his words, then glance around. Felix's hand tightens around our cocks, and I'm getting to that point where I want to tell him not to stop, to keep going until I come, but I need to be inside him. I need to fill him. To own his body and make him forget about anyone who ever came before me.

"Someone might see us," I say. "It's not busy now, but that doesn't mean people won't be by."

"If I'm being perfectly honest, I don't fucking care."

I drop a laugh against his neck and then give his ass a firm squeeze. "Okay. I want you way too badly."

I'm only a little apprehensive as I carry him from the water and back around to where we discarded our clothes. Felix climbs down and fishes in his pocket for the supplies he brought before stretching out along the warm rock, perfect body on full display for me.

"Here." I ball up my shirt and hand it to him. "For your head."

Felix looks at it for a second before reaching out and taking it. "Such a gentleman."

I smirk. "There's nothing gentlemanly about what I want to do to you." I drop to my knees and kiss along every bare stretch of skin I can get to. I run my tongue over his nipple and press my lips to each rib while I hold his hips, pinning him to the rock.

Felix whines when my lips brush his hip bone, and then I turn my head and blow on the tip of his cock.

"Urg. Tease."

"It's not my fault. You look so desperate when I tease you." His cock is red and leaking, veins sticking out angrily and balls pulled up tight. "Where's the lube?"

He blindly reaches for the two packets and throws them to me. "Hurry up."

"You're going to have to tell me what to do." I tear open the lube and dribble some over my fingers.

"Take your finger and destroy me with it."

I laugh and dip my fingers into his crease to run over his hole. "Right here?"

"Yes. Keep pressing."

I massage the area a few times before I carefully press in. His body opens around me, and once I slip inside, I remember the warm, comforting pressure all too well. "Like that?"

"Fucking perfect," he rasps.

His cock has started to flag, so I lean over and suck it into my mouth. I do everything I can to make him feel good as I work him open, following his instructions until I'm three fingers deep, stretching and rubbing, and he's pressing his ass back against me.

"Now. I need you now."

I pull off his cock with a pop and hurry to open the condom and roll it over my dick. My hands are shaky and this is still all so new and I'm so turned on, I can't imagine being able to do this with him anytime I wanted.

I lie over him, weight resting on one arm while I hold my cock steady. Another quick glance around shows we're still thankfully alone, because once I'm inside him, I'm not stopping for anything.

He pushes back against my cock as I start to press forward, and the pressure that surrounds me feels even more intense than last time.

"Goddamn," I mutter, breathless and so *full* of ... of ... *emotion*. It's ecstasy. Like a warm hug for my dick.

Felix wraps his legs around me, just the way I like them, and his heels dig into my ass as he helps me slide in. When my hips meet his ass, we both let out a long breath.

"You gonna fuck me now?" he teases.

"No." I lean down until my lips are touching his. "I'm going to wreck you."

"I'm scared you already have."

A long moan leaves me as my lips close over his, tongue sweeping into his mouth. I lift his hips off the rock to rest on my thighs, and I give a solid, ball-tingling thrust. I can't get over how it feels, how my skin is too tight, my chest ballooning to a point where I'm ready to explode. I set a smooth pace, not too fast, but each thrust hits his ass with a satisfying *slap*, and Felix rewards me with the most delicious sounds.

His hips rock back to meet mine, fingers buried in my hair, and I try to hold him tighter, pull him closer, fuck him deeper. My head is spinning with the pleasure, and it's nowhere near enough.

I'm greedy for everything he can give me, and now I've had a taste, I don't think I'll ever be able to stop.

"You sure you were a virgin?" he gasps, teeth sinking into my bottom lip.

"Is that a compliment?"

"You're pegging my prostate like a pro, and I think I'm going to beat you to the finish line." His voice is strained, a fraction higher than normal, and pride is spreading through my chest.

"I think knowing you feel good turns me on more than having my cock buried inside you."

"You sure about that?" He squeezes around me, and I almost go cross-eyed.

"Close call."

"Now, fuck me like you mean it."

Unlike last time, my hesitance is gone. I might not know exactly what I'm doing, but I pound into him like my life depends on it. And it kinda does because if I stop fucking him, I really think I might die. I'm addicted to him. To his body, to the feel of him around me, to the way he kisses and gasps my name and tightens his legs when I nail him just right.

Felix holds me, and I clutch him just as tight, the rest of the world forgotten as I get lost in how he makes me feel.

"Keep going," he begs. "I'm so, so close."

I haul him upright into my lap. "Make yourself come."

He rides me, and I thrust up into him over and over, drawing closer to the edge. I can't drag my eyes away from his cock. From the precum. His tight balls. The light dusting of ginger pubes. How it bounces as he does.

My thighs quake, knees scraping against the rock as I yank him down to meet my thrusts. His fingers are digging into my shoulders. It's too much, feels too good. My lips meet his chest, his collarbone, his neck. I can't stop touching and kissing and fucking. Sparks race along my spine, my cock throbs, and the pressure builds and builds in my balls until—

"Oh, *shit.*"

Sweet relief rolls over me as I unload into the condom, cock jerking with my release, and a moment later, Felix's ass tightens around me as he chokes back a cry. He comes on my stomach, warm spurts painting my skin before running down to pool where our bodies meet.

He slumps forward, head on my shoulder, breathing deep and hard.

The water has dried and been replaced with sweat, and even though my muscles ache from exertion, I've never felt more relaxed and ready to float away.

My mouth seeks out his, and I sigh into our kiss, stupidly sated, ready to curl up beside him and sleep for the rest of the day.

"We should probably wash this off," he says. "I think we're pushing our luck now."

"Shit, you're right." I ease out of him and pull off the condom, tying the end and stuffing it into my jeans pocket.

Then I lift Felix into a bridal carry and jump back into the water.

"Are we in a hurry to get back?" he asks, wrapping his arms around my neck.

"Nope. We can stay out here all day if you like."

He doesn't answer me, but his kiss is a very solid *yes*.

26

Felix

THE NEXT MORNING, WHEN EARL CALLS MARSHALL AND BOWSER to help, I grumpily throw off my covers and find some clothes too. I pull on a shirt and some jeans and tie as much of my hair back as I can, then stumble after them in the dark.

"You're coming too?" Bowser sniggers.

"Fuck you very much. I'll have you know I'm an extremely hard worker."

"Does that mean I can go back to bed in your place?"

"Don't even try it," Marshall says. "Trust me. Dad will just get you up anyway."

"Yes, I will," Earl says as we get downstairs. He nods at me. "Extra pair of hands, huh? Good."

I'd been worried he was planning to send me back to bed, so that reaction is about as warm as I could expect. We all walk out to the barn in the prelight of dawn, dried grass crunching under our feet.

"We're mucking out stables this morning, boys."

Robbie splutters. "I thought that was a Monday job."

"But you're not going to be here Monday," Early says in a teasing voice. He hands over a pitchfork. "Now, off you trot."

I take mine without complaint, determined to keep up with them all. We let each horse out into the yard as we clean their stalls and haul down fresh hay, and despite the grunt work and the smell and how sweaty I get, I enjoy being outside. I enjoy being around animals. I'm hit with this image, fast-forwarded ten years where I have a vet clinic all of my own and I get to travel out to farms for checkups. I'd always planned to move back to Kilborough after I graduate. San Luco is amazing, but I'm not built for big cities. This slow, country life is in my veins, and while the break from my parents and the chance to grow up is what I needed, in truth, I hate the distance.

But ... I glance over at Marshall and Robbie, ribbing each other and competing to see who can get their stall done first. What does *he* want? Does that even matter? We're not together, and a year is a long time. Plus, with vet school and Marshall wanting to study further, different careers, family in different parts of the country ... there are so many things we'd have to think about, but after yesterday, none of that is important.

I want to keep my marshmallow, and problems are made to be solved.

"Felix?" I glance over at Earl, and he motions to the door. "I could use your help outside."

Me? I'm both excited and nervous as hell to be singled out by him. I want to impress him, but if this is going to turn into one of those "I know you're thirsty for my son, but you're not good enough, so back off" talks, then I'd rather sit this one out.

If only I had the actual guts to ask him first. I set the pitchfork against the side of the stall and follow him. We get to the doors, and he pauses, grabbing a hat that's hanging on a hook and setting it on my head.

He nods, lips trembling against a smile. "There. Wouldn't want nobody getting sunburned."

Is it just me, or ... was that kinda sweet? It's the exact thing Marshall would have done.

Some of the anxiety ebbs away as we walk outside.

"Surprised to see you up this morning," he says as we head toward the henhouse.

"I wanted to be helpful."

"I like that." He rewards me with a grin. "Always made the boys put in hard work. It's important for character."

"From what I've seen, you've done a great job. Marshall's always working hard." *Suck up? Moi?*

Earl's gaze slides to me and away again. "I can, uh, see that."

"See what?"

His loud laugh is clearly where Marshall gets his from. "Y'all went out together yesterday, and you came back with no skin around your mouth. I'm no dummy."

I squeak and slap my hands over my chin, which makes Earl laugh louder.

"Relax, son. I was worried you were going to be one of those city boys at first, all pretty and no substance. Wouldn't know a hard day's work if it looked you clean in the face."

"Well, I *am* pretty," I say.

He huffs with amusement. "At any rate, pretty or not, you've a personality to you and you're here. Not complaining, just getting into it. I respect that."

"Naww." I press my hands to my chest dramatically, but I'm honestly touched. Happy. And so relieved. "That's so sweet, Papa Bear."

"Ah, hell. Why do I get the feeling that name's gonna stick?"

"Because you're a smart, smart man." I unlatch the henhouse, holding the door open for them all to burst outward.

Earl watches the birds, hands resting on his hips, looking like an older version of Marshall, and if that's what Marshall is going to look like in twenty years, I'm liking my decision to keep him more and more.

"So …" Earl rests against the henhouse, then clucks his tongue and points inside.

"Oh, I see how it is. Brought me out here to do all the real work."

"I hate trying to get in there to collect the eggs."

I glance inside. It would be a tight fit for him, but luckily, it should be easy for me. "Huh. Being small isn't looking so bad after all, is it?"

"Suppose it's got some uses."

"I can't wait to tell everyone you found me useful. That I'm better at something than you." I climb in, feeling smug, and Earl's chuckle follows me.

But so does the creak of hinges, and a second later, *thump*. The whole henhouse goes dark, followed by the snap of the lock. I scramble over to the small window and see Earl walking away.

"What are you doing?"

"Good luck telling anyone anything now," he shouts gleefully back over his shoulder.

I watch his retreating form, mouth dropped, wondering what the fuck I do now. I thought we were getting along?

I glance around the dim room, eyes adjusting, and think, *Fuck it.* I came in here to collect eggs, so I might as well. Then when I ever get out of here, I can chase Earl down and throw them at him. Scowling, I set them all in the basket and then decide to try and Hulk bust my way out of here. It was only a little lock. If I give the door enough force …

I throw my shoulder into it, and where I expect the door to

hold firm, it flies open with no resistance, and I catapult out and then slam hard into the earth.

Huh. So ... apparently, it wasn't locked after all.

The sound of four loud laughs makes me look up, and yep. There they all are, just hanging out and watching me.

"I don't think you deserve to be called Papa Bear anymore."

Robbie whoops. "Papa Bear? I love that."

"No." Earl points at him. "You're nowhere near cute enough to get away with calling me that."

I reach inside the henhouse for the basket of eggs and shove them at Earl. "You can get them yourself next time."

"Aw, Fe," Marshall says. "Don't be mad. Dad's played that trick on all of us."

That's when I remember what Marshall told me about from when they were younger. It's something Earl did whenever he was *impressed*.

Robbie holds out his hands. "So, welcome to the family, bro-ite. This is your early warning that Dad thinks he's funny when he's really, really not."

It was ... an initiation. That makes me all warm and gooey and a thousand other things that being pretend locked in a henhouse probably shouldn't bring out.

"Hey, you've never done that to me," Bowser protests.

"Because you're not dating our brother, dumb dumb," Banjo says.

Marshall's whole face floods red, and for one wild second, he looks panicked. Unsure. His mouth opens and closes and opens again, but nothing comes out.

My heart sinks at his reaction, and I manage to say, "We're not dating," because it seems like I'm supposed to.

Even though it sort of feels like we are. Even though I want to be, badly. Even though his whole family assumed we're together.

I half expect Marshall to loop an arm around my waist and

pull me into a hug. To tell them I'm full of shit because we're actually totally madly in love and ready to run away together.

But ... he doesn't. He's frowning, stare locked on the ground, and when I realize he's not planning on adding to the conversation, I turn back to the others. They don't know what's going on, and an awkwardness settles that hasn't been here since the first day. Them on one side, me on the other.

But until Marshall tells me flat out he's not interested, I'm going to do everything I can to get on that side with him. I'll be part of this family, dammit.

"All right." Earl claps his hands. "Back to work."

Everyone breaks and walks in different directions, but I jog after Marshall. He's walking along, typing out a message on his phone, but the second I join him, he locks the screen and hides it in his pocket.

"Is everything okay?" I ask.

"Yeah, of course. Fine."

"Right." I lick my dry lips and can't help asking, "Who were you texting?"

"No one. It was, umm, just looking something up."

I'm tempted to ask him *what* he was looking up, because we both know he's lying. But I just ... can't. I can't find the balls to call him out and possibly push him away.

Because I'm really, really scared of the answer.

I'm scared of the fact he didn't tell his family about us. I'm scared he hasn't asked for more when I've thrown myself at him again and again, and I'm terrified that whoever he was texting was someone he couldn't tell me about.

Is it his someone special? The person Bowser hinted at when he unknowingly called me a cheap hookup to get sex out of the way? Has Marshall found his person?

The thought hurts so much that it gives me a new something to be scared of.

I knew I liked him, knew I was growing feelings.

I just somehow missed that I'd fallen completely fucking in love.

27

Marshall

THE WHOLE WEEK PASSES BOTH TOO QUICKLY AND TOO SLOWLY. It's great being home, it's great seeing Felix with my family, and I love the way he and Brandon get along so well and talk about where they grew up.

But the last few days, something has changed, and it's making me desperate to get back to school. He's almost aggressively affectionate, and I love it, but I'm worried about what's brought on the change. Instead of sleeping on the mattresses on my floor, he climbs into bed with me every night; when we're around my family, he's always close enough for me to wrap my arm around; and when we're alone, he climbs into my arms and refuses to let ago.

I've never felt so needed.

And unsettled.

On the drive back to school, I follow him into the back seat, knees cramping from the small space, and pull his legs over my lap. I rub his calves and attempt to get his easy smiles, but he almost looks ... worried? I can't help but feel like this is tied into his fierce exclamation to my family that we're not together.

When we are.

I know we are.

Felix might be a flirt, but he isn't this clingy with anyone else, and I might be inexperienced, but I know what we have is special.

"What are you doing when we get back?" he asks.

"Nothing exciting. Just, uh, meeting a friend."

I get that weird searching look he's been giving me the past couple of days, and I almost break out in a sweat. I'm not great at lying, and I don't want to be, but I also don't want to spoil my surprise.

Maybe he keeps denying what we have, but he'll do it knowing exactly how I feel about him.

I'm not meeting a friend when we get back though. I'm meeting Mr. Romance so he can help me set up the date, while Bowser takes Felix out and distracts him. My phone is burning a hole in my pocket. I've texted back and forth with Liam a few times the last few days, and I hate disturbing his trip away too, but I'm so anxious about getting this right.

Felix deserves it. So I have to suck up my nerves and get on with it.

The thought of canceling, then going back to school and seeing Felix go out with guy after guy makes my gut feel rotten. I just ... I can't do that. If things end with us, I know I'll have to move out. No way will my heart be able to handle seeing him every day and remembering what I was so close to having.

Felix pulls his legs back to his side and turns to look out the window.

It's hard not to shake some sense into him. I'm sure he has feelings for me, sure he wants to be with me, so I'm clueless why he denied what we had. All I know is I'd been standing there, trying to figure out how to make sure my family didn't overreact to my first boyfriend ever, when he sent me spinning on this course of uncertainty.

But sure thing or not, I'm going to put myself out there. I'm not a risk taker. This goes against everything that comes naturally to me, but I'm going to do it anyway. Because if I have even the slimmest chance of making us happen, it'll all be worth it.

Liam got back yesterday, so we're doing everything tonight. I could have waited until next weekend, but there's no way I wanna drag this out any more. Plus, my nerves won't be able to handle that. I need to know. For real. Do we stand a chance?

While we were away, I was working on a little surprise for him in secret. I'm worried about the execution of it and what he's going to think. Because when I decided to put myself out there, I'm putting myself *way* out there. No holding back. I want him to know everything.

Everything is going to go smoothly. It has to. *Mr. Romance* has planned every last detail.

Except what Felix's response is going to be.

He deserves the date of his life. He deserves someone making a real effort for him. Unfortunately for him, he drew the short straw, and he's stuck with *me* as that someone. The pressure to make this the best date of his life is on.

Bowser pulls up to Liberty Court, and I get that amazing sense of being home. Yet another reason why tonight has to go well. Only when I climb out of the car and glance up, Liam is already here.

I scramble to check the time, and *fuck*, we're an hour later than we were supposed to be.

Liam lifts his hand to wave, catches sight of Felix, and drops it again. Then he spins on his heel and walks away. That wasn't subtle.

Shit, shit, shit. Any chance Felix didn't …

Nope. Felix gets out the other side of the car, and his narrowed eyes follow Liam down the street. He's still watching when he approaches me. "Who was that?"

"Who was what?" My voice sounds panicked.

"*That*." He jabs a finger toward where Liam's disappeared around the corner.

I shrug. "No idea what you mean."

"You're lying."

"I don't know what to tell you." I try for a laugh that almost sounds normal. "Want me to carry your bag in?"

He grabs it from the trunk, pretty eyes flicking back down the street, then tugs his bottom lip between his teeth and leaves without answering.

Not a good sign.

"What was that about?" Bowser asks.

"I wish I knew. He's been acting weird the last few days. I mean, have I done something?" My heart is racing, feeling like this whole thing is steadily slipping away from me.

Bowser looks baffled. "He hasn't said anything to me. I didn't know anything was up—you guys have been attached at the hip all week."

"Yeah, but it wasn't like it normally is."

Bowser swears under his breath.

"I *know*," I say.

"Something's going on. It has to be. I've never seen Felix as silly for a guy as he is with you."

I really hope Bowser's right. He needs to be.

"Look, I'll deal with Felix," he says. "You focus on getting everything set up. Trust me, he's going to flip when he sees what you have planned."

I'd thought so too, but now … who the fuck knows how he's going to react?

We carry our shit inside, and as soon as I'm upstairs, I text

Liam. Thankfully, he's happy to wait around until Bowser and Felix leave. Bowser has already gone upstairs to work on him, and since I can't sit around doing nothing, I tidy my messy room, hoping to distract myself from how anxious I am.

Just a couple of hours. Only a couple of hours until I put myself out there and hope my heart doesn't get shot down and stomped on.

My only reassurance is that Felix would never be that cruel.

It's starting to get later in the afternoon, and if I want this thing ready for sunset, we need to get moving. I pace to my door, back to my window again, then out into the hall. Bowser still hasn't left, and just as I'm about to say fuck it all and go up there, Felix's bedroom door clicks open and they both walk out.

"Ah, hey," I say as they walk down the stairs. I try to act casual, like I'm always hanging out in the hallway. "Going somewhere?"

"A walk." Felix sniffs.

Bowser widens his eyes behind Felix's back. My heart pangs because I never, ever want to make him upset, and there's definitely something wrong with him.

"Okay. Enjoy?"

Bowser thanks me, but Felix keeps walking. As soon as they're out of sight, I groan and scrub my hands through my hair.

Absolutely dreading this whole thing, I pull out my phone and text Liam that the coast is clear, then head down to let him in.

One thing that can be said for him, he's a professional.

Some of the decorations we're using he already had on hand from other dates, and some I've had to pay for specifically. He brings everything with him and helps me set the rooftop up. Festoon lights for when it's dark—hopefully we make it that late —two overstuffed beanbags with a small table between them, flower petals that he sprinkles everywhere, huge round glowing balls that he places all around the edge of the rooftop, and an "ambient" playlist that he sets up on my laptop to drown out the sounds of Liberty Court and the road on the other side.

"You mind if I take some photos of this setup?"

I gesture toward it. "Go right ahead."

"Damn, that's a good view. These are going to look great on my website."

"You've done … this is amazing. I never would have been able to come up with all of this myself."

"You're screwed now. You know that, right?" He's smirking, but I have no idea why.

"In what way?"

"Well, this is your standard now. When you propose to this guy, you're going to have to level up again."

And I know he's teasing, but I can see it. Maybe. One day. If I'm talking about forever here, that's a thing that's going to happen. But there's no point getting ahead of myself until I know where *he's* at.

"I'll keep your number," I say, only half-joking.

Liam pats me on the back. "We're done. The next part is all you. Good luck."

"I feel like I'm about to piss myself."

"Yeah, as your romance consultant, I'd advise against that."

"Good to know."

He smiles, then climbs back in my window. I grab Cactus Everdeen and set her in the middle of the small table, then check the cooler he's tucked away in my room to see what he's brought.

Berries … crackers … some kind of cheese. A bottle of wine. I'm tempted to crack it open and polish off half just to get through the wait, but I tuck it away, hoping like hell that when it's opened, I'll be drinking it with my boyfriend.

28

Felix

THE LAST THING I WANT TO DO IS BE DOWN HERE. THE BEACH IS busy for a Sunday afternoon, and the pier is too crowded to even bother trying to get in there. I love San Luco, and normally I want nothing more than to be in amongst all the fun, but tonight, I'm not feeling it.

Tonight, I want to curl up in bed, hugging Butters to me, while I try not to cry over Marshall. The texting the last few days, followed by that guy showing up today … yeah, I'm not dumb. There's something going on that I'm not supposed to know about, and the only conclusion I can come to is that Marshall's moving on.

So why the fuck didn't he tell me?

I take a deep breath and remind myself that I'm probably wrong. I'm jumping to conclusions. He was only too happy to give me attention in the car on the way home; he *voluntarily* sat in the back even with how uncomfortable he must have been. The mixed messages are making my head spin.

I glance at Bowser. "What would you do if you liked a girl and didn't know if she felt the same?"

"Ask her, obviously."

"Right. Okay." I spin on my heel and head for home.

"Fe, what are you—" He grabs my arm, and I shake him off.

"Taking your advice."

"With …"

He can play dumb all he likes—Bowser knows what I mean. "I'm going to tell Marshall I have feelings for him and want to date him. For real."

"Right *now*?"

"When else?"

He grabs my arm *again*, and again I have to shake him off.

"I don't think that's great timing," he says.

"Why?"

"I just … I thought you were coming to the beach with me. Let's do that, and then you can tell him once you're back."

The desperation in Bowser's tone, the fake-relaxed voice … "You're trying to keep me out of the house."

"No!"

"Do you think I'm an idiot? What's going on?"

"I'm … I'm not—"

Reality dawns on me. I wasn't being paranoid after all. My heart feels like it's breaking as I make my way home, Bowser trying everything he can think of to distract me until he gives up. He pulls out his phone, and I hurry to snatch it off him.

"Nope. You're not sending him a warning text."

"Fe … you don't get it."

Fuck what I don't get. And fuck Marshall. I've never had a real relationship, and yet I can totally see myself having one with him. My sweet, cuddly Marshmallow.

Only maybe not so mine.

And even though I'm preparing myself for it, getting home and almost running head-on into the guy from earlier makes this horrible wounded noise come from me.

"Excuse me," he says with a small smile, then steps past me into Liberty Court.

I almost turn around and tell the asshole to excuse *himself*, but my hands are shaking, and I don't trust my voice to come out right. Did Marshall really choose him over me?

And why the hell wouldn't he say anything?

"Fe …"

I slap Bowser's hand away before he can grab me for a third time and take the stairs two at a time. I'm not quiet, and I storm into Marshall's room with all the force of a goddamn hurricane.

But … he's not here.

Hands come down over my eyes. "You're early."

Marshall's warm voice suddenly in my ear derails the building anger. I want to lean into the sound, to savor it, but I'm too hurt and confused. "What are you doing?"

"You almost ruined the surprise."

"Surprise?"

"Walk forward."

"Marshall, I—"

"*Please*, Fe."

I'm such a sucker for this guy that even though I want to chew him out and throw something at his head, my body doesn't listen. I take a step forward, and another one, hating how steady I am in his hands.

"I'm not sure what's happened the last few days, but if I've done something, I'm really sorry," he says.

Those are the last words I expected. I get the feeling he has more to say, so I bite my tongue, not wanting to ruin … whatever is going on here.

He swallows loudly, the way he does when he's nervous. "I

had the greatest time at home, and I loved that you were there with me. My family adore you, and I knew they would because, well, you're super fucking adorable."

"So why didn't you tell them we were together?" I can't stop my question from coming out, and it's an instant relief to finally ask.

Marshall stops me, and before I can open my eyes, he spins me in his arms. "*You* said we weren't dating."

"Because you looked like you were going to crap yourself over the thought of them finding out about us."

"What? No. I mean, yeah, I was embarrassed, but that was because I know what they're like, and we never would have heard the end of it, but I'm not embarrassed over *you*."

I give it a second for his words to sink in. "You're … not?"

"How could I be?"

There are only about a million ways, but I don't want to give him ammunition. I drag my bottom lip through my teeth, not sure if I should steer the conversation toward the thing that's bugging me more than anything, but I can't help myself. "Who was that guy?"

"Guy?"

Irritation flickers inside me that he's still trying to deny it. "Yes. Guy. The one who was here when we pulled up. The one who just left."

Understanding dawns on his face, and to my surprise, Marshall laughs. "He was helping me."

"Helping you?"

"Yeah." He turns me around again, but this time, he doesn't cover my eyes. "With this."

My jaw drops. The rooftop outside the window is set out like a damn movie.

"After you," he says, taking my hand and gesturing toward the window.

I climb out, still in shock and madly trying to put the pieces together.

When he follows me, I stare, mesmerized, in awe, and hoping that this is what I think it is. "You did this for me."

He nods, hand swiping over the awkward expression he's wearing, and I notice for the first time that he's wearing his navy shirt with the pineapple print. "Yeah. I thought … well, our other dates didn't go so hot. I wanted a do-over. A proper first date. The kind of first date someone as incredible as you deserves."

I look around, not able to stop and focus on any one thing. My throat feels thick and hot, and my eyes are annoyingly prickly.

Marshall takes my hand. "Is this … is this okay?"

"This is …" I use his word. "*Wonderful.*"

Marshall's smile takes my breath away. "It's almost sunset. Come sit with me?"

Try and stop me.

He leads me over to the enormous beanbags. Marshall sits on one, and I think he's expecting me to take the other, but there's no way I'm letting him go now. I drop into his lap, and his arms immediately close around me and pull me in tight. My heart is beating fast, and I'm nervous and excited. I can't focus on any one emotion—I'm too surprised and overwhelmed that he went to all this effort for *me*.

I link my fingers through his, turning to where the sun has started to dip lower, throwing oranges and black over the water and shades of red through the sky.

It's beautiful, and yet … my gaze drifts back to Marshall, and he's already watching me.

"I thought you wanted to watch the sunset."

"Eh. I've found something better."

I squeak and duck my head into his neck.

"Hey … I can't see you now."

"That's on purpose." My words are muffled against his skin.

He eases me back. "Are you embarrassed? By attention? That doesn't sound right."

"I'm not used to *this* kind of attention."

"What kind?"

I don't even know how to explain it. "The sweet kind. Where you look at me and you don't even need to say anything to make me feel like I matter."

His lips hitch up, and he reaches for the other beanbag to drag it closer. "Can you hop over there for a second?"

I glare at the free space. "Why?"

"Because I kinda need my lap."

"For …"

He lets out that booming laugh. "If you move your bony ass, I can show you."

Reluctantly, I get up and drop into the other beanbag. The sound of the inners puffing up around me means I don't hear Marshall picking something up. I eye the instrument he's holding. "Is that a guitar?"

"Ukulele."

And when he starts to pluck out a tune, I immediately recognize it. "You're the one I've been hearing."

"What do you mean?"

"I've been hearing music in the garden, and I had no idea where it was coming from. You were playing it."

His eyes shine. "Did you like it?"

"I loved it."

"Good. Because I've added lyrics." He shifts awkwardly in place. "And I'm going to feel like the biggest idiot singing to you, so please try to hold all laughter until the end."

I pretend to lock my lips tight, and wanting to hear whatever might be coming is the only thing holding me back from tackling him and planting kisses all over his face.

He adjusts his glasses and starts the tune again. "The song is called 'Felix' because I'm super original and all of my creative energy went into writing a subpar song. So you're welcome. And sorry."

The song could be *yeahs* and *ohs* for all I care. He could have a terrible voice and not know how to play that thing, because just having him try to serenade me would send me to jelly. But he does know how to play, and from the very first notes, it's clear he knows how to sing too.

I'm immediately swept up in the relaxed tune and his upbeat deep voice, that I almost forget to pay attention to the lyrics.

F-E-L-I AND AN X
   These are the five things I know best
   About you ...
   This song is all for you ...

F SUITS YOU MOST AND WHAT COMES TO MIND
   Is free, fancy, fresh, flirtatious, fun time
   And fuck ...
   A truckload of fucks.

I LAUGH, AND HE THROWS A GRIN MY WAY.

LIKE FUCK, HE'S PRETTY, AND FUCK, HE'S FUN
   And fuck that guy, he turns me on
   But we've barely scratched the surface ...
   Because fuck me, Felix, you're just so perfect.

· · ·

E'S EAGER AND EXCITABLE
    your butt is pretty edible
    eccentric egotist, I think you're so incredible
    And now I'm getting ahead-ible
    Because we're still on L ...

LIKE LEGENDARY AND LICK-ABLE
    I like and lust and feel so full
    All lazy days and long-ass nights
    Just by your side 'til the morning light

HE SENDS ME A WINK, AND THE WAY HE'S RELAXED INTO IT, THE
words, written all for me ... if I cry, I'm going to kill him.

EXCEPT FUCK, YOU INTIMIDATE ME,
    somehow I irritate you
    Inverse, we're opposites
    Completely incompatible
    And yet ....
    I just can't forget ...

THAT X MARKS THE PLACE I'VE TRIED TO HIDE
    Behind my ribs on the left-hand side
    I'm done faking ...
    You stole my heart and left me aching.

F-E-L-I AND AN X
    Those are the five things to sum up best

What I know to be true
Felix ...
I completely fucking love you.

29

Marshall

I CLEAR MY THROAT WHEN I FINISH, PALMS CLAMMY AND HEART beating a trillion miles a minute. Felix is sitting there with his mouth open, and I'd wanted him to have that same look Brandon did, that look of *he's an idiot, but he's my idiot,* but apparently, I'm not Robbie.

I didn't go big.

Would Felix have preferred that?

I'd tried to think of the perfect date for us, but maybe it wasn't enough. Maybe it only being the two of us didn't make him feel special. Maybe it was too *borin—*

"Oomph!"

Felix throws himself at me, and a wayward knee or elbow hits my diaphragm, forcing the air from my lungs. I have a second to catch my breath when Felix's mouth closes over mine, and he blankets his body over the top of me.

"That was"—he bites my lip—"the single sweetest"—fingers

tangle in my hair—"moment of my entire"—he sucks on my tongue—"life."

"You liked it?"

"You wrote it for me. Just for me."

"I'd do anything for you."

He's blinking hard and fast against glassy eyes, and this time when he kisses me, it's soft and slow, a gentle swipe of his tongue against mine. "I love you so much," he says. "Too much. I'm scared."

"Why?" I pull back so I can see him properly and brush that damn curl off his forehead.

"Because what will I do if I lose you?"

I want to assure him there's no fucking way in hell that's going to happen, but I also said I'd always be honest with him. "Sounds like we're both worried about the same thing."

"Really?"

"I half thought you were going to laugh in my face and leave tonight."

His face falls. "I would never."

I shrug. "Insecurities. What can you do?"

"I find it so hard to believe you have any of those."

I wave a hand over me. "I'm nerdy, quiet, and chunky. People aren't exactly lining up to put me on covers of magazines."

He *hmphs*. "And that's exactly why they're dying out."

"*That's* why?" I chuckle. "Nothing to do with environmental consciousness and the rise of electronic media."

"I'm glad we agree." He nods indignantly, looking so cute that I haul him into a bear hug.

"As long as we both love me as I am, that's all that matters. Only, probably don't leave me for a party-boy gym junkie in a couple of months. I can guarantee that won't do great things for my confidence." And I'm only half-joking because the thought of Felix leaving me is like daggers in my chest.

He lets out a hollow laugh and pulls back to straddle my waist. Then, very goddamn slowly, he runs his hands from my shoulders all the way down to the waistband of my pants, stopping to feel the ridge of my pecs and every bump in my belly. When he glances back up at me, his eyes have darkened in the last rays of sunset, and he takes my hand. "I will never let you go. Ever. You're mine now. Every single inch of you. And if someone tries to take you from me, I'll go fucking savage." Then he rests my hand over his very erect cock.

I squeeze it, my own cock thickening at his words. I'd worried about telling him I love him being too much too soon, but Felix clearly doesn't have that issue. And fuck me, I like it. I shouldn't, but I really, really do.

He rocks his hips into my hand. "You're my boyfriend now, right?"

"Definitely."

"So can I touch you whenever I want?"

"Always."

"And it's not desperate if you come home from work late and I'm already in your bed?"

I lift my eyebrows, and he grins.

"It's almost happened a couple of times," he says.

"You wouldn't have had any complaints from me."

He rocks his hips again. "Speaking of beds, wanna take me to yours?"

"There was a whole picnic and—"

He leans down and nips my ear. "What if I told you we have all night and that picnic will still be there when we're done?"

"Yep." I stand, holding him close. "That'll do it."

Felix climbs inside first, and I can't help grabbing his ass, which makes him squeal. It's awkward climbing back inside with my cock so hard, but as soon as I'm through, I strip off. Felix closes my bedroom door and hurries to follow, and then he's standing there, naked, skin lit up with the multitude of colored lights outside.

His hungry gaze roams over my body, and when his tongue darts out and swipes over his bottom lip, I've never felt so fucking incredible. I close the distance between us, reaching out to run my fingers over his collarbone, then down along the outside of his pec. His muscles are lean but more defined because he's thin, and I plan to inspect his completely naked body at every chance I get.

My thumb circles his nipple, and Felix sucks in a sharp breath.

"That feels good," he says.

"This will feel better." I kiss along his neck to his shoulder, and then I drop to my knees. The one time I got to suck him off was over so quickly that I need to try it again. There's something so addictive about how he reacts when I close my mouth around him, suck him, lick him, drive him crazy. It's like there's a one-way control from his dick to the rest of his body, making him shake and tense, moans filtering through the room as he grips my hair hard.

I've read up on tips and tricks for giving good head, and while those things are great in theory, there's no way to prepare for the stretch of your jaw, the weight of a cock on your tongue, the bitter, salty taste of precum flooding your taste buds and making you drool.

I try to take him deeper each time, remembering to use my hand. When I pull off, there's drool on my chin, and his cock is slick and wet, an angry red that makes my dick throb.

"Fe?"

"Mm?"

"Do you ... do you ever ..." I don't even know how to get the question out. "Do you ever do the fucking?"

He blinks down at me in surprise, and then his expression

softens. His grip on my hair loosens. "Normally, no. I love my prostate being pounded too much to give that privilege over to just anyone. But I've tried it before. And I'd do it for you. If you wanted."

I think I do want it, but I don't want to force him into anything. "Not if it makes you uncomfortable."

He smiles and kneels down too. "It doesn't. It's more about me being selfish, but I'd give you anything. Trust me when I say that topping you will definitely not be a hardship."

"So ... can we try it?"

He reaches around me, and his fingers slide into my crack. "Now?"

"Yeah." My exhale comes out shaky. "I think so."

He kisses me softly. "Get on your back on the bed. I'm not exactly big, but it'll take some prep for that little virgin hole of yours to take me."

"Hell." My face heats.

"Don't worry, we can't all be expert bottoms like me."

I climb up onto the bed the way he wanted me. I'm nervous and excited in equal measure, and even though Felix makes this look incredible, I have no idea how it could possibly not hurt.

He grabs my lube from the bedside table, then leans over to kiss me. "You're in complete control here," he says. "You want to stop, you say stop. Sex should only ever feel amazing. Okay?"

"Yeah."

"Good." He grins. "Now, let's get this marshmallow on a stick."

I choke on a laugh as Felix moves down the bed and settles between my legs. I'm not sure what I'm expecting, but he starts out slow. Soft touches and kisses along my thighs. Where my legs meet my groin. He laps at my balls and presses his nose into my pubes and inhales.

"Shit, you're sexy," he says, voice deeper than usual. His

tongue dips below my balls, and I tense up for a second before relaxing into the feel.

It's … oh, fuck, it's amazing. He gets lower and lower, and I try to stave off my thoughts about whether I should have looked into manscaping or tidying up that area, but then Felix's tongue slides along my crease, flicks over my hole, and he lets out a long moan. I glance down to the sight of Felix's reddish curls behind my cock, his arm moving slowly as he strokes himself, and all my nervousness disappears.

I spread my legs further, tilt my hips so he has better access. I had no clue how good it would feel, but my entire ass feels like it's lit the hell up just from his tongue. My cock is begging to be touched, but I ignore it because I'm not risking getting off before he's inside me.

There's the click of a cap being flicked open, and then Felix's fingers replace his tongue. They're slippery with lube, rubbing circles against my hole.

"I'm going to start to open you up. I just need you to push back against my finger, okay?"

"Yeah." Sounds simple enough.

"Head's up, for your first time, it'll feel weird. I'll go slow, but there might be a tiny sting. It shouldn't be painful though. If it is, you need to tell me."

I nod because the pressure against my ass has increased, and I'm struggling to concentrate on anything but that.

"Push down a little."

I do as he says, and Felix presses a finger inside me. He's right. It *is* weird. The good feelings are mostly background noise now as my brain tries to take over and remind me that it's an *out* hole, not an *in* hole.

"You okay?" he asks.

I take a deep breath, then slowly let it out again. "Keep going."

He follows my lead, working his finger in and out, slowly deeper, and watching my face the entire time. He's right that it doesn't hurt, which is surprising; it's just that overwhelming feeling of weird, so, so *weird.*

"Time for a second."

Again, I push down, and he works the digit in. The stretch is slightly more obvious this time, but it still doesn't hurt. Felix is slow, cautious, ducking down every now and then to lick my cock or suck it into his mouth. It's sweet torture, the slow push and pull, the pleasure warring with discomfort. When he's got both fingers all the way in, Felix starts to move them around. Rubbing and pressing and—

A jolt of lightning hits my balls, and I cry out, totally unprepared for that sensation. When I glance down at Felix, his eyes are wild.

"This is where the fun begins."

He's so, so right.

Felix alternates between stretching me and rubbing that spot, occasionally giving my cock some love too. He gathers the precum I'm leaking up with his tongue, and the moans coming from him are driving me fucking crazy. The fact he finds this as sexy as I do feels almost better than what he's doing physically.

Almost.

Because then he deep-throats me in one go while pressing another finger in, and I swear I see stars.

"I think you're ready," he says a few moments later. "You still good?"

"Very."

He presses a kiss to my inner thigh, then straightens and slowly pulls his fingers out.

My ass tries to grip around nothing, and I don't know how it can feel even stranger being empty than it did when he was stretching me.

Felix grabs the condom and rips it open with his teeth. His jaw is set as he rolls it down his length, and I reach out to stroke his thigh.

"Are *you* good?"

"Just trying not to come," he says. "You have no idea how hot it was seeing you squirming around like that."

I huff a laugh, then pull him down against me so I can reach his mouth. He tastes like pure sex, and every kiss is harder and more desperate than the last. It's hard to stop, and I groan when Felix pulls away.

"I can either kiss you or fuck you. You can't have both."

"Fuck now, kiss after. All night after."

"Deal."

I watch as he rubs lube over his cock, and my ass is desperate for him to get inside me already. For something that started out so hesitant, I'm more than eager. That prostate trick went a long way toward loosening me up, and I totally get why Felix loves to bottom now.

He shifts into position, and I pull my legs back.

"Like this?" I check.

"Perfect." His cock presses against my hole. "It's been so long since I've done this, you're not allowed to laugh if it's over in a minute."

"Why would I laugh? A whole minute has me beat by fifty-seven seconds."

He sniggers and pushes forward.

"Oh, shit." I remember to bear down in time, and Felix clearly did a good job prepping me because other than a tiny sting, it doesn't hurt at all. The threat of pain gone, my anxiousness lessens, and I give in to the feeling of him splitting me in half.

It's fucking amazing torture. He's looking down, watching himself enter me, teeth buried into his bottom lip. Each breath is heavy and tight, the small muscles in his arms standing out, and I have to give my cock a tight squeeze to stop it getting too excited.

When Felix's hips meet my ass, he finally glances up at me. "Still good?"

"Yeah, babe, still good." I run my hand from his bracelets up his arm to his shoulder, then cup his neck. "Ready whenever you are."

He shifts, and pleasure zings through me. Felix starts out with long, slow strokes, and it doesn't take much for my hips to rock back and meet him. My gaze is trained on his face, watching every shift in expression, studying every little thing that turns him on. He builds up his rhythm, and my ass flexes and relaxes against him. I'm simmering with want, my nerves a steady thrum of pleasure that's building in waves over my entire body. My cock is leaking again, begging to be touched, and every sound from Felix, every time his balls hit my ass, every time he squeezes my thigh or digs his nails into my belly is making it harder to hold off.

He's beautiful when he's being fucked, and this is just as hot. He doesn't hide how much he wants me, he doesn't hold back, just takes and touches and plays my body like he was made for me.

My chest is full, the encompassing happiness radiating out to my limbs, driving me wild, making my head spin.

Then Felix plants his hands on the backs of my thighs and lets go. His hips snap forward over and over, pounding my ass and pegging my prostate with every thrust. The pressure is insane, zaps shooting into my balls, and my cock is *throbbing.* Leaking. Begging.

I white-knuckle the blankets to stop from touching myself. To hold off and make this last.

Felix's gaze has gone unfocused, a line of sweat trailing down his throat that I'd lean forward and lick off if I could reach it. But moving from this exact position would be too hard when I can barely think, let alone execute any motor skills.

My balls are tight; they almost hurt from lack of attention. Small pulses are pumping into my cock, and I have to grit my teeth to stop myself from begging Felix to touch me. I want to last. I want to hold out. I want to make sure he never, ever regrets choosing me, and I might be inexperienced, but I'm going to be a fast study.

Felix fucks my damn brains out, and when he finally grunts, "*Nrg*, so close," I've never grabbed my cock faster.

I stroke myself tight and fast, matching Felix's pace, building and building toward the end that I never want to come but desperately need. I'm right at the edge when my dick thickens, and I unleash. Ropes of cum hit my chest, land on my happy trail, and my whole body goes tense as I ride out the high, struggling to keep my eyes on Felix.

"Fuck, fuck ..." He slams his hips against my ass and holds still, head dropping back. His cock throbs and twitches, and his chest works hard to draw in air, and when I feel like I can move again, I reach up and pull him to me.

I cringe as his dick slips out, but the discomfort only lasts a second before his mouth is on mine. He doesn't react to the cum between us, just kisses me like he's claiming me, and it's the perfect end to incredible sex. My whole body feels boneless and loose, and I could easily stay like this for the entire night.

Felix's stomach growls. "Ooops."

"Time for food?" I ask.

"Definitely."

We climb out of bed, my legs jelly, both a little cum drunk as we clean up the mess. Felix ditches the condom, then uses his shirt to wipe the cum from my skin.

"Oh no," he says playfully. "Guess I'm going to have to borrow one of your shirts now."

I snort. "Your room is a couple of stairs away."

He grins as he finds a T-shirt in my closet and pulls it over his head. Then he grabs the hem, rubbing his toe shyly into the ground as he looks up at me through his lashes. "Still want me to get my own?"

"Well, it *is* a long walk." I stalk toward him and run my hands up the backs of his thighs to his ass. "So I'll be charitable and let you borrow it. But *only* the shirt. I can't spare anything else."

He tsks. "I think you just wanna grope me all night."

I laugh and pull on a pair of sweats. "What gave me away?"

"That dick imprint in your pants."

And okay, maybe seeing Felix in my shirt that dwarfs him is getting me chubbed up again. But he's hungry, so I'm going to feed him first. We'll finish our date, and then after, maybe I'll fuck him.

I hold his hand as he climbs out the window, and then I grab the food and follow him. It's full dark now, the lights around us giving everything a soft glow. He waits for me to set the food out, and then when I drop back into the beanbag, Felix crawls into my lap. He sits sideways, arm around me, and we stay like that for hours. Feeding each other and kissing, both of us sneaking hands under clothes but not taking it further. For the first time, we talk, relaxed, not worried about all the outside bullshit, and I fall for him even more.

"I'm glad the night we met was a disaster," I murmur.

"You don't wish it went better so we could have had all these months together?"

"Nope." I peck his nose and slide my hand under the shirt to grab his ass. "I couldn't think of a more perfect first night together than this one."

"Our first date."

"Yeah." My happiness is consuming. "The first of many."

30

Felix

I'M BUZZING WITH MY IDEA BY THE TIME BRADY FINALLY WALKS into Liberty Court. He might hate the constant family comparison, but he looks so much like his pop right now—all muscled confidence and easy smiles—which is kind of perfect for me.

What I'm about to ask of him makes me a shitty friend, but I'm trying to buy boyfriend points with Marshall's family, so surely he'll understand.

I wave to Brady from the hammock I'm lazing in, and he bounds over and dives in with me. The whole thing gives an alarming shudder that has me gripping the sides for dear life until Brady settles, almost wheezing from laughing so hard.

I nipple cripple that A-hole with no mercy.

He hisses. "Fuck, Fe, that's sensitive."

"Oh, *really*?"

"Big night."

"No wonder you're in such a good mood."

He tucks his hands behind his head, and I narrowly avoid being smacked in the face with his elbow.

"This really isn't ideal," I complain.

"We've done this a thousand times. Snuggle in."

I wriggle closer, then hold up my phone to snap a selfie of us. Brady closes one eye and sticks his tongue out, the goofball, and I throw up a peace sign before flicking the picture to Marshall. It's a huge relief that he isn't threatened by my friendship with Brady. I'd offered to not be so clingy and flirty, but Marshall shot that idea down fast. He knows how much Brady has done for me.

"*So ...*" I start.

"Uh-oh."

I laugh. "I love you, but you're going to hate me for this."

"For what, exactly?"

"Turns out Marshall's brother is a big fan. Well, a big fan of Peyton, mostly, but I guess you'll do."

Brady cracks up. "You're right. I hate you."

I smile at him angelically. "He's Marshall's closest brother, and if *he* loves me forever, then Marshall will have to as well."

He groans. "First, I don't think you have any chance of getting rid of Marshall at this point. You two are sickeningly dumb together. Second ... fine. What are we doing?"

I lift my phone and video call Robbie.

"Right *now*?" Brady cries.

"If I don't shamelessly pounce on your generosity, you'll change your mind."

"I hate that you know me so well."

Robbie picks up after a couple of rings. "Hey, bro-ite! This is ... weird."

"I got your number off Marshall," I say, purposely keeping the camera tilted my way. "There's someone who wants to say hi."

"Ah ... yeah, cool." He's clearly confused but rolls with it anyway.

I move the camera so Brady and I are both in the shot. "Rob-dog, you know who Brady Talon is, right?"

His jaw drops. Opens and closes like a fish. "B-Brando?" Robbie calls.

"Yeah, what's—" Brandon comes into view, and when he catches sight of the screen, his eyes fly wide. "Holy fucking shit, Brady Talon."

Brady nods, that public mask of his in place. "Nice to meet you."

I'm trying desperately not to laugh as Robbie and Brandon start talking over each other, proclaiming their undying love for my friend, his brother, and their dads.

And yeah, I get why Brady hates this, but I also think it's kind of adorable to see two big guys completely fall to pieces with hero worship.

I sigh happily. "I'm going to be able to use this moment to my advantage for the rest of our lives. Tracy wants me to clear the table? *Oh, remember that time I introduced you to Brady Talon?* Earl wants me to muck out stalls? *Hey, Robbie, remember when you said Brady was your free pass?*"

Robbie's grin is huge. "You're officially my favorite person."

"I can't even argue," Brandon says, "because you're mine too."

I smile as the three of them talk, Brady being so patient with his PR-ready answers. With Peyton slated to be as big as his dad, and Brady being the one who'll manage him one day, they both know how to handle fans. The fact he's doing this for me without argument just makes me love him a billion times more.

A couple of minutes later, I manage to interrupt and wind up the call. When Robbie and Brandon hang up, the silence is sudden.

"Sorry," I say immediately.

"Nah, they were all right. Didn't ask any of those dumb intrusive questions that I hate."

"Considering Robbie has no concept of personal boundaries, I'm honestly shocked by that."

Brady laughs. "Big family you're taking on."

"In about every way possible. Size, personality—"

"Dicks?"

I snigger. "Not information I need to know."

He's quiet for a moment. "You like them?"

"All of them."

He knocks his head gently against mine. "I'm happy for you."

"I'm happy for me too." I sigh. "Now you're gonna have to man whore it up double time because I'm going to be living vicariously through you. I'm a taken man now. I mean, I'll still have my stories, but telling you I gave the fastest hand job in history at the top of a Ferris wheel loses its charm when you know who I gave it to."

"And great. Next time I see Marshall, all I'm going to be able to hear is the creak of metal from one of those baskets swaying back and forth."

"Actually, it was a seat configuration."

"And no one saw?"

"I'm very subtle when I want to be."

Brady holds up his hand for a high five. "Respect."

"Also, thank you though," I tell him honestly. "I really appreciate you doing that."

"Count yourself lucky. You're the only person I would have done it for."

"I can't believe you flew all this way to meet him," I grumble.

Uncle Heath laughs and throws an arm around my shoulder. And even though he's been married to Dad for a year now, I refuse to stop calling him that.

"This is your *first* boyfriend, Fe. The first guy you're serious about. We want to make sure he measures up."

I sigh. "Really regretting asking if he could come home with me now."

"It was the final straw," Dad points out. "After months of phone calls about this irritating guy you can't stand and then kinda like and are now head over heels in love with, we had to meet him."

I roll my eyes. "It's not even a month until the semester ends."

"Yes, but you were going to see his family first. We were offended," Heath says. His shit-eating grin gives away that there was no offense. At all. They just want to annoy me.

"Only a month," I point out. "Then he was coming to stay with us for a month. My point stands—you could have waited, but you flew out here specifically to embarrass me where Mom couldn't make you stop."

Their matching sniggers prove I've got it in one.

"The ground rules are that you don't mention my childhood, don't mention how I came out to you, and definitely do not mention how many times I've said he's my future husband and father of my babies."

"Twenty-seven," Heath counts.

I flip him off.

"Relax," Dad says, nudging me. "We only want to meet him. We'll be nice, welcoming, congratulate him on having a massive d—"

I groan loud enough to cut him off.

"Don't blame us," Heath says. "Your dad has asked you plenty of times to stop oversharing."

"I can't help it." My smile gets giddy as we approach the door to Shenanigans. "He makes me so happy."

"And that's why, no matter how much shit we give you both, we're going to love him anyway."

I smack a kiss on my dad's cheek. "There was never any doubt."

I sent Marshall a heads-up text that I was meeting him for his break about half an hour ago but didn't tell him why. Dad and Heath surprised me by turning up before lunch and demanding to be taken to my boyfriend.

And even though we've been together over a month now, that word never gets old.

I walk in and immediately spot my behemoth. Not even because of how he sticks out in a crowd, but I swear the way he lights up when he sees me is a magnet for my attention whore self.

He stands straighter and opens his arms, so I jog over and jump into them. Having him carry me around is one of my favorite things, and he doesn't seem to be getting sick of the constant cuddles and neediness. Marshall presses a kiss to my hair, and then a throat clears behind me.

Marshall goes stiff, and I slide down out of his grip.

"Marshmallow, this is Dad and his husband, Uncle Heath."

Heath bats at my head. "Little shit."

"Ignore them," Dad says and holds his hand out to Marshall. "So you're the guy sticking it in my son."

Marshall's eyes fly wide, his blush setting in faster than anything I've been able to achieve so far. "Ah …"

I know what Dad's doing without even needing to ask, so I curl my lips between my teeth and try not to laugh, while poor Marshall looks like he wants the ground to open up and swallow him whole. They never did see the funny side to Earl locking me in the henhouse.

"I thought you said he takes control in the bedroom?" Heath asks, eyeing Marshall with concern. "He doesn't seem all that confident to me."

Dad makes a noise in agreement. "Definitely can't picture him with a paddle. Are you sure this is the right guy?"

The three of them turn to look at me, and I know they expect me to go along with them, but I can't do it anymore.

A laugh tears from me as I wrap my arm around Marshall's. "Aw, Marshmallow, don't be mad. It's Dad's way of welcoming you to the family."

Realization dawns on him, and he gives us all a flat look. "That wasn't funny."

"Kinda was," I correct as Heath pinches his fingers together and agrees with me.

Marshall bends down and buries his face in my neck. "Just let me know when they're gone, and I'll come out again."

"Sorry, Marshmallow, you're stuck with us for a week," Dad says. "But we promise no more talking about sex so long as you can get Felix to shut up about it."

Marshall draws back and pins me with a look. "Tell me that's another joke."

"I *would*, but I can't."

"We'll be talking about *that* later."

Heath brings his hands together loudly. "Oh, there it is. That sounded bossy."

"Sorry, Marshall," Dad says. "I can promise *I* won't talk about sex anymore. Those two are a lost cause."

"This is not how I pictured meeting you," Marshall says.

"Makes sense though," I point out. "Our first meeting needed a do-over, now your first meeting with them needs a do-over. All this symmetry is wild."

"And suddenly, I'm dreading meeting your mom." But Marshall is smiling. It's one of the things I love about him—he's a good sport. Easygoing. Reliable. Quietly snarky when it calls for it and amazingly protective. Plus, he can handle *me*, which says more about his character than anything does.

And not once, even for a moment, have I seen a glimpse of that *boring* side he's so worried about.

I link my fingers through his and lead us all to a table. "Dad and Heath own the resort we're staying at. I asked them to make sure a cabin was reserved for us. *Away* from the other rooms. We wouldn't want to disturb the other guests, after all."

"Fucking hell," Marshall mutters, swiping a hand over his face as though he can wipe the embarrassment away.

"Ignoring them," Dad says. "Fe mentioned you're into history. I think you'll like Kilborough. The whole town is built around it."

"Yeah, I've read up on the prison. I can't wait to see it."

And like that, Dad and Marshall take over the conversation. It warms me to my toes to see them talking, getting along, bonding over Kilborough and everything to do there. My chin is resting on my palm as I watch them, and when I glance over at Heath, he looks as lovestruck as I feel.

He sends me a quick wink, and this shivery feeling ripples through me.

Pure fucking contentment.

This is my family. Mom and her boyfriend too. Then Earl and Tracy and all of Marshall's brothers.

And Marshall.

All mine.

All completely, fucking *mine*.

EPILOGUE

Marshall

Ten Years Later

THE FRONT DOOR SLAMS OPEN, AND I CHUCKLE AT THE LOUD footsteps coming down the hall. "Little bro? Bro-ite? Where you at?"

"Through here."

Robbie walks in, cap backward, my two-year-old nephew in a carrier on his chest and five-year-old niece on his shoulders.

"Aren't they getting too old for that?" I ask.

"Fuck no." He pulls Lahna off his shoulders and airplanes her to the ground, then does the same with Trey. "You and Fe still cool to watch them while Brandon and I are away?"

"As long as you don't mind them being hopped up on sugar while you're gone." I grab two cookies from the cupboard, and the little monsters practically pounce to grab them from me, then tear down the hall.

Robbie laughs and pounds me on the back. "You're going to regret that later."

"Dude, who doesn't give their kids sugar? We lived on Cheerios and Cap'n Crunch growing up."

Even saying that, I admire the way Robbie and Brandon are raising those two. They moved a few streets away from us in Kilborough, and already my niece and nephew know more about farming and growing food than I ever will.

No, instead, Fe and I have animals. Lots and lots of animals. After Felix worked for a few years as a vet, we opened a wildlife sanctuary where we rehabilitate injured animals and try to get them back into their natural habitats. Felix gets to be around animals, which he loves, and the grants and donations we receive cover most of our costs, so I get to spend my days researching and writing papers on how the Technological Era is shaping civilization.

"I gotta go," Robbie says.

"Have fun at your reunion."

"Thanks." He heads for the door before calling out, "I think the kids are trying to ride the goat."

Shit. "She's only got three legs!"

I hurry outside, but they're both sitting on the back step, finishing their cookies like the adorable little angels they are.

Fucking Robbie.

I leave them and walk down to the New England Cottontail enclosure. Felix has been trying to increase the population in the area, and any free time he has, I always find him there. He has a soft spot for rabbits.

He doesn't see me approaching, so I manage to sneak up behind him, and he jumps when I swamp him in my arms.

"Hey," he says softly, leaning back into my chest, trying to get as close to me as possible. It's one thing about him that hasn't changed, and I still love his neediness as much as when we first met. "We've got our first kits," he says.

"No way."

"Yep."

"Are you sure?"

He pinches my arm. "*Yes*, I'm sure."

I hug him closer, reaching down to the bracelet his dad made him and rubbing my finger over the *M* carved into it.

Felix lets out a long, content sigh, nuzzling his head back into me. "Did you get the paper finished?"

"I did. Robbie just dropped off the kids."

And as expected, he lights up. "They're here? You didn't tell me."

I chuckle and kiss him right over his pouty lips. "It was literally a few minutes ago."

He hurries to take off his gloves and set them on his examination table, but I grab his apron string before he can get any further.

"Before you go …" Nerves ripple through me. "You love them."

"Lahna and Trey? Duh."

"You love spending time with them."

He tilts his head, suspicion crossing his features. "Marshmallow …"

"Well, I was thinking, maybe, how would you feel about some proper kits of our own?"

His jaw drops. "Really?"

"Robbie gave me the number of—"

I can't even finish my sentence before Felix launches himself into my arms. His legs close around my waist, and he kisses every part of my face he can reach. The constant string of yeses coming from his mouth blur together until they make no sense, but I know exactly how he feels.

Kids are a big step, but we're ready.

Suddenly, Felix groans. "Trey is trying to ride the goat."

"Fuck." I drop him and run outside, trying to coax Trey away from the poor creature, and only the promise of more sugar is able to do the trick. He's already a little tank and takes after my brother to a T, which means as soon as the cookie is gone, he's off chasing animals again.

So maybe Felix and I have a bit to learn before we bring an actual child into our lives, but we've got the time to learn it.

We've got our family around for support, lives we love, and most importantly, each other.

"I have one condition," Felix says. "You're not allowed to love the child more than me."

"Sorry, I think that's unavoidable."

He puffs out a breath. "*Fine.* But you're not allowed to think they're cuter than me."

"Have you *seen* a baby?"

Felix scowls. "I think I've changed my mind."

"Really?"

"Nah." He grins. "But you *do* have to promise to tell me I'm pretty at least once a day."

"Deal."

And it's the easiest deal I'll ever make, because I already do it.

Every day.

I promised myself that I'd make sure Felix knew how special he is, and I've followed through. In return, he encourages and supports me in just … being me. No boredom. No stress. We're there for each other in everything we've faced.

And we'll be there for each other no matter what else comes.

Thanks so much for reading The Dating Disaster!

If you're curious about Charlie (Mr. golden-retriever) and Liam (Marshall's date guru) make sure to grab their story, Mr. Romance!

Want more from me?
If you're after more college guys, check out my Frat Wars series (which includes Marshall's brother Robbie).
And to keep up with my releases, come join my Facebook group, Saxon's Sweethearts.

MEET ALL THE COUPLES OF FRANKLIN U!

Brax and Ty's story:
Playing Games
Marshall and Felix's story:
The Dating Disaster
Charlie and Liam's story:
Mr. Romance
Spencer and Cory's story:
Bet You
Chris and Aidan's story:
The Glow Up
Cobey and Vincent's story:
Learning Curve
Alex and Remy's story:
Making Waves
Peyton and Levi's story:
Football Royalty

MY FREEBIES

Do you love friends to lovers?
Second chances or fake relationships?
I have three bonus freebies available!
Friends with Benefits
Total Fabrication
Making Him Mine
This short story is only available to my reader list so follow the
link below and join the gang!
https://www.subscribepage.com/saxonjames

OTHER BOOKS BY SAXON JAMES

FRAT WARS SERIES:

Frat Wars: King of Thieves

Frat Wars: Master of Mayhem

Frat Wars: Presidential Chaos

DIVORCED MEN'S CLUB SERIES:

Roommate Arrangement

Platonic Rulebook

Budding Attraction

NEVER JUST FRIENDS SERIES:

Just Friends

Fake Friends

Getting Friendly

Friendly Fire

Bonus Short: Friends with Benefits

LOVE'S A GAMBLE SERIES:

Good Times & Tan Lines

Bet on Me

Calling Your Bluff

CU HOCKEY SERIES WITH EDEN FINLEY:

Power Plays & Straight A's

Face Offs & Cheap Shots

Goal Lines & First Times

Line Mates & Study Dates

Puck Drills & Quick Thrills

PUCKBOYS SERIES WITH EDEN FINLEY:

Egotistical Puckboy

Irresponsible Puckboy

FRANKLIN U SERIES (VARIOUS AUTHORS):

The Dating Disaster

And if you're after something a little sweeter, don't forget my YA pen name

S. M. James.

These books are chock full of adorable, flawed characters with big hearts.

https://geni.us/smjames

WANT MORE FROM ME?

Follow Saxon James on any of the platforms below.
www.saxonjamesauthor.com
www.facebook.com/thesaxonjames/
www.amazon.com/Saxon-James/e/B082TP7BR7
www.bookbub.com/profile/saxon-james
www.instagram.com/saxonjameswrites/

ACKNOWLEDGMENTS

As with any book, this one took a hell of a lot of people to make happen.

The cover was created by the talented Natasha Snow and edits were done by the comma-queen Sandra Dee from One Love Editing, with Lori Parks proofreading the bejeebus out of it.

Thanks to Charity VanHuss for being the most amazing PA I could have ever dreamed up. Without you I'd be even more of a chaotic disaster and there isn't enough space to cover the many hats you wear for me.

Eden Finley, you constantly under-sell yourself but I've learned so much from you. You're the bestsest disaster bestie I could ask for, and a queen of a co-author. You're also stuck with me.

Lucky you.

To Louisa Masters, thanks for constantly reining in my spirals of doom and reminding me to "stop borrowing trouble". I'd be an anxious mess in the corner at least half of the time without you.

Karen Meeus, AM Johnson, Riley Hart, thank you so much for taking the time to read. Your support is incredible and I really appreciate it!

And of course, thanks to my fam bam. To my husband who constantly frees up time for me to write, and to my kids whose neediness reminds me the real word exists.